CHIMERA

TOR BOOKS BY WILL SHETTERLY

Dogland

Nevernever

Elsewhere

CHIMERA

Will Shetterly

TOR ®

A Tom Doherty Associates Book
New York

CHIMERA

This book is printed on acid-free paper.

A Tor Book
Published by Tom Doherty Associates, LLC
175 Fifth Avenue
New York, NY 10010

www.tor.com

Tor® is a registered trademark of Tom Doherty Associates, LLC.

Design by Jane Adele Regina

Library of Congress Cataloging-in-Publication Data

Shetterly, Will.
    Chimera / Will Shetterly.—1st ed.
      p. cm.
    "A Tom Doherty Associates book."
    ISBN 0-312-86630-5 (alk. paper)
    1. Genetic engineering—Fiction. I. Title.

PS3569.H458 C48 2000
813'.54—dc21   00-027673

First Edition: June 2000

Printed in the United States of America

0 9 8 7 6 5 4 3 2 1

For Brandi and Brian

ACKNOWLEDGMENTS

John M. Ford and Emma Bull contributed enormously in suggesting characters and plot elements for this novel, but neither of them should be blamed for any shortcomings in the final work. I'm also very grateful for the advice I received from my editor, Beth Meacham, and (in alphabetical order, because all their suggestions were wise, even if my execution was not) Michael Engelberg, Alex Epstein, Don Helverson, Randy and Jean-Marc Lofficier, Erin Maher, Ricardo Mestres, Kay Reindl, Terry Rossio, and Marv Wolfman. And everything I write owes something to my fellow members, past and present, of the Scribblies: Steven Brust, Nathan A. Bucklin, Raphael Carter, Kara Dalkey, Pamela Dean, Patricia C. Wrede, and the already mentioned (but never mentioned too often) Emma Bull.

CHIMERA

1

Zoe Domingo walked into my life in the back room of a casino on the edge of Crittertown. If I hadn't had my mind on more important things, I would've turned and looked when a woman asked in a voice like a husky purr, "Chase Maxwell? Your phone message said—"

I knew what it said: "Maxwell Investigations. Please leave a message. And if this is Eddie, you bum, no more excuses. Bring my money to the high rollers' table at Wonderland." It did not say that anyone, no matter how nice her voice, should interrupt the game. But I didn't point out that she wasn't Eddie. I merely said, "I'm playing here," and nodded across the table at the Egyptian cowboy.

He nodded back and said, "I surely hope so."

The game was seven-card stud. The night had not been especially good or bad to me, but that was about to change. Technically, I was playing with three people besides the Sinai Kid: a Japanese salaryman, a chromium-haired borgette with all the latest implants, and an old Nigerian woman who was probably the best player at the table. But this hand didn't belong to any of them. All three had folded, leaving it for the cowboy or me.

He kept looking at the woman behind me. I wondered if they were partners. In my business, paranoia's either an occupational hazard or a recipe for success. Then I realized she couldn't be signaling my hand. The dealerbot would catch any body language or electronic communication between them. The cowboy had been leering at the borgette earlier. All his gaze meant was that the woman who didn't respect my playing time was worth looking at.

But the cards in front of me were more deserving of my attention. I held three big boys who would pay for last month's rent, and the next few besides.

The dealerbot, who looked remarkably like Clark Gable with translucent blue skin, turned to me. "Sir?"

"Let's make this a little more interesting." I pushed all my chips into the middle of the table. "A hundred and fifty K."

The woman behind me said, "If you want to be left alone, why tell clients where you are?"

"Because the normal ones leave a message." I grinned at the cowboy. "What'll it be, pard? You gonna see that, or fold?"

The cowboy flicked his eyes back to the table. He gave me another lazy smile and said, "Think I'll raise. Say, another two hundred K?" He had the drawl down. Going by the voice alone, you'd think he was one of the folks who had voted to privatize Texas rather than one of the petroleum princes who had bought it.

He slid two towers of chips across the table, smiled again, and scratched his ear.

People like him get to play the game that way. People like me get to decide whether we'll be good losers or bad ones.

The dealerbot said, "Do you wish to meet the raise or fold, sir?"

Sometimes people like me manage to find option number three. "Hold on." I turned in my chair and saw her for the first time.

You have to forgive the cowboy for staring. A pair of cheap sunglasses hid her eyes, but that only called more attention to her other features: cheekbones like a Mayan princess, full lips, a small, wide nose, skin the color of pale copper, a mop of hair in tangled skeins of black and gold and brown. Her clothing consisted of a short, iridescent sea-green jumpsuit and low silver boots, leaving her lean, tan arms and legs bare. Her only jewelry was an elegant silver watch on her wrist. Due to her proportions and her effort-lessly perfect posture, she appeared to be tall, but the frame of the doorway revealed that she was actually quite short.

I saw the bust of Nefertiti once. If the two women could stand side by side, Nefertiti would look like Zoe Domingo's geeky kid sister.

Many thoughts went through my head. The one that came out of my mouth was, "How much cash have you got?"

She frowned, pulled a handful of crumpled bills out of her pocket, and riffled through them. "A little over a hundred K. But that's—"

I snatched her money and slapped it on the table. "Con-gratulations. You've hired a detective."

The dealerbot wrinkled its translucent brow. "Sir, you may not increase your stake during a game."

I looked at the cowboy. He shrugged and said, "Hell, this is a private game. We can run it how we want." I could've kissed him then, until he went and spoiled it. He smiled at me. "Go ahead, sport. But that was a two hundred K raise."

The woman who wanted to hire me said, "Gee, too bad," and reached for her money.

I caught her wrist. As she tensed to pull free, I had an instant to register that she was stronger than she looked. Then she relaxed and raised her eyebrows in a question or a threat. She smelled like jasmine, with a hint of something else, something woodsy and wild. I said, "You want to hire me or not?"

"I think so."

"All right, then."

I slid her watch off her wrist, added it to the pile of cash, and pushed it all into the center of the table.

"Hey! That cost a hundred and thirty K!"

"Trust me." She obviously didn't. I whispered, "He scratches his ear when he bluffs."

The cowboy was appreciating the show. I met his sphinx smile and asked, "Good enough?"

He held the watch up to the light, whistled, and turned to my new client. "Cartier. A hell of a timepiece for a little thing like you."

She leaned her head to one side and smiled. "It was a present."

"And I'm sure you deserved it." He put the watch back into the pot, capping the pyramid of chips and cash before us.

The dealerbot said, "Show your cards."

I snapped my three kings down on the table. "Balthazar, Melchior, and Caspar. Merry Christmas, pardner."

I reached for the pot—and the cowboy showed his cards: five diamonds.

He said, "Diamond flush. And a happy New Year to you."

The dealer raked the pot toward the cowboy. I watched it go with that feeling that God has just had a good laugh at your expense. When I looked at my client, I saw my reflection in her shades and closed my mouth. Her expression did not suggest she was as impressed with my gaming skills as she might've been.

The dealerbot said, "Ante up."

I stood, dropped a K on the table for the rabbit chimera who had kept bringing me drinks, picked up my jacket from the back of my chair, and headed for the door. My client started after me.

The cowboy called to her, "Hold on, missy. You play poker?"

She shook her head.

The cowboy smiled. "Play anything else?"

She nodded. "Cowboys and Indians. You can be Custer."

I waited for her in the twilight zone between the quiet

darkness of the high rollers' hideaway and the carnival madness of the main room. Like most places to spend major money in Crittertown, Wonderland was strictly "humans only," though a few customers must've been gene-checked at the door; I saw two borgies who could've passed for humanform bots at a distance, and a wilder who looked as bestial as any chimera from a discount genomerie.

Wonderland's support staff was evenly divided between bots and chimeras. The bots had most of the positions of trust: dealers, tellers, strolling one-armed bandits. The chimeras provided entertainment and services where flesh made a better impression than metal or plastic. It all follows the laws of profit; no one's going to tip a box that shines your shoes, but I was happy leaving one of my last Ks for the rabbitwoman who had smiled at me as she brought my drinks.

An announcer screamed, "Let's have a big hand for the Chippendogs!"

A troupe of canine chimeras in tear-away tuxedos took the stage at the center of the room. Most of the players ignored them, but I clapped. The client caught up to me then, so I said, "Someone deserves a big hand tonight."

She turned her shades toward me. "Maybe he scratches his ear when it itches."

"I don't want to hear about it." I headed into the crowd.

She followed. "Hey, you want to bet the farm on three kings, *no problemo*. Where are you going?"

"Out for a smoke."

"What about my case?"

"My usual retainer's two hundred K a day."

"That was all my money."

"Then you get a day's work. Nothing illegal. No guarantees of success. No refunds if I deliver in less than a day. What's your name?"

"Zoe Domingo."

I'm paid to be curious about clients' cases, not their

names. "Ms. Domingo. Call me tomorrow to—" I finished the sentence with an "uh-oh."

Coming toward us through the crowd was Arthur Madden, a middle-aged man whose expensive suit and equally expensive grooming made him look like a respectable businessman. The effect was enhanced by the black disk of a datacle tucked in his left eye, feeding him market reports or porn. But a respectable businessman wouldn't have at his heels a glowering, two hundred pound chimera.

You didn't need to see Bruno's forehead tattoo to know his genetic heritage. Even in a suit that must've cost as much as Arthur's, Bruno looked more dog than man, with a nose and a jaw that met my definition of a muzzle, feral black beads for eyes, and short, black Doberman hair that covered most of his visible body.

I grinned, thrust out my hand, and said, "Arthur! Good to see you!"

He ignored the hand. "Max. I hear you dropped half a meg tonight."

I shrugged. "You know how it is. Some nights Luck smiles. Some nights she frowns."

"When you passed my office on the way to the game, did you think of that little loan you haven't paid back?"

"I'm on it. The lady here brought me a big case." I turned to acknowledge her.

She dipped her chin graciously, and Arthur began to smile. The smile faded when Bruno sniffed loudly, then announced, "I don't smell money. Just cat pee."

I frowned at the dogman, then at my client. Hiding an ID tat gets a chimera a minimum of two years in prison, guaranteed. Erasing the tat might get a chimera put to sleep. I couldn't see anything on her forehead. But for all that Bruno was bred for brawn, not brains, I knew he wasn't stupid enough to call a human a chimera if he wasn't sure.

Zoe Domingo leaned toward Bruno and put two fingers

under his chin. "Tease a cat—" Her fingernails extended like claws unsheathing, answering any doubts anyone might've had. "You might get scratched."

Bruno sprang back with a snarl that would've done his grandparents proud.

Arthur looked at me and shook his head. "Max, you want to rent a critter girl, that's your business. But passing her off as a client—"

I could've walked away from the case then. Some people would say I should've. From a moral standpoint, the cat-woman had misrepresented herself. From a legal one, we hadn't signed a contract—and even if we had, under South California law, I couldn't be bound to a contract with a chimera.

But I had taken the cat's money and given her my word. Plus I hated the idea of telling Arthur I hadn't recognized Zoe Domingo for what she was. And maybe, in the part of my soul where there still lived a knight in grimy white armor, I didn't want to turn away a damsel in distress, even if that damsel was only half human. I said, "She hired me, Arthur. You'll get paid."

He frowned. "You think I'm a shmuck?"

"I know your policy on critters. I'll get her out before anyone notices." I patted his shoulder, took the cat's arm, and started for the door.

Arthur said, "You do think I'm a shmuck." Before I could protest, he turned to man's worst friend. "Bruno. Break two of his fingers."

The dogman's heavy hand caught my shoulder. I turned back toward them as graciously as I could.

Arthur smiled at me. "If you're afraid you'll scream, we can go into my office." I really wished I knew what his datacle was showing him then.

I looked around. As I feared, the rest of the Terrible Trio were coming our way.

The larger was hairless and flat-featured, with sharp teeth and a whale tat to tell you he had orca genes. The other was maybe fifty pounds lighter, which wasn't any more reassuring. His coarse white hair and bear's head tat said polar bear plainly enough. They wore conservative business suits like Bruno's—Wonderland was, after all, the kind of place where the family that plays together, stays together. They passed through the gamers and the gaming tables, remarkably discreet for two creatures who looked like they'd enjoy nothing more than the chance to turn a few humans into a late night snack.

I looked back at Arthur. "We don't need to go anywhere."

"You're sure? If you make a scene, it'll cost you more fingers, maybe some ribs."

"C'mon, Arthur. I only need a couple more days—"

"Sorry, Max. But to show we're still friends, you can pick the fingers."

I looked down at my hands. Broken fingers heal, I told myself without much comfort. If I went to a free clinic, they might even heal straight. Letting Bruno play with two fingers might buy me a week, but which two? You use your little fingers less than the others, yet there would be an advantage to having both injuries on the same hand.

While I was weighing options, the catwoman said, "Bruno. You like being a lap dog?"

He grinned at her, baring teeth as threatening as the orca's. "When dog bites man, pussycat—oh, yeah."

I said, "Arthur. What do you expect me to do?"

He shrugged. "Choose two fingers, Max. Or give me my money. I hate making life harder for you. But you must see that you have responsibilities."

Bruno turned his grin on me as Arthur added, "I suggest the pinky and the ring finger. Tape them together, and you'll hardly notice the inconvenience."

Very aware that the cat was watching me, I said, "You're

too thoughtful, Arthur," and extended my right hand, index finger pointed at Bruno. "If you've got to, start here."

Arthur nodded at Bruno. The dogman grinned and reached for my finger—

—and the air around my right wrist went crazy as space warped. The 9mm SIG Recoilless flew into my waiting hand—

—and the bearman grabbed my wrist and wrenched it behind my back. I grunted to let him know that if all he wanted to do was hurt me, he was done now.

Bruno said, "Where'd a low-rent peeper like you get an Infinite Pocket?"

I shrugged. "I'm lucky with gumball machines."

Arthur said, "Outside. Hurt him."

He and his pets had all their focus on me. My cat client showed them that was a mistake by leaping onto the bear's back and raking her claws down his face. With a roar of pain and anger, he released me to flail at her.

I tried to show them that was another mistake by aiming the SIG at Bruno. Before they had time to be impressed, the orca slugged me, knocking me back across a blackjack table. Chips, cards, and customers scattered in my wake. The tabletop buckled, spilling me hard onto the floor.

The world became brighter and clearer then, in that way it does when your body knows you may die soon. I felt like I was moving through clear gel; I could smell and see and hear everything precisely, as if my senses had heightened to save me. But my poor body couldn't move quickly enough to make use of the information flooding my mind.

I saw my SIG kicked further away from me by a fleeing gambler who never noticed it. Casino patrons screamed and shoved to get clear of the fight. Someone shouted, "He's got a gun!" I wondered who they were talking about, until I realized that it'd taken that long for the rumors of my action to cross the packed room. Arthur was running for his office, for no reason that I wanted to wait around to learn. The orca was caught in the crowd, without a clear path for attacking my client or me. Bruno's position was better. I saw him working my way.

I wanted to dive under a table and crawl for the doors. I might've, if I didn't have the cat to consider. Call that my second chance to drop the case. Credit the decision to stay to professional pride or professional self-preservation: detectives who abandon clients in times of trouble don't get many referrals.

The client in question was no better off than me. The bearman yanked her off his back and threw her at least ten yards away. Her sunglasses flew off her head, but I was too far away to see her eyes. She twisted in midair to land nimbly on her feet on a card table, sending chips and startled players in all directions.

The casino would get a lot of free publicity tonight, I thought. Yet I doubted we'd get any thanks from Arthur.

The bearman growled and charged the cat. She leaped onto the stage, and dancers fled. A heavily muscled dogman dancer glanced wildly from her to the bearman, then dove under the curtain at the back of the stage.

Bruno had made his way to me by then, so I gave him my personal gold star for effort. I'd like to think my sensei would've approved of my punch, a clean snap from the hips that drove my entire weight through my fist into his chin.

He dropped like a brick. I flexed my hand, grimaced, and said, "Cheer up, Bruno. I think you got your two fingers."

Never be clever in battle. The orca tackled me from behind, and we crashed against a roulette table. I couldn't let him get a good grip, so I rolled desperately, catching glimpses of the madhouse around us as the orca scrambled after me.

Most of the customers had fled the main room. Onstage, the cat was climbing a side curtain. Below her, the bear roared and ripped the curtain down, and I figured the fight was over for both of us. But the cat kicked out, releasing the curtain. She landed lightly beside us and rose with a side kick to the orca's chest that knocked him off me.

I scrambled across the floor, snatched up my SIG, and aimed it at the charging bear. Proving he was smarter than he looked, he halted.

I glanced at the cat. "Thanks."

She nodded. "Likewise."

Her eyes were golden brown, with black slitted pupils. They suited her. Her jaguar hair fell in tangles around her face. The tip of a pointed, lightly furred ear protruded from her wild locks. She gave me a defiant look and tucked her hair behind her cat ears.

We backed across the deserted room toward the front door. Arthur's three guardians watched sullenly. I kept my pistol high to remind them that what some people called the great equalizer should be called the great promoter; with the gun in my hand, I was the most deadly species in the room.

I told the cat, "I don't work for chimeras. Nothing personal. It's my policy."

She said, "Fine. Where's my refund?"

She had me there. I couldn't think of a way to get out of the job that would leave any white showing in the poor knight's armor. "All right. One day's work."

Police sirens approaching Wonderland cut off any response she might've had. We turned our backs on Arthur's pets to run for freedom—too late. Steel fire walls dropped soundlessly in every window and archway, sealing the room.

Bruno and his buddies trotted toward us. I spun around with the SIG to let them know that nothing was going to happen to us until we'd talked to the cops. As they skidded to a halt, I said, "Why don't you boys wait on the far side of the room?"

They didn't like that, but when Bruno nodded, the other two gave in. All three retreated.

I whispered to the cat, "I'm not a priest or a lawyer. If you've done something illegal, don't tell me."

She pulled a tissue and something else out of her pocket, keeping them close to her body. "Can you hide this?"

I thought she was hiding the second object from Bruno and company, but realized later she was keeping it out of sight of the casino's surveillance system. I let her drop it in my hand.

While she vigorously scrubbed makeup from her forehead with the tissue, I glanced down at what she'd given me: a perfectly spherical black opal, with two thin, gold rectangles passing through it like knives, attached to a gold earring hook. The opal and its rectangles looked like something from a Beverly Hills jeweler, but the earring hook looked cheaper. There was a small imperfection in the solder joining the hook to the opal, as if someone had altered or repaired it in a hurry, without the skill of the artist who created the opal and its intersecting rectangles.

I nodded at the black opal earring. "What's this?"

"That's what I hired you to find out."

"Did you steal it?"

"No."

I pointed at a smudge of makeup on the cat's head tattoo on her brow. "You missed a bit."

"Thanks." She scrubbed the tissue across her forehead again.

This wasn't the time to push for answers. I opened the Infinite Pocket and released the SIG. It flew into the shimmer of space at my wrist as if sucked by a super magnet. I dropped the earring in after it and closed the Pocket.

The cat watched the process with an eyebrow raised. "How did you get that thing?"

"A long, dull story. Sorry about your watch."

"Counterfeit. Twenty K in Ensenada."

She didn't crack a smile, so I didn't, either. "Huh. Which means I only owe you half a day's work."

"Sure. If you want to reimburse the cowboy for the watch."

"Hmm."

"A full day?"

I nodded. "A full day."

The fire walls rose. Two copbots entered, followed by four human cops, all with sleepguns out and ready to fire. I put my hands up. The cat kept staring at the bots, as if she was ready to run without warning. I elbowed her, and she imitated me.

A hard-looking Asian woman stepped forward. "I'm Sergeant Ling. You two look guilty."

I lowered my arms very slowly so she would have plenty of time to tell me to keep them up, if she wanted to. "Can't go by appearances, Sergeant. We want you to know we're not armed and would do nothing that might seem threatening to a guardian of public safety." If you think it's hard to say that with a straight face, you've never had to deal with a police force provided by the lowest bidder.

Behind me, Arthur said, "He has a pistol in an Infinite Pocket in his wrist."

Well, in Arthur's place, I wouldn't have done me any favors, either. I grinned as he came up beside me. The effect was spoiled when a copbot grabbed my right arm and jerked up the sleeve, revealing the pale circular scar on my inner wrist.

"Open it," Ling said. "Carefully."

"Damn," I said. "It's jammed." As Ling frowned, I added, "Don't worry. It'll stay closed."

Ling said, "It better."

I said very nonthreateningly, "I'm a P.I. I'm licensed to carry. Want to see the ID?"

She did. I drew the card from my hip pocket with my left hand and gave it to her. The second copbot stepped in front of me for a blink test. When my soulful browns jibed with CityCentral's records, the bot stepped away and nodded at Ling.

She handed the card back to me. "Doesn't say anything about an Infinite Pocket."

"Or anything about where I can carry."

"If a gun appears while we're around, you'll carry it up your ass. Sideways." She looked at the bot holding me. "Let him go. Tranq him if he gets annoying." Then she asked Arthur, "What's the story?"

I massaged my wrist as I glanced at the overturned furniture and the torn stage curtain. I had the feeling that my day's work for the cat would consist of sitting in an L.A. County cell trying to look like I didn't need a boyfriend.

"We don't serve critters," Arthur said. "When I asked her to leave, she and her friend decided to make trouble."

I thought it was decent of Arthur not to mention that the cat had been passing. Then I realized he had nothing to gain by revealing it now, and he could always mention it later if it seemed useful.

Ling glanced at the cat. "Scan her." As a copbot read her retinas, Ling asked Arthur, "Do you want to press charges?"

He looked at me. "You broke a table."

"With my back," I said.

"Can you pay for it?"

"You know I'm good for it—"

"Right."

"I can't make money in jail, Arthur."

He considered that. It's not precisely true. Even before trial, you can join a prison work force. But they pay a hundred dollars a day, and food, laundry, and rent cost ninety-eight. It's a great system for prison barons, but not so good for creditors.

"True." Arthur turned to Ling. "Thanks for responding so promptly, Sergeant. The club won't be pressing charges."

Ling nodded.

I said, "We're free to go?"

A copbot stepped up beside Ling. "Sergeant?" It put its head by her ear, and she glanced at the cat.

The cat looked around the room, then at me. I shook my head slightly. I would help her against Arthur's little carnivore club. I wasn't about to take on L.A.'s finest, what our Libertarian mayor proudly calls "the best police that money can buy."

Ling said, "Zoe Domingo?"

The cat said, "Yes."

Ling looked at Arthur and me. "She comes with us."

The cat said, "Don't I get any say in this?"

Ling looked at her with surprise. "Where are you from?"

"Minnesota."

"Oh, yeah. They passed some kind of critter rights bill, didn't they?"

The cat nodded.

Ling said, "You should've stayed there."

"I'm here as a visitor—"

Ling said almost kindly, "We won't sell you, girl. Not if you're innocent, anyway."

The cat glanced at me. That was my third and final chance to drop the case. But she had helped me with Arthur's pets when she didn't have to. I said, "I'm responsible for her."

"You haven't been doing that great a job." Ling shrugged. "All right. You can come along. But you're both getting searched, and any activity from the Pocket will be treated as a potentially lethal threat. *¿Comprende?*"

I raised my arms. A human cop patted me down, then smiled a bit too much as he headed for the cat.

Ling said, "I'll do it," and searched her. They didn't find anything interesting on either of us.

Arthur said, "Would you mind taking them out the back way?"

"Not at all," Ling answered, and I remembered that the casinos are major contributors to the Police Officers Association.

Bruno and his friends with fangs smiled as we passed. I ignored them and asked Ling, "What do you want her for?"

"Questioning."

I glanced at the cat. She looked away.

As we went through the back doors, a band began a Ragtime Revival tune in the main room. Chimera janitors and cleaning bots hurried in to begin tidying up. Within a few minutes of our departure, customers would once again be happily presenting their hard-earned money to the priests of the gods of chance.

A cruiser pulled up in the alley to meet us. Its doors sprang open and Ling said, "Hop in." The cat and I climbed in front, the doors closed and locked, and the cruiser drove silently away.

I looked back at the cops in the alley. "She didn't even wave."

"Can we get out of this thing?"

"If for some reason we wanted to—" I met the cat's slitted eyes. "We'd find the windows are shatterproof and the drive-box can't be opened without special tools. But since we're just trying to help the police with some problem they have, it's reassuring to know that we're safe in here. And if, God forbid, something put us in danger, we're fortunate that the car's microphones will pick up our cries for help."

"My. That is a relief." The cat leaned back in her seat, brought her knees up to her chest, and hugged her legs as she watched L.A. speeding by the window.

I watched the scenery, too. I know this town well, but it

was odd to travel the streets without stopping to pay to use any of them. The cruiser slid into the automated lanes of the Ventura Tollway, and we raced silently at two hundred kilometers an hour toward downtown.

2

It was a night for back doors. The next on the tour belonged to the new police headquarters. Two cops—one human, male and beginning to wrinkle, and one bot, sexless and stainless—met our cruiser. There's nothing impressive about the rear entrance, beyond the fact that its smooth surfaces must be easy to clean. Below a Christmas wreath, someone had slapped a small sticker on the glasteel door that read "Garbage in, garbage out."

The copbot directed us through the building with simple commands: "Forward, left, halt." The cat kept me between her and the bot, and she watched it constantly. A few states had banned copbots, but I couldn't remember if Minnesota was one.

The human cop never said a word as we walked a long hall, then rode the elevator. Since we weren't exactly prisoners and we weren't exactly guests, his compromise between intimidation and civility was that all-purpose emotion of the underpaid civil servant, boredom.

They left us in a small waiting room with a holovision set. I looked out. A copbot stood at attention in the hall. I tried the door. Locked.

The cat dropped onto a couch and said, "Any idea how long we wait?"

"They have any reason to be nice to you?"

"No."

"Me, neither."

So we watched HV. Adam Tromploy, KCAL's digicaster, who seems as artificial to me as any human news anchor, gave us the day's events, starting with the proposed Chimera Rights Resolution. It was facing fierce challenges in the U.N.'s General Assembly; the likelihood of passage was "not good."

"Some surprise," the cat said, curling up on the couch and closing her golden eyes. "Like the genomeries would free their property out of the goodness of their hearts."

The next news item brought her to the edge of the couch—a werewolfing in an Italian restaurant in New York City, the fifth in that city this year. The restaurant's securitycam caught most of the action.

A shaggy apeman in a busboy's uniform was carrying dishes through a room filled with human diners when he staggered. His tray slipped from his hand. Plates, glasses, and cutlery clattered onto the hardwood floor as he doubled over, clutching his chest. Customers turned and stared. A human in a white jacket, probably the maitre d', hurried up to him, looking angry. Then the apeman reared up. Before the human could speak, the apeman snapped the guy's neck, threw him against the dessert cart, and tore into a man and a woman at the nearest table.

In less than thirty seconds, the ape killed four humans and a dogwoman waiter who tried to stop him. Her sacrifice gave everyone else time to get out. When the cops arrived, they opened fire with bullets, not sleep darts. The first shots barely slowed him. He tore open a copbot before he finally fell under the hail of police fire.

As medics carried out the dead and wounded in the background, a man in a bloody shirt gave the usual werewolfing victim's spiel. One, it attacked anything that moved. Two, how could anyone want to give critters equal rights when one of them might begin a killing spree at any time?

In the interest of the appearance of balanced reporting, some guy came on with a subtitle proclaiming him a real scientist. He gave the usual chimera expert's spiel. One, statistically, genetically enhanced creatures are not significantly more likely to go berserk than humans. Two, we've given chimeras our virtues; should we be surprised if they have our vices, too?

The cat's eyes closed again when Tromploy began talking about AIs competing for the world chess championship in Jerusalem. I could've dozed then, too. The contest may've officially been between Indigo 74 and AI-LL23C, but it seemed more like free advertising for Chain Logic and Apple IBM, the companies that designed them.

I looked out the door again. So far as I could tell, we had been forgotten. I said, "Why me?"

The cat answered without opening her eyes. "I didn't take you for the philosophical type."

"I wasn't asking why I had to have my game interrupted—"

"Which you would've lost anyway."

"Without getting in hock to you."

Her eyelids flicked open as she gave me a sideways glance, dark slitted pupils at the edge of golden eyes. "Refresh my memory. When did I force you to take all of my money?"

One point for the cat. I turned back to the HV.

We watched the usual unpromising news about efforts to restore the ozone layer and another border dispute between North and South California over homeless people heading north for welfare benefits. The Chief Justice announced that the Supreme Court would consider whether the laws of the Arizona theocracy were in violation of the First Amendment, Arizona's Christian Party governor announced the state legislature would consider whether the Supreme Court was in violation of the Decentralization Amendment, and the President's spokeswoman said no federal troops would be sent to impose the will of nine old men and women on the free people of Arizona. Then the chairwoman of one of the human football leagues complained about the growing popularity of the chimera league, saying that for their safety, chimera players ought to wear helmets and padding like their counterparts in the human leagues.

"*Que* altruist," the cat said.

When Elvis and Marilyn sims began singing about the cocaine being back in Coca-Cola, I turned to the cat and tried again. "What I meant was, why'd you come to me? Or is that something you'd rather not talk about now?"

"I called some other agencies. The first three were very friendly until they heard I was calling for myself, not my owner."

"You've got an owner?"

"No. I called four more detectives with the camera turned off. None of them would work for cash."

"Why'd you think I'd be any different?"

"I was calling from a bar in Crittertown. The Tavern of Dr. Moreau."

It's a small place on Lankershim with cheap beer, no decor to mention, and, every Tuesday night, a house band consisting of four chimeras and a human on sax that played the finest wildsong in L.A. They didn't welcome humans, but they didn't discourage us, either. One afternoon, I overheard a chimera ask, "What's a skin doing in a fur bar?" and the weaselman behind the counter answered, "Keeping his tab paid up. Which is more than I can say for some."

I didn't think anyone at Moreau's knew my name, but the cat anticipated that question. She said, "I asked the barman if he knew any detectives who would work for chimeras. He said there was a skin that might be worth a call. He dug your card out of a big glass bowl, some kind of drawing for dinner for two at Beauty and the Beast's. That's when I got your recording."

"I hope you put the card back in after you called."

She smiled at that. "Relax, Mr. Maxwell. I did."

"Call me Max."

The smile faded.

"Or don't, Ms. Domingo. You're the client."

She nodded. "It's nothing personal. You have a policy about working for chimeras. I have a policy about humans with policies about chimeras."

"I broke mine."

"Because you can't afford to pay me back. If you'd known what I was, would you have taken my case?"

There were a lot of things I might've said. I settled for the truth. "No."

"I don't see any reason to compromise my principles, Mr. Maxwell."

"*You're* claiming the moral high ground, when you presented yourself as—" I remembered that the room had to be bugged and stopped the sentence there. I glanced twice at the ceiling to remind her that they would love for us to give them something useful.

She glared at me, breathed once in exasperation, then breathed again more calmly and said, "I needed to get to you as soon as possible."

"Ah. Necessity is a principle now."

"What would you know about necessity?"

"I know that principles you abandon in the face of necessity don't deserve the name."

"That's easy for a human to say, Mr. Maxwell."

I looked at my watch. Zoe Domingo would be my client for another twenty-two hours and ten minutes. I said, "Did I mention I get eight hours off for sleep, an hour each for meals, and as many bathroom breaks as I want?"

She smiled, baring very white teeth. What do you call the canines in a cat? Her teeth, like so much of her, passed for human at first glance. But her fangs, like those of her forebears, had been designed to rip flesh from her prey. "If we're both lucky, Mr. Maxwell, it won't take you long to find what I'm after."

A home repair show followed the news. Neither of us got up to see if it was possible to change the channel. If I ever have a house with gutters, I'll be able to take great care of them.

A human cop saved me from learning how to take equally great care of tile grout. She was short, stocky, and a little more communicative than her predecessor. She seemed to have decided to treat us like guests you could shoot if they misbehaved. "Mr. Maxwell? Zoe? This way, please."

The cat kept her eye on the bot backing up the human. I began to wonder about Minnesota's policy on bots in general. Some people don't like them, the way some people get the creeps from dolls and puppets. But copbots are humanform in silhouette only. Okay, they have optics where a human's eyes would be so they can send stereoscopic images to CityCentral. Still, they look as lifelike as a wooden artist's mannequin. No one would look at a copbot and see any kind of mimicry of life.

Then I thought about the way house cats chase light from laser pointers. I had no idea what Zoe Domingo saw when she looked at a copbot or what she considered a mimicry of life. Bots move, don't they? The apeman that werewolfed in New York had torn into a copbot with the same berserker glee that it had shown its biological prey.

The second cop duo brought us to a small room with a table, four uncomfortable plastic chairs, and a monitor mounted high on the wall. Classical music played in the background, something almost soporific. The walls were sky blue, a soothing color, but that and the music did not make this a soothing room. The closest thing to decoration was a "No smoking" sign bought cheap from an office supply site. I'm sure there's a room in police headquarters where they would bring the governor if they needed to question her about something. This wasn't it.

The cat took a chair and closed her eyes. I was getting envious. I watched her nap and wondered what I had gotten into. I had just decided to light a cig and see whether the smoke would summon anyone when two men entered.

"Mr. Maxwell? I'm Detective Vallejo. This is my partner, Detective Chumley." Vallejo was a small, round man in a business suit that absorbed light. My first thought was that he wore it to look thinner. But nullight is expensive—if he'd wanted to be thinner, he clearly could've afforded the occasional visit to a body shop. His voice was pleasant, with a hint of an accent, his tone was polite, and his smile looked sincere. I knew I was supposed to like the guy, but I did anyway.

Chumley looked like he'd walked out of a museum exhibit for the theory of human evolution. If he grew a beard and got a forehead tat, your only question would be whether he had gorilla or baboon genes. My vote would've been for gorilla. I first thought his suit was cheap because he hit a body shop every week. Then I saw that his hands were hard like a fighter's and decided that his muscle came the hard way, and the cheap suit was a badge of honor. Or maybe it was to annoy his more fashionable partner. Or maybe it was just to say that he didn't want to get anything on good clothes, like your blood.

Chumley's expression of perpetual constipation told me I wasn't supposed to like him. Stifling the impulse to assure him he was doing one hell of a job, I stood and offered my hand. "What can we do for you, detectives?"

Vallejo's grip was firm, to emphasize that he was more than a dandy. Chumley's was gentle, to let me know that he didn't need to use his strength to threaten me.

The cat had risen when I did. Both detectives ignored

her. Vallejo indicated the chairs. "We need to ask Zoe some questions."

She nodded. "Of course."

I said, "And everything we say in here's going to be run through a lie detection program."

Chumley grinned coldly. "What do you think?"

I shrugged. "No one's got anything to hide."

As we all sat, Vallejo asked the cat, "You realize that it's a crime to fail to report a crime?"

She frowned. "What do you mean?"

Chumley said, "Should he try again in Spanish?" When she blinked at him, he added, "We pulled your file. We can tell you your litter number at Bionova's Panama branch and the names of everyone you were sold to. No one wants to keep you long, do they?"

She said, "English is fine. What crime did I fail to report?"

Vallejo said, "Tell us about Janna Gold."

"If you're asking, you already know."

Chumley said, "Humor us."

"She was my friend."

"Friend," said Chumley. "You've had the same address for two years. After you ran away from Fulltime Entertainment, she bought your papers and gave you your freedom. I'm guessing she was a little more than a friend, huh, pussycat?"

The cat studied him. "You don't know a lot about friends, do you, Detective?"

Vallejo smiled as he looked away from his partner.

Chumley said, "You and the doctor have some kind of spat? If there was trouble between you two, we'll find out about it."

"No," said the cat. "You can't think I'm responsible for—"

"You didn't report it. You abandoned your *friend*—"

Vallejo interrupted. "Given the circumstances, that might be understandable."

Chumley frowned at him. "Yeah, right."

Vallejo said, "Did Dr. Gold have any enemies?"

"No," said the cat.

"There's no reason anyone would want her dead?"

"Not that I know of." When the detectives simply kept watching her, she added, "Doc tended to under-tip. That's no reason to kill her."

I wanted to tell her that her experience with necessity must not have included waiting tables, but I kept my place in the peanut gallery.

Vallejo said, "Who would benefit from her death?"

"She has a sister in Havana with a couple of kids. But they were close. They visited often. I can't believe her family had anything to do with it."

"If you're looking at people who inherit," said Chumley, "put yourself at the top of the list."

That was the first time I saw the cat look completely surprised. Her jaw dropped to speak, her eyes opened wide, her ears swivelled forward, and her head drew back as she stared at the detectives. It lasted an instant. She closed her mouth, narrowed her eyes, and relaxed her ears and shoulders, reverting to the dispassionate mask that most chimeras present in public.

Vallejo asked the obvious—one of the marks of a good detective. "You didn't know about the will?"

"I never thought to ask. Who's in it, and how much do they get?"

Chumley said, "Gold's not dead four hours, and you want to know what you've won."

The cat leaned forward. I prepared to tackle her if she went for Chumley's throat. She said, "I want to know who else might benefit. Doc may've under-tipped, but she could be generous, too."

Vallejo said, "There's three meg to you, three more to the

sister and each of the kids, and two meg to the Clean Seas Society. Everything else goes to the Chimera Advancement League. That includes her patents and copyrights."

The cat looked at her hands in her lap. I felt bad that the three of us were studying her so closely just then, but if you're not willing to feel bad, you shouldn't be in our line of work.

Chumley said, "Disappointed she didn't leave everything to the house pet?"

The cat flicked her gaze to him. "Most of it went to the C.A.L., right? I think she did."

Chumley nodded. That may've been the closest thing to embarrassment that he could manage.

Vallejo said, "Why'd you come to L.A.?"

"For a vacation."

"That's all?"

"So far as I know."

"Who do you know here?"

"No one."

"What about Gold?"

"She said there was someone we would visit. She didn't say who."

"You weren't curious?"

"Like a cat." She smiled, not so much at him, I thought, as at a memory. "She didn't want to tell. She could be like that."

Chumley said, "Secretive."

The cat shook her head. "She liked to surprise me."

Chumley jerked a thumb at me. "How'd you hook up with him?"

"He was the first detective I found who would work for a chimera."

Chumley turned to me. "You're not too discriminating."

I shrugged. "Look who I'm hanging out with now."

Vallejo said, "She hired you to find Gold's killer?"

I could feel the cat watching me. I nodded. "That's about the size of it."

"What've you learned?"

I laughed. "Hey, I got the job in the casino. You've known about this longer than I have."

Chumley turned back to the cat. "You went right to the phone and hired a detective rather than call the police."

"I don't like cop—" She held his gaze for the tiniest moment before she finished. "Bots."

Chumley scowled. Vallejo caught his arm and shook his head. "Let her have that."

Chumley grunted softly in agreement. "Tell us about the trip out here."

The cat shrugged. "We took a train out of Minneapolis this morning, caught the Daytripper in Chicago, arrived in L.A. at five-thirty local time."

"Uneventful?"

"I'd say so."

"Would the conductor agree?"

She frowned. "I got up to get Doc some water and left my ticket behind. The conductor thought I was supposed to be in third class. Doc told him I was with her. It was no big deal."

"He said you have an attitude problem."

"Well. He thought I should've been grateful for the chance to blow a real human in return for riding in first. Learning I had a ticket was a problem for his attitude, not mine."

Chumley grinned, not a pleasant sight.

Vallejo coughed, said "I see," drew a remote control from his jacket, and clicked on the monitor. "We have some interesting video from the security cameras. Care to tell us about it?"

The cat's eyes narrowed. She glanced at me. I gave her a tiny shrug, and she nodded to the detectives. "Why not?"

3

The monitor showed a still image of L.A.'s Union Station waiting room all decked out for Christmas, with holoangels carrying gift-wrapped packages back and forth below the ceiling. The waiting room was full of passengers, mostly human, but a few non- as well: a bot at the elbow of an old man, a plump pigman in a business suit, a trio of white ratwomen in nurses' uniforms. Two porters crossed in the foreground, a bot cart and a small, hairy man with a monkey tat. I refrained from asking if the monkeyman was a relative of Chumley's.

Vallejo put the remote control's pointer on the cat and an older woman who appeared to be entering from Track Nine. I glanced at the cat beside me as Vallejo zoomed in on her image. She watched the monitor impassively, as if she had shown enough surprise in this room.

The onscreen Zoe was dressed like the one sitting beside me, in the same short, iridescent green jumpsuit and silver boots, but she wore a black backpack. A suitcase rolled close to her heels like a faithful collie.

The older woman with her reminded me of my Aunt Dakota. That meant I was inclined to respect her without especially liking her. No taller than the cat, she looked sturdy. Her gray hair was clipped short, she wore no makeup, and she had let her skin wrinkle naturally. She wore a tweed suit and brown walking shoes, as if she'd rather be in England's

Lake District than L.A. A dozen earrings in each ear were her only concession to vanity.

"Well?" said Chumley.

"That's us," the cat agreed, then said, "Wait!" She jumped up, went to the monitor, and pointed at a man in the background who was watching the news in a rental holochair. "Can we see his face?"

Vallejo put the crosshairs on the man and hit reverse. The man got out of the chair and raced away backward. Vallejo hit play, and the man walked forward in perfect silence.

I said, "Who erased the audio?"

Chumley looked at me like I was a bug on a just-washed windshield. "We've got audio."

Vallejo said, "Mostly crowd noise and P.A. music. If you want to hear that—"

"No thanks." The music in the stations consists of ads disguised as technofolk dance tunes. Someone could make a fortune selling ear plugs to commuters. But while I was glad to miss the latest creations of the jingle meisters, I was also sure the cops had more useful audio than they were admitting. Sound filtering and lip-reading software would give them large pieces of what was being said onscreen. I hoped the cat realized that nothing would please them more than catching her in a lie.

She still stared at the man on the display. He looked young and physically fit. There was nothing special about his beige water-look suit. Perhaps the most distinctive thing about him was the pair of mirrored See-alls hiding his eyes.

"Doyle," the cat said, with an edge to her voice. Vallejo freeze-framed. Doyle had conventionally handsome features and short brown hair parted on the side. He looked like someone who would be encouraged by his friends to become an actor or a model because he photographed well. He wasn't memorable enough to become a star. He looked like the nice guy that the girl dumps when she realizes she's destined for a wonderful life with the male lead.

"You'd met him earlier?" Vallejo asked.

"No," said the cat. "I didn't realize we were being watched."

Vallejo hit play. When the cat and Janna Gold reentered the waiting room, he clicked the crosshairs on the cat. The computer began tracking her. She waited while Gold looked around the room, then said something to her. The cat pointed at a subway sign. As they headed toward it, passing a café with a "Humans only" sign, Chumley said, "Well?"

Vallejo let the video play while the real-time cat answered, "Doc wanted to know if I'd like to get a cab. I told her the subway would be—" Her voice caught. She closed her eyes, bit her upper lip, took a deep breath, then looked back at the detectives. "—more fun."

Onscreen, at the entrance to the subway system, Gold fingered the largest of her earrings, then released it and glanced over her shoulder. As the cat raised both eyebrows her way, I recognized the black opal earring that I now carried in the Pocket.

Gold smiled reassuringly at the cat and followed her into the subway tunnel. The rush hour traffic included a copbot heading in the same direction. As the cat disappeared from view, Doyle stood and walked away.

Another camera picked up the cat in the tunnel. She waited while Gold tapped her thumb twice against a scanner. Then they proceeded into the station.

A third camera caught them stepping onto a slidewalk that carried them down a long tunnel. On the walls, posters flickered to life, advertising guardbots, sex clubs, rates on indentured servants, and the opportunity to live in domed communities. The onscreen cat winced as they passed a poster with attractive G-stringed chimeras shimmying on a stage. I knew the cat was new to the city then; Angelenos no longer notice the announcer shouting, "At Dr. Do-Lot's, you don't just talk with the animals!"

The cat and the older woman met a flurry of commuters heading in the opposite direction, which meant they had just missed a train. At the end of the tunnel, they stepped off the slidewalk and turned the corner toward the platform. As they went out of sight, the copbot followed them into the tunnel.

Vallejo over-rode the computer tracking so we could watch the copbot. It opened a plate on the wall and flipped the switch inside. A steel gate slid out to block the tunnel, sealing the bot in with the cat and Gold. A sign on the side of the gate read "Temporarily Out of Service."

I frowned. A copbot closing off access to a subway platform suggested an official operation in progress. But if the police wanted Gold and the cat, why hadn't they been arrested in the waiting room?

The image cut to a subway platform, empty except for the cat and Gold. As Gold looked down the tracks for a train, the cat led the powered suitcase to a bench, then shrugged off her backpack and set it on top of the suitcase.

Gold returned to the bench. She and the cat began to talk, apparently quite casually. The detectives and I looked at the cat in the room. When she looked away, Vallejo stopped the video. "I know this is difficult—"

The cat sat up as if stretching her spine. "Let it play." As the silent conversation resumed onscreen, she provided the narration. "Doc said she was going out after we checked in. I asked her what I'd be doing. She said I never had trouble finding some fun. I told her I thought we'd both be finding some fun on our first night in town. But she said she had to talk to a friend about a project."

The image froze again. Vallejo asked, "What project?"

The cat shook her head. "Doc worked on lots of things.

When I asked her about them, the language got technical fast. I quit asking."

"She must've mentioned some names."

"All the time. But I don't know who she was referring to then."

Chumley said, "She worked for the big robotics firms: Seimens, Chain Logic, Singer, Sony. Any of them come up?"

"Not like there was anything special about any of them."

Vallejo hit play, and the cat continued narrating. "Doc said she wouldn't be long. I said, 'Fine, I'll tag along.' She said she wanted her friend to tell her she was imagining things, and then maybe we could all get a drink together. I asked— Stop it."

Vallejo paused the two in mid-discussion. The cat said, "Can we skip the next part?"

Chumley shook his head. "We need to know you didn't forget something."

She looked at me. I didn't like it, but I nodded. This was her best chance to convince the police she was innocent— and her best chance to convince me, too.

She said, "Okay. I asked Doc if I would like her friend. She said she thought so. Then—" Zoe bit her upper lip. On the display, Gold smiled as she said something. Her smile died without warning when something small zipped by her and smacked against the far wall. The next one struck her neck— a police sleep dart. Gold's mouth opened in surprise and fear. Then she sagged as the drug took effect.

The onscreen cat gasped something, probably Gold's name, and caught her. She pulled the older woman behind the shelter of the bench, plucked the sleep dart from her neck, and, staying low behind the bench, looked around.

Vallejo zoomed out so we could see what she saw. The copbot stood at the entrance to the platform, one arm raised, its dart gun extended from its wrist.

Chumley said, "It give any warning?"

The cat shook her head. "No. After it shot Doc, it said something like 'Citizen, step away from the bench.' I yelled that we weren't doing anything."

That's when I began to realize how much trouble the cat was in. Maybe that was when she had begun to realize it, too. In the playback, she stayed crouched beside Gold. The back of the bench shielded them from the security cam as well as the bot, but I could see the cat grip Gold's hands, then shake her.

Vallejo said, "What's going on?"

"I was trying to wake her. I couldn't." As the bot moved toward the women's bench, the cat told us, "It said this was my last warning to move away from the bench."

Chumley said, "Why didn't you?"

Vallejo hit the freeze-frame as the cat answered. "Even in South California, cops are supposed to warn you before they shoot, right? If you're human, anyway?"

Chumley nodded. "If you're human, anyway."

Vallejo said, "What did Gold give you?"

"What do you mean?"

Vallejo hit the rewind and zoomed in. On the bench, Janna Gold brought her hand to her head, then seized Zoe's hands. Then her hand fell limp as her eyes closed.

Chumley said, "There. It looks like she gave you one of her earrings. What's the story?"

The cat shrugged. "I wish I knew. What's the big deal about an earring?"

Vallejo said, "That was my next question. Why do you think she gave it to you?"

"Maybe she thought it was lucky."

"Where is it?"

"I don't know."

Vallejo's frown suggested that being nice now didn't mean he would be nice forever. "Oh?"

"It disappeared later on. There was a lot going on."

"A dying woman gives something to you, and you lose it."

"You don't have to try to make me feel worse. I want it back, whatever it is."

Vallejo and Chumley were quiet. My bet was they had audio implants updating them on what the lie detection software made of the cat's statements so far. I hadn't noticed any outright falsehoods. Apparently their software hadn't, either.

"Seeing what kind of luck it brought Gold," Chumley said, "you might've been lucky you lost it."

Vallejo hit play. Onscreen, the cat glanced at the copbot marching toward them. Her eyes were wide with fear or desperation. She shook Gold, then put her fingertips to Gold's throat, then put her cheek beside Gold's, listening, perhaps, or hoping to feel a breath. Then she flung her head back. Her mouth opened wide, contorting her face in what must've been a terrible roar of rage and loss.

I started to ask if Gold was really dead, but the cat looked away from the viewer at that moment, giving me my answer. I said, "Any idea what was in the rogue bot's dart?"

Chumley's glance said I should remember that my presence was tolerated, not welcome. Vallejo said, "Standard sleep serum. But not the standard dose."

On the viewer, a train pulled into the station as the copbot reached the bench and peered over it. The cat, crouched by Gold's still body, looked up. The copbot's dart gun swung down toward her.

The cat vaulted the bench, knocking the bot's arm aside and driving the heels of her silver boots into its pristine torso. The bot crashed backward. The cat leaped onto it before it could rise. She straddled its chest and slammed its steel skull against the pavement again and again. One of its optics cracked. So did the tile beneath its head.

The bot flailed an arm, hitting the cat's shoulder. She skidded across the platform toward the subway car's opening doors. A few passengers bolted for the safety of the tunnel, but most stayed huddled in the train. A copbot was struggling to control a chimera. The conclusion was obvious.

The bot rose smoothly and advanced on the cat. She scrambled to her feet and sprinted to the nearest car. The bot fired as she jumped inside. Its darts shattered against the closing doors.

The monitor image cut to the train's interior. The bot jammed a steel arm between the closing doors. They sprang apart, and the bot stepped in. The doors bounced shut behind it.

The train started with a lurch. The cat squeezed by frightened passengers as she ran for the rear of the car. The copbot aimed its dart gun toward her, and a passenger opened his mouth in a scream. Given the crowd and the moving train, any shot at the cat was more likely to hit a human.

As the bot retracted its dart gun into its forearm, the cat continued the narration. "It said something like 'Warning, that chimera has werewolfed.'" Their worst fears confirmed, the passengers panicked, madly pushing each other out of the way as the cat ran for the next car.

Another camera caught her entrance there. A boy fell in the aisle in front of her. She leaped over him. A young man lunged for her arm. His dreams of being the nightly news's hero of the hour died when the cat caught his wrist and shoved him back at the copbot.

She flung open a door marked "Unaccompanied chimeras must ride in the last car." The aisle before her must've been twice as packed as the previous ones. Most of these chimeras—dogs and cats primarily, but also apes, rodents, and swine—wore workers' uniforms: janitors, nurses, doormen, waiters, maids. Though their faces were marked with ID tats or covered with fur, they saw a copbot pursuing a chimera and responded with the same fear that the humans did. Werewolves don't discriminate.

The camera in this car showed the cat plunging into a sea of chimeras that parted madly before her. She knocked the few stragglers aside, only to reach the end of her course. The next door was the last. Beyond it lay the ever-receding, dimly lit tunnel.

The copbot stopped in the aisle and raised its arm. The dart gun extended itself—no chimera would file a complaint about police negligence if it was hit by a sleep dart, and maybe that was all the bot was shooting, now that Gold was dead.

Without looking back or slowing down, the cat wrenched open the final door and lunged through. A dogwoman gasped, then covered her mouth when the copbot turned its featureless head toward her. This was clearly a police matter. It was no business of hers if a suspect chose suicide over surrender.

The copbot ran to the rear door, leaned out, and turned its head from side to side, scanning the darkness for Zoe's body. Then it tilted its head upward.

A silver boot lashed down from above, striking the bot in the forehead. It staggered and nearly fell, then caught the door frame. The silver boot struck again, but now that the bot was braced, it didn't even shiver as the boot heel drove into it. It snatched the cat's ankle to drag her down.

A second silver boot thrust against the inside of the bot's elbow. The metal arm twisted under the impact, and both silver boots drew back up into the darkness.

The bot went through the door and scuttled up toward the roof like a steel spider—

—and Vallejo froze the frame.

"Hey," I said. "Do I deposit two Cs for the next install-ment?"

Vallejo asked the cat, "What happened up there?"

She pursed her lips and glanced at me. I shrugged. I

wanted to know the same thing. She told Vallejo, "We played chase."

"How?"

"There are things to grip on the roof. Maintenance hand-holds, air conditioners, stuff like that."

"How long did this chase last?"

"Not long. I got lucky."

"Oh?"

"It fell off."

"Yes. In front of a passing train."

"That was the luckiest part."

Chumley said, "You sure you didn't help it fall?"

The cat glanced downward in a fair imitation of innocence.

Vallejo said, "What happened next?"

"I hung on until the next station."

Chumley said, "Would've been easy to lose the earring up there."

The cat hesitated. "Sure. But it disappeared later."

Vallejo clicked the remote again. Passengers walked quickly away from a train leaving the North Hollywood stop. As it picked up speed, the cat dropped from the roof of the last car to land lightly on the platform.

She stood, brushing herself off. Something bumped her from behind, and she jumped three feet away, crouching as she whirled to face this new danger. It was only a Ti-D-Bot after a gum wrapper at her feet. It swept up the gum wrapper and rolled away.

The cat straightened up and smoothed her hair as if she had intended to jump. She looked around, saw no one in sight, then took something small and dark from her pocket. Walking toward the exit, she fiddled with it like a kid with a toy with moving parts.

She stopped abruptly. The man from the waiting room, in his opaque See-alls, stepped onto the platform. Two copbots followed him. The cat took a step back and glanced over her shoulder. Before she could bolt for the train tunnel, he held out a police ID.

At Chumley's glance, the cat explained, "He identified himself as Inspector Doyle. He said the bot that killed Doc was malfunctioning, and Doc was helping him in an official investigation."

Vallejo said, "Of what?"

"He didn't say." On the viewer, the cat lowered her hand to her side and took another step back from Doyle. "He wanted Doc's earring. I asked him if he had a warrant. He said he didn't want to arrest me."

Chumley said, "Nice guy."

"Yeah." The onscreen cat raised her fist as if to throw down the thing in her hand. "I said I'd rather not see if it broke if I stomped on it. But if he didn't back off, I would."

Doyle lunged for her wrist. The cat straight-armed him, knocking him back into a copbot, and turned to flee. The second copbot grabbed her arm. She jerked free. Something small, dark, and round fell from her hand.

The cat dove for it. The copbots reached for it, too.

The black sphere hit the floor with a click. The bots froze like statues. One toppled onto Doyle, breaking his See-alls and pinning him down.

Vallejo paused the action. Chumley said, "Make a wild guess as to what stopped the bots."

The cat said, "They ran outta gas?"

"Funny. Now think what fun you'll have doing five to ten for concealing evidence."

"What evidence?"

Vallejo zoomed in on the black sphere on the subway floor. Chumley said, "Sure looks like Gold's earring."

The cat said, "I told you. It disappeared."

"In the station?"

"Later."

"Where?"

The cat glared at him in exasperation. "I had it in the station. It's gone now. It disappeared somewhere in-between. Is that so hard to figure out?"

Vallejo said, "We're trying to help you, Zoe."

"Do you take turns at Good Cop, or did he lose today's coin toss?"

Chumley smiled. "Nah, I'm an asshole by nature."

Vallejo said, "Most of Gold's work was in artificial intelligence. What's that suggest?"

I said, "That there isn't enough real intelligence to go around?"

Chumley frowned and asked Vallejo, "Why'd we let him stay?"

Vallejo glanced at me. "Because we're trying to do this like nice guys."

He zoomed out and hit play. Onscreen, the cat snatched up the earring, looked at it with surprise and curiosity, then looked up as Doyle shoved the toppled copbot aside and stood. His broken See-alls fell from his face, revealing faceted sensors where his eyes should be.

For a second, I thought it must be a borgie fashion statement. But if Doyle was a borgieboy, he wouldn't hide optical enhancers under See-alls. He would wear them proudly or leave them home. A human who wasn't borg-obsessed and needed eyes would get donors or synths. Only one reason for Doyle's eyes made sense. No wonder the cops were concerned.

Vallejo and Chumley had viewed the video at least once while we were sitting in the waiting room. The cat had already lived it. I was the only one watching now who was surprised. The onscreen cat must've been as surprised as I was, but she only tightened her lips and narrowed her slitted eyes.

Doyle drew a Beretta Recoilless 9mm from a shoulder

holster, aimed it at the cat's heart, and spoke. The cat filled in, "He said I could see why the earring shouldn't get in the wrong hands. I started to ask him if it shut down bots, why didn't it affect him, but I figured that out."

So did I. Doyle wasn't controlled from CityCentral. He was an artificial intelligence passing as human.

Doyle gestured for the earring with remarkably human impatience. The cat tossed it toward him, just a little beyond his reach. As he stretched for it, she grabbed his arm and wrenched the Beretta from his grip.

Doyle lunged for her. She fired, shredding synthskin from his shoulder, baring a network of cables and wires, but failing to slow him. He grabbed her arms and slammed her against a pillar. She grunted, then, bracing her back against the pillar, brought up both feet and kicked against his chest. He flailed backward, releasing her.

She landed easily and aimed the Beretta at him. He stood erect, smiled, then stepped toward her. The cat said, "He said he was backed up. He asked if I was."

Doyle took her throat in both hands. She emptied the Beretta into his neck. Synthskin tore, then polycarbon struts broke away. Sparks fountained like an Independence Day display as bullets ripped through power and data lines in his carbon-fiber spine.

The cat kept squeezing the Beretta even after bullets quit coming from it. Doyle still stood grinning at her, his fingers tight around her throat. If she hadn't been sitting beside me, I would've sworn it was over for her.

Then Doyle's head wobbled. It swung around once. The last of the synthskin ripped from his neck. The head fell at the cat's feet, bounced across the platform, and came to a stop five yards away. The body remained upright, still clutching the cat's throat.

She gulped air as she pried Doyle's fingers away. She jumped back, caught her breath, then gave the body a tentative push with the barrel of the Beretta. The body rocked and fell backward, hitting the floor and vibrating like a frying pan dropped in the kitchen.

The black opal earring lay half under Doyle's severed head. The cat crept up on it, ready for the head to speak or bite or morph into something deadly. A spark spat out of its neck, and the cat jumped aside like, well, a startled cat.

She reached out, picked up the earring, then poked the head with the Beretta. When Doyle remained dead, she lifted the head high by its hair, peered into its blank eyes, and said something. At our collective glance, the cat, looking a little embarrassed, repeated her line, "Hasta la vista, Yorick."

She dropped the head and ran for the exit. A hall camera revealed a sliding gate blocking her way and a gaggle of frustrated commuters standing in front of it. She jumped onto the gate, scrambled up and over it, and landed among the commuters. The cat said, "I told them you'd think someone'd check more carefully for passengers before shutting a station down."

The monitor went blank. Vallejo turned to the cat. "After that?"

"You must know the rest."

Chumley said, "Indulge us."

"I caught a cab to Crittertown, found a phone, and called Mr. Maxwell."

I waggled my hand. "That's me."

Chumley said, "Honest people would call the cops after something like that."

I said, "Copbots kill her friend and go after her, and she doesn't go to the police? Golly."

Chumley looked at me. "We don't have to do this with you here."

Which was true. I said, "Carry on, McGruff."

Vallejo told the cat, "We have video of you getting into the cab. You say you lost the earring after that?"

She nodded.

"We checked the cab."

"If I lost it there, another passenger could've found it."

"We're checking on that."

"It could've disappeared in the casino. All I know for sure is that I don't have it now."

Chumley turned to me. "Hey, Mr. Answers. Where do you think it is?"

"You got me."

"Let me get this straight. You don't know where this earring is?"

Had he asked if I knew how to get it, I don't know what I would've said. That one was easy. "You're getting it. I don't know where the earring is."

Their lie detection program must've suggested that we weren't being entirely forthcoming, but they didn't need software to figure that out. And that didn't necessarily mean anything. Everyone's got something they'd rather not discuss with the police. Chumley looked at Vallejo, then at the cat. "Let's hear the story again. From the top."

She said, "With feeling?"

Chumley frowned at her.

I said, "She's told you everything you don't have on video. It's time to charge us or watch us walk."

Vallejo said, "You're free to go anytime."

Chumley said, "If you don't want to help the police."

I said, "The security cam shows Gold being killed by a copbot. Which then attacked my client. What more do you want? She's a victim, not a suspect."

Vallejo said, "We've got the bots that went after her. Someone reprogrammed them."

The cat said, "I didn't think anyone could reprogram copbots."

Vallejo said, "Neither did we."

Chumley said, "But if anyone could, Janna Gold could."

I said, "You're suggesting suicide?"

Chumley said, "I'm not suggesting anything yet. But if Gold could reprogram copbots, maybe kitty learned how, too."

The cat gave him a "what rock did you crawl out from" look. I said, "For the lousy three meg she would inherit?"

Vallejo said, "People kill for less."

Chumley said, "Maybe she wanted the same gadget that Doyle AI wanted. Something that shuts down bots would bring a hell of a price. Enough that some people wouldn't mind killing off an old lady or two. Especially if you could keep your hands clean by having a bot and an AI do it for you."

Before the cat could respond, the door opened. One of the most beautiful women I have ever seen stepped into the room. Her short hair was Scandinavian pale, her skin was Mediterranean dark, her cheekbones were Asian sharp. She was tall, and she moved with an athlete's grace. She wore a tailored black suit and opaque, charcoal-gray See-all's. If the Greeks had needed a goddess of high fashion, she would've had the job.

The cat sprang up. I saw her reaction and rose, tensing my wrist for a few milliseconds' advantage in case I needed the SIG.

4

The newcomer smiled and lifted both hands. "Don't shoot, I'm on your side. Kris Blake, Technology Crimes Division." If she had been an actress, her agent would've told her to deepen her voice and lose the hint of a coastal Californian accent. I liked it. You can only stand so much perfection in a person. I didn't like it enough to relax, but I held off on opening the Pocket.

The cat stepped back from Blake. "Ditch the shades."

"My eyes are sensitive."

"Ditch the glasses, or you'll be sensitive in lots of places."

Chumley moved toward the cat. "Sit down, critter—"

Before I could decide whether to intercept Chumley—the cat could clearly take care of herself, but that would only make things worse—Blake shook her head at him. "You saw the video, Detective. In her place, I'd suspect anyone hiding their eyes, too."

Blake removed the See-alls. Her sky-blue eyes watered as she blinked, but they were normal human eyes. Or perhaps I should say they were, like the rest of her, perfectly human, but decidedly better than normal. "Okay?"

The cat nodded. "Thanks."

Blake replaced the See-alls and shook hands with Vallejo. "Sorry I'm late. This isn't my usual shift."

Vallejo said, "Your office called. We appreciate the help. I'm Manny Vallejo."

Chumley took her hand next. "Dick Chumley. You saw the video?"

Blake nodded. "On the ride over. Anything to add?"

Chumley shrugged. "A lot of nothing. She doesn't know what the earring was, why Gold was coming here, or where the earring is now. Says she lost it after leaving the station."

Blake held out her hand to me. "Mr. Maxwell." Her grip was firm, warm, businesslike. "Have you been able to offer any insights?"

I smiled. "None that anyone's appreciated."

She smiled back. One of her teeth was a bit crooked, but otherwise her bright whites and pink gums were a testimonial to South California dentistry. I wondered how many men had suggested she become an actress, and decided I wouldn't be one of them.

"I'd like to show you and Zoe something." She glanced at Chumley and Vallejo. "If you boys are done?"

Vallejo nodded. "We've got nothing that can't wait."

Chumley told us, "Keep in touch."

I said, "How could we not?"

Blake opened the door. The cat and I glanced at each other, then headed out. I nearly bumped into her when she paused at the threshhold, looked back at the two detectives, and smiled. "I was never interrogated before. It was fun."

Chumley sighed. "Fun. Don't tell anybody, okay?"

Blake said, "This way," and headed down the hall. She had a walk that I could've followed anywhere, but I had other things to think about.

Blake was far enough ahead to be out of earshot. I stopped the cat with a hand on her arm. A few officers and a copbot passed by, paying us no mind. I whispered, "Interesting video. You were going to tell me about all that, right?"

"In my copious free time."

"What was Gold to you?"

She pulled away from me. "The only human I could trust."

I let her go. If she was telling the truth, I understood why she would do what it took to get Gold's killer. If she was lying, she was a better actor than most.

Blake waited for us at the elevators. As we descended, she said, "What do you know about the bot that was passing as human?"

The cat said, "Doyle? It wasn't a bot. It was an AI."

"Well, what's left is a chassis. Most of the circuitry's fried."

I said, "Any clues where it came from?"

Blake grinned. "You stole my question. It was pretty convincing as a human?"

The elevator stopped, and we got out. The cat said, "As human as any cop. But the eyes are the windows to the soul, right?"

Blake laughed. "Touché."

A short walk brought us to a door labelled "Laboratory." Blake looked into the blink box, and the door opened. She led us in.

In a small white room, a short, bald Indian man and a lab bot that looked like mobile emergency room machinery were peering into a headless humanform body laid out on a table. Cables had been pulled from the bisected chest like organs in an anatomy exercise.

The body was not meant to survive close inspection. It had nipples and a penis, but they were no more convincing than a department store mannequin's. Its skin was too smooth. It had no hair. Only its hands showed the attention to detail that would make you buy the illusion. They were weathered and chapped, like those of a guy who spent his weekends outdoors.

Judging from the video, the head was as good as the hands or better. Dressed and animated, Doyle had been convincing. Walking quickly through a crowd, he wouldn't inspire a second look. To the untrained eye, he would've been human; obviously, he had fooled the cat. On video, he had fooled me. But as I studied his artificial form, I doubted he would've fooled me in person.

Blake said, "Hey, Prof."

The man grinned. "Kris Blake. We finally meet."

"This is Zoe, the chimera that thing attacked. And Chase Maxwell, who she hired to look into this."

Prof nodded at us. "I won't be saying anything conclusive for a few hours yet, I suspect."

"Mind if we take a look?"

"Just don't forget to tip your tour guide."

"Thanks."

The lab bot wheeled backward so we could move closer. The cat said, "Where's its head?"

Blake said, "U.N. Security wanted it."

I said, "UNSEC? This is big time."

Blake nodded. "A copbot killed an unarmed human. Big time's an understatement."

"Did you get a look at the head?" I asked.

"Impressive work," Prof said. "Best animatronics I've seen. UNSEC probably can do more with it than we can, especially if it comes out of Japan or Europe."

Blake asked the cat, "Does seeing it remind you of anything you didn't tell Chumley or Vallejo?"

The cat shrugged. "It was more convincing dressed." She stepped closer to Doyle's body for a better look.

The lab bot said, "Electrical activity—"

The body sat up and flung out its arms, knocking Prof and the lab bot across the room. As the body swung its feet to the floor and turned toward the cat, I flexed my hand. The SIG slammed into my palm and fired. I held the trigger down. Slugs tore into the body's chest, stomach, and groin. The body twitched, but kept coming.

I stepped between it and the cat. The body snatched the

SIG from my hand and threw it across the room.

"Run!" I yelled. That's a thing you do at a time like that, as if you think the idea hasn't occurred to anyone else.

The laboratory door had closed behind us. I don't know whether it would've opened if the cat had tried it. She didn't. As the body reached for her, she kicked it in the chest.

It stumbled back. I shoved it, trying to knock it over. The body slapped the cat aside. One hand pinned me against the wall. The other hand gripped my gun arm as if to snap it off. Maybe it thought I carried a backup pistol in the Pocket. I did, once, until I hocked it.

All I could do was yelp in pain. Whatever I might've done next was made moot when Blake grabbed the body from behind and spun it away from me. It backhanded her as it fell, knocking her against the lab bot.

The cat and I circled the body. It rose and turned between us. I wanted to make a dash for the SIG, but that would've left the cat with no one to distract it.

Useless clever notions flashed through my mind. Start a fire so water from the sprinkler system would get in the body's damaged casing and short-circuit it—but I didn't see a way to make a fire, and the emergency system probably didn't use water. Trick the body into crashing through a window—but the windows were most likely glasteel. Keep the body moving until its power drained—but there was no sign that its batteries had been damaged. Hope the cavalry arrived soon—but I would've bet that the door was soundproof and almost no one passed by the lab at night. Pray for a miracle—but God just gets giggle-fits whenever I could use a miracle.

The body headed for the cat. As she jumped back, I started forward—to do what, I don't know; maybe to spit down Doyle's neck. The body whirled toward me.

Blake shouted, "Stand back!"—advice that I was already

taking. She'd unreeled a cable from the array of equipment built into the lab bot. As I dodged, she whipped it at Doyle's body.

The head of the cable struck the body's abdomen, slipped down, then stuck magnetically to its thigh. As the body closed a hand on the cable to rip it away, Blake jabbed a button on the lab bot's chest.

The head of the cable sparked. The body spasmed repeatedly, then took two drunken steps toward Blake. She held down one of the lab bot's power buttons, upping the output. The cable sparked more brightly. The body snapped upright, then toppled. It lay as still as it had been before.

The lab bot honked. We all turned toward it, except for Blake, who kept watching Doyle's body. The lab bot's indicator lights went out, and the cable connecting it to the body fell limp.

Blake said, "Prof."

A few tendrils of smoke rose from the open neck and multiple bullet holes in Doyle's body. Prof grabbed an extinguisher from a cabinet and sprayed foam down the body's throat.

I said, "So much for the electronic evidence."

Blake said, "Maybe I should've let it get you."

I glanced at her. "You're bleeding."

She touched a cut on her cheek and winced. "Just a scratch." She smiled. "I always wanted to say that." It was a nice smile.

I rubbed my arm.

She said, "You're hurt."

"Only my pride." I returned her smile with interest. "I always wanted to say that."

The cat, scowling, dusted herself off. "Well, whoopee for the Danger Twins. Is Robbie really dead this time, or should I add him to my Christmas card list?"

Prof said, "Twenty thousand watts to a machine with

damaged shielding? I think that's as dead as an AI can get."

I asked Blake, "You were sure the floor was non-conductive, weren't you?"

She shrugged and gave me another smile. "Pretty sure."

The lab bot's indicator lights came back on. Prof, pulling out a medikit from a cabinet, said, "You okay?"

Blake said, "I'm fine."

"Wasn't asking you."

The lab bot said, "I've rebooted. Next time, please turn me off with the shut-down command."

Prof took antiseptic and a swab from the medikit and headed for Blake. She held up a hand in protest. "That's really not necessary."

He nodded. "That's modern medicine for you."

The cat and I kept glancing at Doyle's body, but it never so much as twitched. I told Blake, "So, we've got an AI that could pass as human, and at least three copbots doing its bidding."

"Bidding," the cat said. "That's good."

I ignored her. "One of them definitely had no compunctions about killing people, and it didn't look like the others did, either. Any theories?"

Blake squirmed as Prof cleaned and bandaged her cut. "The neatest one's a Frankenstein scenario. Gold builds Doyle, an AI that can pass as human, but something goes wrong. He escapes and captures copbots that he programs to kill his maker. Gold suspects what he's up to, so she comes after him. Only he gets her first. But Zoe escapes, so the copbot sends a warning to Doyle, who's waiting at the next subway stop in case something goes wrong."

"How'd he get there so fast?"

"He must've had a flyer waiting for him. I doubt he would've hired one, but we'll check the records."

The cat said, "What if there's more than one Doyle? One at Union Station, one at North Hollywood?"

Blake winced more than she had when Prof applied the antiseptic. "Then my theory's not so neat. But the flyer's plausible."

I nodded. "Sure."

"So, under the single Doyle theory, he meets Zoe at the next station with all of his backup."

I said, "You're working mighty hard for this theory. There could be more altered copbots out there."

Blake shook her head. "Three copbots went missing around five P.M. today. One thing we're sure of is they're all accounted for."

The cat said, "Unless Doyle reprogrammed some others that still look like they're working normally."

Blake turned to Prof. "Can we run complete checks on every copbot in South California? Immediately?"

Prof said, "You've got it," and headed across the room for a phone.

Blake said, "Assuming there's one Doyle, any Trojan Horse copbots will need an activation code that'll never come. We should know in a few hours if any of them are infected."

I said, "What's the rest of your best-case scenario?"

"What you saw on the North Hollywood video. Doyle tries to get the earring from Zoe and fails. The only loose end is the earring itself."

"And evidence for the theory."

"There is that. Or should I say there isn't that?"

The cat said, "If Doc was working on a human-looking AI, why would she keep it secret?"

I said, "She must've had a nondisclosure agreement."

Blake added, "Most states have laws against making non-humans that can pass."

The cat said, "Sure. But if one escaped, she would've no-tified someone, law or no law. She wouldn't let something like that run around loose."

Blake said, "I know you'd like to think so. But our files are full of people who panicked and tried to cover up something they shouldn't have."

I said, "Gold said something about checking on a project with a friend. Finding the friend looks like the next step to me."

"Me, too." Blake looked at the cat. "Can you give us a list of the people you know she worked with?"

"As far as I know, none of them are in South California."

"Maybe one moved here." Blake indicated a computer terminal. "You can type it up there."

The cat nodded, took a seat, and began typing.

I asked Blake, "What's your worst-case scenario?"

"Absolute worst?"

I nodded.

"A private detective gets in the way and winds up dead while the bad guys escape."

"Ask Jody Frye in Missing Persons about me. I play fair, and I'm no glory hound."

"That's about all we can ask for."

"So what's your second-worst scenario?"

Blake glanced at the cat, bit her upper lip, then smiled and shook her head. "All right. Suppose there are more Doyles. Whoever built them might be changing their appearance as we speak. Maybe the bad guys are using them to remove anyone they see as a threat. If they think Zoe was Gold's partner, she just moved to the top of their list. And if they know you're working for her, you're just another loose end. I want her to have police protection. You should consider it, too."

"Ah, it's nice you care. But I can't."

"Why not?"

"It's part of the detective's code."

"Which part?"

"The part that says thou shalt not let the police hold thy

hand when thou art frightened, lest those who would become thy clients think thee an utter wuss. Letting a client accept police protection is different, of course."

The cat glanced up from the computer. "Thanks, but no thanks."

Blake said, "Accept it, and you're pretty much free to go where you want. Refuse, and I'll have a judge lock you up for your own safety."

The cat frowned at Blake. "I thought people could take any stupid risk they wanted since the Libertarians got elected."

"Just about," Blake said. "But you're not people."

"You've got my records! I'm free!"

"In Minnesota, maybe. Here that just means you can't be picked up as a stray and claimed by whoever finds you."

The cat closed her eyes for a moment. "I see."

"You'll accept police protection?"

She looked at me. I said, "What can it hurt?"

The cat nodded. "Okay." She sat back from the computer. "That's the list."

"If you think of anyone else—"

"Yeah. I'll let you know."

Blake looked at the monitor, then at me. "What's your e-mail?"

I told her, and she sent me a copy of the cat's list. We both knew the cat could recreate it with ease, but it was a nice gesture.

Prof returned from his phone call. "Virus scans are underway. If you're concerned, we could have every copbot examined over the next five days."

"No sooner?"

"You could pull them all at once, if you don't mind cutting the police force in half. We might have them back on the streets in less than a day."

Blake shook her head. "Okay, five days." She looked at

us. "You'll sign promises not to talk about this. Break the promise, and you both get put under protective custody somewhere unpleasant."

I said, "I love sweet talk."

Blake said, "My bosses might think I shouldn't give you a choice."

"Don't worry. I'll sign."

Blake and I looked at the cat. She sighed. "Ditto."

Blake glanced at the cat and me. "C'mon."

We headed for the front entrance. I took that as a good sign. The cat said, "When do I get my luggage back?"

"When we've finished going over it for clues." Blake heard the cat's sigh and added, "Tomorrow afternoon, most likely. We'll call when we're done."

"Well. It could be worse."

In the lobby, Blake said, "I need to make a few arrangements. Wait here."

While Blake went up to the main desk, the cat and I each took a different bench in the corner. We had the place to ourselves, which would've been nicer if it hadn't smelled like a drunk had slept there recently. I said, "What hotel were you going to stay at?"

"The Queen of Angels. Why?"

"Whose name was the reservation in?"

"Oh."

"None of the big hotels take unescorted chimeras. There's always the Range in Crittertown."

She frowned, and I remembered that the Range had a reputation for more than good restaurants and the best chimera entertainers. That's where furries—men and women who like sex with chimeras—prefer to go, either with a chimera date or in search of one.

I said, "I can't vouch for the rooms, but the main restaurant's great."

"It's not cheap."

"No. But you don't want a cheap hotel in Crittertown."

"That's all right. I know someone who said I should stay with her. I'll take her up on it."

I pulled out my phone. "Want to give her a ring?"

The cat hesitated.

I said, "If it's local, I won't even put the charge on your bill."

"No. She said to show up anytime."

Blake returned with a copbot in tow. The cat said, "You said police protection. You didn't say anything about a walking toaster."

Blake said, "Prof already checked this one. You can trust it."

The cat narrowed her eyes in doubt. Blake ignored that and handed me a computer and stylus. I signed a promise not to talk about the case until an arrest had been made or the department took it public. Then Zoe signed the same promise. Blake folded up the computer and put it in her pocket.

We left by the front door, with the copbot bringing up the rear. I put myself between it and the cat, but that didn't seem to make her any more comfortable. I understood why Blake had pulled a bot for guard duty—a human would've expected time-and-a-half—but I wished she had found an alternative. At that moment, keeping the cat in police custody and letting me spend the next day alone on her case sounded pretty good to me.

A Personal Rapid Transit station was in front of police headquarters. Three or four perts sat on the station's side rail, waiting for someone to press the call button. Blake did just that. A pert rolled forward. She put a pass in the card slot, the door slid open, and she gestured for us to get in.

The cat and I shrugged at each other and took the forward-facing seats; Blake and the copbot, the rear-facing ones.

The car said, "Destination, please?"

Blake glanced at us. The cat said, "I'm in no hurry. You go first."

I pressed the TALK button and said, "Lankershim and Vineland."

As the pert slid out onto the main rail, Blake said, "Crittertown?"

I nodded.

The cat said, "Hey! The person I'm staying with is just around the corner from there."

Blake said, "You're not getting a hotel room?"

"I'd rather not be alone."

"I thought you didn't know anyone here."

"I haven't met her. She's a friend of a friend."

"What's the address?"

"It's in my suitcase."

"Then what's her name?"

"Cyn Wharton. Only she's subletting."

"So how do you expect to find her?"

"My friend showed me a picture of her house. It's half a block from Lankershim, near Vineland. She said the neighborhood's total-hep."

I said, "It's cheap. Do Grove or Huston sound familiar?"

The cat said hopefully, "Huston?"

Blake sighed. "It's a nice night. Why shouldn't we spend it walking around Crittertown?"

I reached into my jacket for a pack of cigs. "Anyone mind if I smoke?"

"No," said Blake.

"Yes," said the cat.

"They're decarcinized," I said.

"They stink," the cat said.

I checked my watch. Just under twenty-one hours to go.

5

No one spoke for most of the trip to Crittertown. I was as content as anyone could be who desperately needed a nicotine fix.

I love cities when they slumber, when the streets are clear and quiet, and you can imagine what a place would be if its resources met the needs of its population. I love the PRT system, sliding along at seventy kilometers an hour, five meters above the ground, never slowing until you reach your destination. Riding a pert in daytime has its charms, especially at rush hour when you glide above the roofs of traffic-jammed commuters who think sitting alone in a steel box that you own is superior to public transportation that you use when you need it and someone else services and maintains. Of course, I might've felt differently if I could've afforded a steel box of my own.

Not everyone slept—cities may nap, but they never sleep. A kid in a second-floor bedroom waved as we passed, and the cat waved back. There are always at least a few cars on L.A.'s streets. One raced ahead of us to show its speed, only to stop and fall behind at a red light and never catch up to us again. Another pert joined our track, far ahead of us, then zipped away toward the Pacific. I had a pang of jealousy. If I wasn't on a case, I could've taken a pert up past Malibu and spent the night at a campground by the ocean.

We crossed the Santa Monicas, following the 101 Tollway

past the dark ruins of Universal City, then scooted up Lankershim. I couldn't enjoy the ride as much as I normally would. I was tired, the unmoving presence of the copbot was distracting, and I had an ever-growing list of questions to ask the cat when no one else was listening.

She had curled up in her seat as if to sleep, but when we passed a street light, I saw that she watched everything through slitted lids. What did she make of the city she saw? What sort of city would cat people make, if left to themselves?

I shifted my glance to Kris Blake. She also watched the city slip by. Shadows fell softly across her cheekbones and neck like a lover's caress. The top two buttons of her shirt were open. I admired the hollow of her throat, the rise and fall of her chest. She flicked her eyes in my direction, saw me looking at her, and smiled.

"The night's so clear," she said, and it was. A slight ocean haze had dimmed the downtown sky, but it hadn't climbed the Santa Monicas.

"One benefit of life in the Valley," I agreed.

"You like living here?"

I nodded. "I saw two owls on Ventura Boulevard a few weeks ago. A movie crew had cleared the street for a night shoot, and the owls were sitting up on a drugstore roof, just waiting to see if we were going to give the city back to them."

"They must've been disappointed when the shoot ended."

"Owls are patient."

"Would you like that? To give the city back to the wild?"

I shook my head. "I like cities, so long as there are plenty of parks in them. Give me clumps of cities and clumps of wilderness over global suburbia any day."

"Thomas Jefferson thought we should be a nation of farmers."

"He had his share of odd notions."

"Like being opposed to slavery, and never freeing his own slaves?"

"That's one."

"It's hard to have the courage of your convictions."

"If you can't act on them, what kind of convictions are they?"

Blake shook her head. "You set yourself a hard moral code."

The cat said, "Name an easy one."

Blake glanced at her as the pert switched to the Lankershim-Vineland side rail and slowed to a stop. The door opened. Since I was closest, I stepped out first and tapped a nic stick from its pack.

A couple of chimera kids waited on the platform. They were dressed nice, he in an iridescent red suit, she in an off-white gown. They must've danced until Pied Piper's had closed. Their faces were decorated with complex black and red designs that framed their forehead IDs—the law may've forced one tattoo on them, but it didn't stop them from getting more. The monkeyboy's face was fairly furry and semi-simian—his extra tats merely emphasized that he knew what he was. The doggirl had very human features—so far as I could tell, only her eyes would have prevented her from passing. Her extra tats let everyone know she had chosen her side.

I see kids who are passionate, arrogant, and optimistic, and I feel nostalgic. I smiled as I brought my cig to my lips. The doggirl must've thought I was being condescending. And maybe I was, a little bit. She scowled. The monkeyboy caught her arm. She said something dismissive about "skins," and that might've been the end of it.

But the cat was next out of our pert. The doggirl saw her, then glared at me. "Fucking furry!"

I shook my head and removed the cig. "Congratulations. That's inaccurate *and* redundant."

The monkeyboy told his date, "Leave it."

She told the cat, "Cousin, don't whore for skins."

Blake got out. "What's going on?"

I said, "It's just the welcome wagon."

The doggirl said, "Skins aren't welcome—" She stopped when she saw the copbot, last to leave the pert. "Forget it." We stepped aside so she and the monkeyboy could take the pert, but I knew that didn't make her feel any better. When you're sure the world's against you, it's hard for the world to prove it doesn't know you exist.

I pulled out my Swiss Army knife, clicked the lighter, and saw the cat looking at me. "Mind if I smoke outdoors?"

"Yes."

"Then walk upwind." I brought the flame to the tobacco and inhaled deeply, filling my lungs with sweet relief.

Blake, watching the chimera kids leave in the pert, said, "You get that often?"

I laughed. "Relax. We're going on four years without a riot in Crittertown. We just ran into one of the human-looking ones who—" I noticed the cat watching, realized I was halfway through one of my less diplomatic observations, and figured the best I could do was finish it. "Needed to prove she's more critter than thou."

I concentrated on smoking after that. It was a fine, fine cigarette. I had waited for it long enough, and it didn't disappoint me. I should've given it a name, say, Lucious Lucinda. Sometimes it's easier to remember a smoke or a meal than a person you once loved, badly, madly, sadly. Maybe the best times I had had with my wife were when we sat smoking together.

The old, white-furred catman at the newstand saw me and called, "Hey, Max, that copbot following you 'cause you had too good a time?"

"That copbot, Felix? It's not following me. Must be after you. Aren't you Mr. Goodtimes?"

He laughed. "That's me, all right. Mr. Goodtimes, uh-huh." He winked at my client. "That young skin get tuckered out, you come find me here, missy. In all my years, I never heard a complaint."

"That's because you're selectively deaf," I said.

Felix cupped his ear. "You say something, Max?"

We all laughed. I waved and said, "Not me. See you later, Mr. Goodtimes."

"Everybody does. I'm the Eighth Wonder of the modern world."

We walked up toward Huston Street. Blake said, "Quite a character."

"Uh-huh," said the cat. "A regular Uncle Tomcat."

"Ah," I said. "A real chimera would've arranged to be kept by a rich human, I suppose."

She gave me a cool smile. "I'm not going to fire you, Mr. Maxwell."

"Damn."

As the four of us trudged north, I hoped the cat would find this house of a friend of a friend quickly. She looked at the park and frowned. I wondered what she saw, but the only things there were trees, benches, a playground, and several hundred people sleeping on the grass.

"What's so interesting?" I asked.

"Homeless humans. But no homeless critters."

"There are stray critters around. But they aren't going to sleep where they can be rounded up easily."

"Why doesn't anyone round up the humans?"

I couldn't tell if that was a joke. I said, "Because they're free."

"Free to die of hunger or exposure."

"That's freedom."

"And the rich are free to keep all they can grab."

"That's part of freedom, too." I nodded at the camp of sleepers. "They own their bodies. The healthy ones can sell a kidney or a lung, or indenture themselves for a few years."

"You think that's right?"

"Right doesn't have much to do with the way the world is." I liked the sound of that line, but she kept looking at me. "What?"

"Nothing." She turned away with a grimace, as if she had bitten into something disgusting. I checked my watch. Twenty hours, twenty minutes. I would never go into debt on three kings again.

At Huston, we turned right. When we walked half a block, the cat said, "Hey. I knew this street sounded familiar."

She was looking at a small pink stucco house with a gravel walkway going around back. All of its lights were out.

Blake said, "Looks like your hostess went to bed."

The cat started toward the door. "Cyn said she might be out tonight. But she hid a key by the back door."

I said, "I'll walk you up."

The cat shook her head. "If she's in, you'll wake her. Leave Mister Transistor on the porch. I'll be fine."

Blake nodded. "We'll wait until you're in."

"I don't want to turn on the lights if she's asleep. I'll wave when I find the key."

I said, "Call me in the morning. First thing."

The cat said, "Don't worry. I'll get my money's worth."

The copbot followed her up to the porch as Blake and I watched. The cat told it, "Stay," and walked around back. The bot took a sentry's stance by the porch.

A moment later, the cat stepped out from the back of the house, waved once, then ducked back out of sight.

I said, "That's a relief."

Blake glanced at me. "You don't like your client?"

"I don't like a lot of my clients."

"I like her."

I blinked at that. "You do?"

"I'm always a sucker for a smart-ass." She smiled as if she didn't have any particular smart-ass in mind.

I began to believe this might be a great night after all. "I was going to say you didn't have to stick around. But if you'd like a cup of coffee—"

"Tea?"

"An excellent choice. Maxwell's All-night Cafe serves the best cup of tea that you can find in the Valley at—" I checked my watch. "Two thirty-three A.M."

She cranked the smile up another notch. "Perfect."

Heading for my apartment, I asked, "Mind if I smoke?"

"Not at all."

I tapped out another—I confess, I don't remember the sister as well as Lucious Lucinda, but she still took good care of me. After that first puff of heaven, I said, "Thanks for stopping the headless horselessman."

"You're funny."

"There's something a guy likes to hear."

"And you're fishing for compliments."

I shrugged, a little embarrassed at being caught.

She laughed and relented. "It would've been a shame if the bot damaged that nose."

"That's more like it. Why're you a cop?"

"A recruiter approached me in college. I liked the idea of using my computer skills to help people. That sounds hokey."

"Not at all. I'm glad you're staying for tea."

She grinned. "Hey, part of my job is making sure you haven't had unexpected company."

"No one's tried to kill me lately."

"Oh? What about the critters at Wonderland?"

"They just play rough. Dead men don't pay debts."

"Someone might think the cat passed you the earring."

"You think that's what this is about?"

"Could be."

"Maybe the earring's evidence of another crime."

"Such as?"

I shrugged. "Maybe we'll find out." I pointed at my building, a classic California two-story, complete with a dingbat on the front. "Home, sweet home."

I let her go upstairs first. Gentlemen say this puts you in position to catch the lady if she falls. Gentlemen know this puts you in position to admire the lady's butt. Kris Blake's was well worth admiring.

At my door, I said, "You really think there's cause for concern?"

"Better safe than sorry."

"True." My SIG leaped from the Pocket into my hand.

She stepped back in surprise, then laughed. "You're trying to make me jealous."

"Anything to impress the girls."

"Isn't that a bit scary—opening a Pocket so close to you?"

"I only open it when something else is scarier. And there's a cut-off to shut it down if living flesh is too near the field."

She drew her pistol from a shoulder holster. I almost admitted that I had fantasies about women with shoulder holsters, but discretion or embarrassment won out. She showed me hers. "Eleven-millimeter Vetterli Dual-Chamber Recoilless. Sleep darts in one chamber, explosives in the other."

"Could've used explosives on Doyle's body."

"Wouldn't have left much to study." She shrugged, a rather charming action. "Not that what I did was much of an improvement."

"You stopped it. I won't quibble about your method."

She smiled, then nodded at my SIG. "I hear Infinite Pockets are standard issue for UNSEC special forces."

"Mine was a blue-light special at Kmart."

She said more quietly, "Anyone inside will know we're coming."

I doubted anyone was in my apartment. If someone had opened a door or window since I left, a tiny red indicator light was supposed to glow on the access plate. But anyone who could tamper with copbots would laugh at a consumer home security system.

"I was giving them time to change their minds and leave." I gestured for her to back away, squatted down, then touched my left thumb to the access plate. The door slid open. Still crouching, I peeked in, gripping the SIG firmly in both hands and scanning over its sight.

I only saw familiar furniture. None of it threatened more than my reputation for good taste. I stepped in. Blake followed, Vetterli extended. We would've made a great instruction video for how to enter a potentially dangerous environment, but no one was there to admire our style.

I tapped the light switch twice to bring on every light in the house. Darkness would've been an asset against amateurs, but amateurs wouldn't have gotten past the security system.

The combination living and dining room (are there people who really think that living and dining are separate things?) was clean and almost bare—which was why it was clean. It held a wood-frame futon couch, a shelf unit full of research discs, an end table with a lamp and a couple of sailing magazines, and a folding kitchen table with two chairs. I liked knowing I could move out in an hour.

I waved for Blake to check the balcony while I glanced in the apartment's tiny kitchen. You would've had to send nanotech assassins to hide anything dangerous in there.

I saw movement out of the corner of my eye and turned fast. It was Blake, reflected in the glass door of the microwave. I let my breath out, caught her eye, and indicated the hall. She nodded and followed.

I gave the bathroom a glance, then jerked my chin toward

it to let Blake check the shower stall while I peeked in the hall closet. That put me in position to enter the bedroom first, which would let me pick up any dirty underwear I might've left on the floor.

The bedroom held a futon bed, a chest of drawers with a portable HV on top of it, and a noticeable shortage of ninja-bot assassins. I glanced in the closet, but no one was hanging out with my extra suit.

Blake came in as I looked under the bed, aiming the SIG in case I spotted killer dust bunnies. Instead, I spotted Blake looking under the other side of the bed. We both jumped a little. I shook my head. "We don't need caffeine."

She grinned. "Nope. We're permanently wired."

The bed was between us like a challenge, or a promise. I said, "Cocoa?"

"Why, Mr. Maxwell. I'd love some."

"Right this way, Ms. Blake."

We headed back for the kitchen. She said, "Do your friends call you Chase?"

"Only my mom. And then only when she's annoyed with me. People who're really annoyed call me Chase Oliver Maxwell the Fourth. Or Olly, which might be worst of all."

"You prefer Max?"

"I prefer O God of My Waking Dreams."

"Max for short?"

"Yeah."

She laughed. "Max?"

"Yeah?"

"Kristal Agatha Blake."

I shook my head in sympathy. "Anyone ever call you Aggie?"

"I'll remind you that I'm armed."

"Yes, ma'am, Ms. Blake."

"Kris."

"Kris."

When I took the soy milk from the fridge, she said, "Soy milk?"

"I'm afraid that's it."

"Are you allergic to dairy?"

I shook my head, then said, "Well, I'd probably have trouble digesting cow's milk now."

"You're a vegetarian?"

I nodded as I poured out two mugs and put them in the microwave.

"Health reasons, religious ones, or you don't like hurting animals?"

"Change 'religious' to 'spiritual,' and I'll go with 'D. All of the above.' "

"You're an odd private eye."

"I've never met a normal one."

"It's just that, well, you carry a gun. But you don't want to hurt animals."

"I'll rethink that when I get mugged by a cow."

The microwave went off, so I got out the mugs, dumped the contents into the blender along with four wedges of Ibarra chocolate, and punched "High."

"What made you a vegetarian?"

"Seemed like a good idea at the time." I poured hot chocolate froth into the mugs and handed her one. "How's this?"

She took a sip, then smiled. Dark foam lined her upper lip. "Delicious."

"The Aztecs had chocolate and human sacrifice. That's got to balance out on the karmic scale."

She took another sip. "I'd say so."

I reached out and wiped chocolate from her lip with a forefinger. She frowned. I showed her the foam on my finger. "Chocolate moustache."

She licked the finger. I said, "Oh, my."

"You've got one, too." She leaned forward and licked my upper lip.

"Your way's nicer," I said, and we let our cocoa get cold.

The curse of being a detective is that it's almost impossible to completely quit being the observer. Her kissing was bold and inventive, yet a tiny bit practiced, like dancing with a professional dancer. But then, perhaps mine seemed that way, too. I wasn't doing this because I was falling in love, and I was sure that she wasn't either. We were doing this because it seemed like a good thing to do at the time. When I realized that I was analyzing the cinnamon taste of her mouthwash or her toothpaste, I decided this was a fine time to let Detective Max go to sleep while Mammal Max had fun.

We lost most of our clothes in the kitchen. Beneath her suit, she wore a red silk lace bra and matching panties—I prefer black or white, but I was still appreciative. She was appreciative, too. I don't know if her panties or my boxers hit the floor first. It's a miracle we didn't tear anything.

Naked, she revealed more human imperfections, a scattering of small brown moles across her shoulders, a pimple on an otherwise perfect buttock, a few pale hairs around delectable nipples. They were not defects; they were details unique to her. The scar on her shin said she had a childhood. The half-grown toenail suggested that something had fallen on her foot in the last few months. These observations may not have inspired anything like love in me, but they inspired affection and the certainty that there was more to learn about Kristal Agatha Blake. They made this competent and carefully guarded woman seem, like me, a person who had found someone to trust enough to let fall the walls of civilization and free the wild self within.

We took turns being the one who leaned back on the kitchen counter and the one who knelt on the linoleum floor. When I found myself wondering at the taste of her douche and wishing she hadn't, I told the detective to go back to sleep. I was amazed by her passion—not so amazed that I questioned it, but enough that I commented on it. She said she hadn't fucked in months. I liked that, the combined suggestions that she recognized her needs and didn't give into them with just anyone.

We had each other first at the kitchen table, with her lying on her back, then with her leaning on her elbows with me behind her. Afterwards, we laughed and separated. I put the mugs in the microwave to reheat them, but we had begun again on the sofa before the timer sounded. Still joined at the groin, I carried her to my bed where there was more room to roll, and we took turns being on top.

I came twice in that hour, once in the kitchen and once in the bedroom. She was a screamer—by my count, she came at least three times. After her second, as I was doing my best to catch up with her, she said, "Thank you, O God of my Waking Dreams." All I could do was grin. Well, grin and keep doing the things that seemed to have inspired the comment.

When we took a break, I returned to the kitchen and re-zapped the chocolate that we had left in the microwave. Though I kept my belongings limited, I had a candelabra that I claimed was for power outages but only came out when a woman I liked was in my home. I lit the candles and carried the reheated chocolate back to the bedroom.

She said, "You look like a man who isn't ready to sleep."

"I can always sleep."

"Is that all you can always do?"

"Gods, woman. You're insatiable."

"How would you know? You've barely tried to satiate me."

"Drink up. Then we'll see who satiates whom."

"What's the winner get?"

"The loser. And vice versa."

She tossed back her chocolate. "How about a back rub?"

"You do know how to treat a guy." My chocolate was too hot for my taste, so I sipped it and set it aside.

I nearly fell asleep in the soft, rumpled bed, in the glow of the candlelight, with her hands firmly massaging the tight muscles of my back and the scent of chocolate and sex thick in the air. I said, "That's nice."

"Glad to be of service." She kissed the back of my neck. "In whatever way I can."

"I didn't know this was part of a bodyguard's job."

"Some bodies are better to guard than others."

"Mmm. You're good at your work."

"There are things you're good at, too."

"We aim to please."

"Max?"

I smiled into the pillow. "Kris?"

"Why did the cat hire you?"

Her strong hands continued to work on me while I lay there, trying to think of an answer that would end this line of discussion. The best I could do was a reminder that sex did not grant us total intimacy. "You know I can't answer that."

"You can if you think she's involved in a murder."

My obligation to my client made me ask, "Do you?"

"Try not to tense up."

It was too late. I rolled over and caught her wrists. "If you want to grill me, let's do it back at the precinct."

"Sorry. But as long as she has that earring, or anyone thinks she does, you're both targets. I'd hate to see you get hurt, Max."

"Is this an interrogation?"

"No." She slid her hands down my chest. "The precinct's a lousy place for what I have in mind."

She leaned down for a passionate kiss. After a long, lazy, tired, comfortable, almost painful time, we each added another Big O to our scores.

I fell asleep in her arms after blowing out the candles and woke when she slipped from the bed. Moonlight silvered her limbs. She seemed so inhumanly beautiful then that I shuddered. I said, "You can stay, you know."

"People will wonder if I go to work twice in the same clothes."

"Tell them you got lucky."

She leaned over and kissed me lightly on the lips. "I did."

"You can borrow some of my clothes."

"Now there's a helpful suggestion. Good night." She kissed me again and headed naked into the hall.

I got up and followed her into the kitchen, where she was pulling up her red lace panties. She looked at me and said, "You didn't have to get up."

"Hmm. Sleep, or watch you get dressed? That's not as nice as watching the reverse, but it's still a good show. Maybe when I remember this, I can play it in reverse."

She rolled her eyes. "Men."

She dressed much too quickly for my taste. When she finished, I applauded. "Encore!"

"Dream on."

"Want something to drink before you go?"

"I'm fine."

I didn't press her. We'd had great sex; we didn't really know whether we could stand to spend more time together. I was sleepy and, since I hadn't bothered to put on a robe, cold. I kissed her goodbye at the door. Warmth alone might've explained why I felt so good in that embrace. "Kris?"

"Yes?"

I wanted to show her the earring, to get her help in learning what it was and why anyone wanted it. I said, "Don't be a stranger."

"I won't be. And, Max? If you happen to find that earring—"

"You'll be the next to know."

"Good."

She gave me a last cinnamon kiss, then strode into the night. I closed the door and headed for the hall, grinning sleepily with the warm glow of the well laid. I didn't know whether I liked Kris Blake, but I knew I liked what we did together, and I sure wouldn't mind if we did a little more. All I wanted at that moment was to put on my robe, have a last smoke, and crawl back into that warm bed to fall asleep in less time than it takes to finish this sentence.

Something scratched at the balcony door, and a cat meowed to be let in. I muttered, "What the hell," and pulled back the drapes. Just beyond the glass, with an insufferable grin, stood Zoe Domingo.

6

I yanked the drapes together, realized I couldn't leave the cat on the balcony, then wrapped the end of a drape around my waist and opened the door. She stalked into the middle of the living room, looked around, and shook her head sadly. Before she could comment on the decor, I said, "How long were you out there?"

"Long enough to wonder if you were ever going to stop. Is the girlfriend coming back tonight?"

"Kris?" It was too soon to think of Blake as a girlfriend, but I liked the possibility that I might someday soon. "Not unless she forgot something."

"Good."

"Why?"

"She smells funny."

"You don't like her because she smells funny?"

"I don't like her because she's a cop."

"Speaking of cops, where's your guardbot?" When the cat shrugged innocently, I could answer my own question. "Watching the wrong house. That *was* all your money. And you don't have any friends in town."

"Wow, you are a detective."

"Would you mind looking away? I want to get a robe."

"Afraid you'll blind me with your godlike splendor?"

"I should be so lucky. Turn around."

She sighed and started reading the spines of my disc boxes. "Are you ashamed because you don't have fur? The

Wild Church says that's what God took from you, when he kicked you out of Eden."

I ducked into the bathroom and grabbed my robe off the back of the door. "I'm not ashamed. I'm cold."

"And how's that affect whether I see you naked?"

"Look, it makes me uncomfortable."

"Why?"

"I'm an old-fashioned guy, okay? If we were on the beach, I wouldn't mind."

"Are there any critter beaches in L.A.?"

"That was rhetorical. There's a mixed beach up past Malibu. I didn't think cats liked to swim."

"Why do you think zoo cats get ponds? And you're not the only one who can be rhetorical."

I decided that if she had been human, I still wouldn't like her. Which reminded me that the only reason I had to put up with her was business, and our dealings went much better when we focused on that. "When they notice you're missing, this is the first place they'll check."

"They shouldn't think it's odd if I sleep until noon. We'll be on the case well before then."

"I will be, anyway."

She frowned. "And I stay here?"

"Wherever you wish." I reached for the phone.

"What're you doing?"

"Calling information. There's got to be a decent hotel with a room for a chimera."

"I thought you were broke."

"Now that you're straight with the cops, you can use a credit card."

"Anyone who can reprogram copbots can track a credit card transaction."

If it'd been earlier in the day, I would've thought of that. I hung up.

She headed into the kitchen. "I guess you're stuck with a house guest."

I tailed her. "How'd you get a name like Zoe Domingo?"

"It was a twenty-six cat Sunday at the ol' in vitro lab." She opened the refrigerator and scanned the basics: soy milk, beer, soy cheese, hummus, tofu, orange marmalade, maple syrup, salsa, tomato-mushroom spaghetti sauce, spicy garlic and black bean stir-fry sauces, potatoes, broccoli, carrots. Her frown grew as she checked the freezer: onion bagels, corn, spinach, peas, soy beans. "No meat? Not even a pack of bologna?"

I shook out a cig from a pack near the stove and lit it on a burner. "No cat litter in the bathroom either."

"Very funny."

"I don't eat meat."

She stared at me in disbelief. "A vegetarian nicotine addict."

I took a deep drag on the cig, exhaled, and grinned. "I can quit any time."

"Uh-huh." Her nostrils flared as she grimaced.

"But since you're not comfortable—" I stubbed out the cig in the sink.

"Thanks." She took out the package of cheese, sat on the counter, ripped the plastic open with a fingernail, and proceeded to break pieces off and eat them.

I said, "Help yourself."

She looked at the cheese as if she'd just realized what she was doing. "Well. Your three kings ate my lunch money."

Since we were staying up, I got a beer and opened it. "Want one?"

"Water'd be nice."

I pointed at a cupboard. "Glasses." As she filled one with tap water, I said, "What did you expect your lunch money to buy?"

"I told you. The earring."

I opened the Pocket. The earring shot into my hand. Viewed up close, its gold rectangles had patterns of tiny holes and indentations. The black opal flashed in rainbow colors. It was pretty, but people rarely kill for pretty. Being able to shut down copbots—that you might kill for. I set the earring on the kitchen table. "Sure you want me to start hunting?"

"Why not?"

"Because here's the story so far. Dr. Janna Gold, AI expert, is D.O.A. in L.A. Someone knew she was coming. Her companion escapes unhurt with a mysterious and valuable doodad that she hides from the police."

The cat set aside her cheese and water. "Meaning?"

"The companion could've set Gold up, double-crossed her partners, and hired a cheap detective to make her story look good. Or to be her fall guy."

The cat's claws extended. She bared clenched teeth.

I said, "That's high on the cops' list of possibilities. They have a dead body, and you. They have to start with you. So do I."

"I wouldn't let anyone hurt her!"

"Guess you fucked up, then."

She reached for the earring. "You're fired."

I put my hand over hers to stop her. "Thought you said you wouldn't fire me."

"You've lucked out."

I kept the hand over hers. "Why'd you really hire me?"

"I want to know who killed Doc!"

"Why? What did a skin ever do for you?"

She kept the glare on me, full burn. "She adopted me. She was my mother." As tears formed in her eyes, she grabbed the earring off the table and turned to go.

I caught her shoulder. Her look said that wise men don't do that. I said gently, "The cops didn't know that."

"The papers haven't gone through. Satisfied?"

I wasn't, not entirely. Still, I sighed and turned toward the hall. "The couch doesn't look like much, but it's comfortable."

"You'll help me find her killer?"

I looked back. She seemed very small and very alone under the kitchen light. "That's what you paid me for, isn't it?" I left her standing there.

I used the bathroom and put the seat down before I left, a gesture that I doubt she noticed. Bed wasn't what I'd hoped it would be. I couldn't sleep. I thought about Kris Blake, and I liked what I thought, but that kept leading me back to the cat and her case.

The only thing I knew for sure was that I wanted a smoke, but I couldn't think of a way to do that without her smelling it. Mind you, I couldn't think of a reason why she shouldn't smell it. She wouldn't think any less of me. Maybe that was why I didn't want her to smell it.

I studied the shadows cast by the street lights, finally muttered, "Oh, hell," threw the covers back, and got out of bed. I tapped a cig out of the pack on the dresser, brought it to my lips, pulled out my pocket knife, snapped the lighter on, then stopped. I don't know why. She was just a chimera who would be out of my life in seventeen hours—sooner, if I found what she wanted.

I took the cig out of my mouth, scowled at it, and dropped it back on the dresser. I could go twenty-four hours without smoking. The next time someone said I couldn't, I would know they were wrong.

Warm soy milk seemed like a good idea. I threw on my robe and headed out.

I stopped at the archway into the living room. Street light through the front windows showed Zoe Domingo under a blanket on the couch. She was asleep, one hand under her cheek.

If I went any further, I would wake her. She was a damn

cat with nothing on her conscience; she would go right back to sleep. I told myself to go ahead and get the soy milk. In the morning, she wouldn't remember I'd disturbed her.

Then I sighed, defeated. One day's work. I went into the bathroom. Tap water tasted good enough. Something wet must've been all I needed. I fell asleep easily after that.

The alarm was set for eight-thirty. The cat went off at eight. The knock at the door was easy to ignore. A shouted "Hey, Mr. Detective, I don't think there are any clues to my case in your bed" was not.

I found a shirt, socks, and underwear that still looked clean and threw them in the zapper to kill anything that might be growing on them. While they zapped, I showered and shaved, which began the process of waking up. My suit may not have looked expensive—because it wasn't—but the cloth was Everclean. I shook it, pulled it on over the fresh-zapped underclothes, and voila! Instant detective. Just add coffee.

Which I smelled in the hall. That pulled me faster than usual to the kitchen. The cat, in her sea-green jumpsuit, sat on the counter, finishing a bowl of ginger granola.

"I have chairs."

"I like heights. It's genetic."

"Suit yourself. Thanks for making coffee." I poured a cup, then popped a bagel in the toaster.

"I figured the machine wasn't there for looks. If I knew the rest of your addictions, I'd have them laid out for you. I couldn't find any cigarettes."

"I only smoke when I feel like it."

"From the state of the ashtrays, you feel like it a lot."

"I only clean house when I feel like it, too."

"Do you only work when you feel like it?"

"I try. What's the rush?"

"It's getting late."

"Eight twenty-five?"

"The cops may decide against letting a critter get her beauty sleep."

If I solved her case in an hour, I could go right back to sleep. I smeared apple butter on the bagel, took a big bite, then said, "Do you have a computer on you?"

"Why? What do you want to bet it against?"

"We should start with some cyber-sleuthing, and my DigiPal's in hock."

The cat pulled out a pocket computer, a micro-thin PowerPad with a scuff mark on one corner. As I reached for it, she said, "If they can reprogram copbots, they can tell when I'm online."

"We'll use my line and my account." I jacked the PowerPad's data cable into the side of my phone and pressed its ON-OFF button. A holographic screen and keyboard appeared in the air. I began typing on intangible keys.

The cat said, "Where do we start?"

"With Janna Gold." I found her bio on SciFiles. The screen filled with scrollable text and a picture of Gold. I read the highlights aloud, in case anything sparked something useful from the cat. "Expert on comparative neurology. Human brain mapping. Development and storage of identity in machine intelligences. Received a Chain Foundation grant." I glanced at the cat. "Chain Logic's headquartered out here. Was she coming to see them?"

"Maybe. The project she wanted to check on could've been one of theirs."

"Who else might she know in town?" I typed LOS ANGELES + MACHINE INTELLIGENCE + CHAIN FOUNDATION. A picture of a distinguished, white-haired man with thick, black eyebrows appeared onscreen. "Well, of course. Oberon Chain himself. Looks pretty good for his age."

"Being filthy rich can't hurt."

I checked to see if he was doing anything that'd made the news. He was. "He's throwing a charity event today."

I tapped the MORE button at the bottom of the screen. The next page said "Picture not available." All it had was a name, an e-mail address, and a brief, enigmatic description—no street address or phone number. I read it for Zoe. " 'Mycroft. Consultant. Specializing in sapience, politics, xenogenetics, and chimera matters.' Mustn't be very good if he can't afford a last name."

"Never heard of him."

"Well, just in case—" I typed and sent a quick e-mail message: "Dear Mycroft, I'm investigating the death of Dr. Janna Gold. Her daughter—" I didn't look to see what the cat thought of that word choice. "And I would be grateful for a few minutes to speak with you about the last time you saw her. Sincerely, Chase Maxwell, Maxwell Investigations."

The third page showed a middle-aged black man and pages of text. Impressed, I whistled. "Amos Tauber. USCLA's Balisok Law School. Nation's foremost expert in nonhuman rights—"

"Thank you. I've heard of Amos Tauber."

"The doc ever mention him?"

"I don't think so. You think she worked with him?"

I tapped the phone icon by Tauber's name. "Let's ask."

A chromium humanform bot appeared onscreen. Its round eyes and smooth curves were extremely nonthreatening. It looked like a top-of-the-line household model that you would find in a Sears robotics department. It said, "Professor Tauber's residence."

"Tell him Chase Maxwell's calling. I'd like to ask him about Janna Gold."

"I'm sorry, he's at the university. I'm Jefferson 473, his personal robot. May I help you?"

"Was your boss expecting a visit from Dr. Gold?"

"Why do you use the past tense?"

"She's dead."

"Oh, my. Is Professor Tauber in danger? He's gotten death threats, but he refuses to take them seriously."

"I don't know. He's at the U. all day?"

"Yes, sir."

"When does he get lunch?"

"Between one and two."

"Tell him we'll try to catch him then." I hit DISCONNECT and grinned at the cat.

She didn't grin back. "Why not now?"

"Because we're going to a party."

The Libertarian Revolution hit South California before the PRT system had reached the Huntington Museum. The system's buyers followed the first law of capitalism—"Sure profit now beats potentially greater profit later"—and halted work on the Pasadena line, so we had to transfer to an electric bus in Burbank that took us the rest of the way.

I love Angelenos—no one looked twice at us on the bus. Okay, they looked twice, but they never said a word.

I had changed to a crisp, summer-weight suit, the second-best thing in my closet, and a Hawaiian shirt, the best piece of clothing I owned. When my old man died, the creditors said I could have one item, so I took his favorite shirt. People who knew Hawaiian shirts would know I wore money; the buttons were hand-carved wood, and the pocket patch had been cut to perfectly match the pattern of the shirt. I couldn't pass as a rich man who cared how he looked, but I could pass as one who didn't.

The cat looked uber-chichi in a short red dress, sunglasses, and a white turban that hid her hair and ID tat. That her silver boots suited the red dress was pure good fortune. None of the individual parts of the outfit said money, but the assembled pieces said she was someone whose primary cares were her looks and her fun.

Our styles didn't match, which only made us more plausible. Whether you assumed I was a shlub whose money had attracted a showgirl, or she was a child of privilege with a taste for bad boys, we looked like insouciant beneficiaries of sweet, fickle fortune.

We stepped down from the bus outside the Huntington grounds so no one would see that we didn't arrive in a sports car that cost enough to put a couple of poor kids through college. The cat's fashion-model perfection disappeared when she tugged at her hem. "All right, how did a client leave her dress in your apartment?"

"It's a long story."

"And you don't get paid at the end of it."

"Well. Not in dollars."

"Eeuwww."

We walked up the driveway without talking. The cat looked around her like a kid approaching Disneyland, and I felt a little of that thrill. I wished I was there on a date with Kris Blake instead of on business with the cat.

When Los Angeles was young, Henry Huntington became an astonishingly rich man by providing the city with an efficient network of red trolley cars, one of the world's great public transportation accomplishments. The automobile industry destroyed the trolley system—remember the second law of capitalism, "Eliminate your competition"—but Henry Huntington left another legacy to the city. His home and gardens house one of the world's great museums.

Approaching the grounds made me remember my first year of marriage. We would come here for high tea, linger in the Shakespeare garden, and stroll through the collections of paintings and books.

I was jerked back to the present at the main entrance, where a plump, cheerful woman sat at a table with a list. She looked at us as though we had come to bring her sweepstakes winnings and said, "Your names?"

I glanced at the list. There was no check mark beside "Johnson, 2." I gave her my best smile and pointed there. "We're the Johnsons."

She frowned. "The sisters?"

I pride myself on being unflappable, but that flapped me. Before the instant of silence could grow, the cat said, "Maxine decided to change her look. Come along, dear."

I smiled weakly at the woman and followed the cat in.

The event was already in progress on the museum's elegant lawn. A band and a podium were set up under a banner that read UNITED HEARTS INTERNATIONAL: CURE WEREWOLFING NOW! Cloth-draped tables surrounded a portable dance floor. Perhaps two hundred guests in designer suits and dresses faced the podium, where a middle-aged woman in teal, that season's most approved color, told them, "The terror of werewolfing inspires pity in us, not fear. We gather here in the spirit of love to help those who must live with this nightmare."

I scanned the crowd as people applauded. The spirit of love moves differently at the heights of society. When the underclass wants to help someone, they march or build or clean or dam. The overclass eats finger food.

Oberon Chain stood near the podium with several important-looking people. He appeared heavier than in the online photo—not fatter, but stockier, stronger. Maybe the fashion for the physique of the wealthy had changed since the photo was taken. Chain radiated dignity, kindness, confidence, and a straightforwardness that made you want to trust him. He seemed positively presidential, but people with his money rarely run for office. They buy someone to do the job for them.

The garden party had been roped off with white cords. At a gap in the cords, a bot greeted us. It looked like a four foot tall cross between a chess pawn and a bowling pin. Camera-like eyes in its dark, translucent head settled on us. "Welcome, madam and sir. Your names?"

The cat smiled. "The Johnsons."

I added, "Sent us in their place. We're the Maxwells."

The bot said, "One moment, please. I must call—"

I said, "No need," and grabbed the cat's arm. "Darling, there's Oberon!" I pulled her into the party and headed toward Chain.

The bot rolled after us, calling, "Please, sir, madam—"

The cat turned and put a finger to her lips. "Shh!"

On stage, the speaker was saying, "Until there's a cure for werewolfing, until humans feel safe in the presence of chimeras, the Chimera Equal Rights Amendment will never pass. As you work for the cure, you work for justice for all creatures. Please, give generously."

That brought stronger applause. As the speaker left the podium, Chain stepped up to shake her hand. The band started a Ragtime Revival tune that made me fear Ragtime Rev was already dying; the band's take was technically perfect, but it didn't make you want to grab your date and leap onto the dance floor.

The bot at our heels said, "Sir, madam, please, if you would just—"

I grabbed my date and leaped onto the dance floor. When I took the cat in my arms, she raised an eyebrow but didn't protest. We Castle-walked through a cluster of dancers, leaving the bot at the edge of the floor.

The cat said, "You dance better than you gamble."

"Careful. I can still stomp your toes."

We swirled across the floor and ended with a turn that sent her perilously close to Oberon Chain. As he frowned and glanced at us, I said, "Oberon Chain, Zoe Domingo."

He turned away from the people he had been speaking to, said, "A pleasure," then looked at me. "Have we met?"

"Chase Maxwell." I offered my hand. "We're crashing your party."

The cat said, "It's important."

Chain studied us with a calm face that must have reassured many investors during financial crises. The bot greeter caught up to us then. "I tried to stop them, sir—"

"It's all right." Chain asked the cat, "What brings you here?"

"Was Janna Gold coming to see you?"

"Dr. Gold? We haven't spoken in years. Why do you ask?"

I said, "She was murdered yesterday."

He frowned. "I'm sorry to hear that. What's your connection to her?"

The cat said, "She was my mother."

Chain's eyes narrowed. "I heard she had adopted a critter."

The cat removed her dark glasses.

Chain's frown grew deeper. "I see."

I said, "I understand Dr. Gold had worked on a project for you."

Chain turned the frown to me, then smiled. "I'm sorry, Mr. Maxwell. Successful companies stay successful by keeping secrets. I'm sure you understand."

"Could those secrets have had anything to do with her death?"

He pursed his lips in deliberation, then shook his head. "I can't see how. If I thought there was the slightest chance they had, I'd notify the police immediately. No business secret is worth a human life."

If there was another question I should've asked, it didn't occur to me then. "Well. Thank you for your time, Mr. Chain."

"Good luck." Chain nodded and turned his attention back to the people he had been speaking with.

I took the cat's arm to lead her out of the party. As we passed, people noticed her eyes. A matronly black woman stepped aside and whispered to her friend, in the loud way of the deaf and the oblivious, "I know what this charity's for, but I never thought they'd let one in!"

The cat turned, yanked off her turban to show her ears and tattoo, and grinned coldly. "Cat ears, lady. No secret's safe from us." She slam-dunked the turban into a trash bin and strode away. I followed her through the exit and down the driveway. She may have been small, but I would've had to run to catch up with her.

She waited at the bus stop, making no movement except for the slow clenching and unclenching of her hands. A bus was approaching as I came up beside her. She gave me a fierce glance, then looked away.

I said, "That went well, don't you think?"

She didn't answer. Scowling, she boarded and took a bench near the middle of the bus. A few seats beyond her was the standard notice: "Unaccompanied chimeras must sit behind this line." I'd never paid attention to it before.

The bus at mid-morning wasn't crowded. Several humans sat in the front. At the back were a few chimeras and a couple of Riders, homeless people whose favorite place to sleep was public transportation. Across the aisle from the cat and two rows behind her sat three young borgies, two Hispanic boys and one white girl. They looked like ordinary teenagers who didn't want to look like ordinary teenagers. Their add-ons showed heavy scar tissue, like you'd expect to see from a neighborhood Frankenstein shop.

I sat and asked the cat, "What do you make of Oberon Chain?"

"He smells funny."

"You think everyone smells funny."

"You smell okay." She caught my glance and added, "When you're not smoking."

Behind us, the smaller male borgie sniffed loudly. "What's that stink?"

His large friend said, "Are we passing the zoo?"

The small borgie nodded. "It sure is hard to keep animals clean."

The cat inhaled slowly and deeply. I said, "Should I—"

She shook her head. "Ignore them."

The large borgie called, "Hey, furry. What's she smell like when she's wet?"

The small one said, "Bet it's pretty funky."

I looked back. The large male was bigger than me; the other was tiny. The borgette was thin and pasty. Their arms were bare, showing hardware and the corded muscles that come from a discount body shop. I couldn't tell whether they were high on anything other than gang stupidity. I said, "All right. You've had your fun."

If I'd thought about it, I would've realized that was a challenge. The big one stood, grabbed the rail above our seat, and leaned over me. "I'd buy a pretty critter like that. What do they go for?"

His pack slid into the seat behind us. The borgette poked me in the back. "Hey, mister. You recommend the breed?"

The big borgie grinned. "Yeah. That a good breed for breeding?"

The little one stroked the cat's hair. She jerked away and looked back at him. He smiled. "Nice pussy."

I thought about popping the SIG, but there were three of them, and if they were being this bold, they were probably all exercising their legal right to bear arms. Their add-ons mostly looked aesthetic, not functional, but they could be packing sound, light, and projectiles, and hoping for an excuse to try them all. I put a hand on the cat's shoulder and said, "Careful, fellas."

The borgette said, "Yeah? Why?"

I gave her astonishment. "You haven't heard that chimeras werewolf under stress?"

The big one snorted. "No one knows why critters werewolf."

The little one reached for Zoe's hair again. "Hey, pretty pussy, you gonna—" He stopped talking when the cat twitched. As we all watched, she growled softly, then grabbed the back of the bench in front of her.

I said, "Easy, Zoe!"

The little borgie said, "What's wrong with her?"

"They're nice kids." I glanced at them. "Aren't you?"

The cat growled softly. The borgies looked at each other. The cat's hands stayed on the back of the bench, but claws like tiny stilettos unsheathed themselves. The three borgies nodded hesitantly.

I said, "Say it!"

The borgette said, "We're . . . nice kids."

"Tell her you're sorry."

They looked at each other again. The cat stared at them, breathing raggedly. Her upper lip drew up, exposing very white, very sharp teeth.

"Come on, guys! If she doesn't calm down—"

The big borgie said, "Hey, we're sorry."

The little one said, "We didn't mean nothing."

"You're just dumb fucks, right?"

The little one said, "Yeah. We're just dumb fucks, that's all. We're just—"

The cat snarled, loud enough to make me want to run for it.

The borgette said, "Oh, shit!" The little one hit the overhead stop bar. All three scrambled for the exit, fighting to be the first out as the bus pulled up to the next corner.

The borgies stumbled onto the sidewalk, then looked back at us. I said, "Wave goodbye to the nice kids, Zoe."

We both grinned and waved through the window at the borgies on the sidewalk. They stared back with expressions of painful enlightenment as the bus pulled away.

The cat and I leaned back in our seats. I asked, "Better?"

She nodded. "Better."

We caught a pert in Burbank. I told it to take the Mulholland Drive rail along the spine of the Santa Monicas, then shoot down Beverly Glen, which only added a few minutes to the trip. The San Fernando Valley on our right was smoggy—the original inhabitants called it the Place of Smokes for good reason—and Los Angeles on our left was foggy, but it was still nice to ride the hill crest and see what was there to be seen.

Actually, I hoped it was nice for the cat. I napped. Perts aren't designed for that. You can't expect a lot of comfort in a pod designed to be cleaned with high-pressure hoses, and, like the seats in fastfooderies, the seats in perts are designed to be comfortable while you sit up and uncomfortable if you stretch out. The reason's the same in both cases; the owners want you to make room for the next customer.

We nearly paid for taking the scenic route. Amos Tauber was shutting his door as we walked up the hall to his office at USCLA. Though there was more gray in his hair and goatee than in his online picture, he carried himself like a man half his age—not stiffly erect, like a military man, but supplely, like a lifelong student of yoga or tai chi. Most famous people seem smaller in real life. Amos Tauber's carriage made him larger.

The cat said, "Professor Tauber?"

I held up my P.I. license. "Chase Maxwell. This is Zoe Domingo. We'd like to talk to you about Janna Gold."

He blinked at us, then nodded. "I was just going to lunch. Would you care to join me at the cafeteria?"

The cat said, "We'd be delighted."

"I see you've never eaten there." As we headed down the hall, Tauber asked, "What's this about?"

The cat said, "Your life may be in danger."

An elevator arrived, and we stepped inside. Tauber said, "Then you do know the cafeteria."

As we ascended, I said, "You heard that Dr. Gold was killed?"

"It was on the morning news. It's a great loss."

"What story did they give?"

Tauber frowned. "There's more than one?"

"Usually."

"A tragic accident. The police are investigating. What are the other stories?"

"It wasn't an accident. Someone killed her. We don't know who."

"You believe I can help?"

The cat said, "We hope so. Was she coming to see you?"

Tauber nodded. "I expected to hear from her last night."

I said, "Do you know what she wanted to talk about?"

"I'm afraid not. She said she'd rather discuss it in person."

"Was that unusual?"

"I didn't know her well enough to say. I thought it a bit odd, but many interesting people are a bit odd."

The cafeteria on the top floor of the Mahr Building was half full of students and faculty, mostly human, but including a few chimeras. During the last round of student protests, someone had argued that a public university under an administration aggressively pushing privatization shouldn't turn away students who met the academic standards and could pay their own tuition. But the increase in werewolfings had brought the school's policy under scrutiny again, and the number of human applicants had declined. The betting money believed this was the last year for chimeras at USCLA.

I carried a tray with lentil soup, a whole wheat bagel, and a glass of apple-cranberry juice to one cashier while Tauber carried his—spaghetti and herbal tea—to another. The cat took longer than us, though not from indecision. I overhead her at the steam table, giving a pigwoman attendant her order: "Turkey. Chicken. Some tuna. Come on, you can get more than that on a plate!"

Tauber and I took a table at the back of the cafeteria, away from other diners. I said, "Do you have any idea who might want to kill Dr. Gold?"

"Not at all. Is there any reason why I should?"

"Perhaps not. But people have threatened to kill you."

"Of course. I'm the public face of a string of unpopular positions." That was an understatement. For twenty years, he had been hated by humans when he championed chimera rights, and in the last five, he had won nearly as many enemies among chimeras who felt abandoned when he began promoting AI rights.

"Would the same people go after Dr. Gold?"

"I doubt it. She lived in the world of ideas. The people who hate me don't have much truck with those."

The cat joined us as I said, "Do you have any notion why she wanted to see you?"

"No. She said she wanted my opinion on something that was probably nothing, but it'd be an excuse to visit."

The cat said, "She didn't act as if it was nothing."

I added, "Have you considered hiring a bodyguard?"

Tauber laughed. "Are you here for a job?"

"No. But you should think about it. I can recommend some good agencies."

"I won't ask someone to stop a bullet for me, Mr. Maxwell. If anyone wants to kill me, let him look me in the eye and shoot."

"What's to keep someone from doing just that?"

Tauber shook his head and smiled. "People are afraid of equal rights for machine intelligences. Frightened people stop thinking. If I give in to fear, I'd have to join 'em. And I rather enjoy thinking."

"Nice speech. Why waste it on me?"

"Because I believe it. Caution didn't free my people. It hasn't freed Ms. Domingo's. It won't free MIs."

His use of "MI" threw me for a second. AI activists argue that "AI" is misleading—if sapient programs are truly intelligent, their intelligence can't be "artificial." I decided to stick to the discussion at hand. "Martin Luther King didn't die in bed. Your bot's afraid you won't, either."

Tauber jerked his head back in surprise. "My what?"

The cat said, "Your housebot. It's worried—"

"Ms. Domingo, even Robert E. Lee freed his slaves. How could I keep one?"

Alarm bells sounded in my mind. I said, "A bot calling itself Jefferson 473 answered your phone this morning."

Tauber frowned. "You must've gotten the wrong number."

"No. Someone intercepted—"

Behind us, Kristal Agatha Blake said, "Hello, Max, Zoe."

We turned. The woman with whom I had shared my flesh and my inhibitions, if not my soul—and perhaps even that, on a short-term lease—slid her See-alls down her nose to show her eyes. In my mind's eye now, they're steel blue, but that may've only been the reflected sunlight from the window. She grinned pleasantly. "Amos Tauber. Pleased to meet you."

I said, "Kris! What brings you here?"

She said, "Loose ends," drew her 11mm Vetterli Dual-Chamber Recoilless, and shot Tauber. His chest exploded. Whether his mouth fell open from surprise, shock, or the relaxation of voluntary muscles, I will always wonder. I like to think he died instantly. He collapsed in his chair, slumping forward to strike the table and his plate with his forehead. The plate flipped like a tiddlywink, strewing spaghetti on top of gore.

For what seemed an impossibly long, silent moment, Tauber lay in that pool of blood and spaghetti sauce. I looked at Blake and expected to see—I'm not sure what. Maybe her looking as appalled as I felt, as if she had meant to shoot him with a sleep dart as some sort of joke and the joke had gone horribly wrong. Or smiling as Tauber sat up and the host of *In your Face!* came out to announce that this had been staged to entertain a billion bored HV viewers. What I saw was no expression at all and the Vetterli moving, ready to fire again.

The nearest diners turned toward us, looking for the source of the explosion, not yet thinking of the deadly possibilities. Funny how you don't, even when it's the most logical explanation. Then someone saw Tauber and screamed. The cat sat rooted to her chair, still waiting to find out she was on HV, but losing hope fast. I tensed my wrist. I felt as if I was watching myself as the SIG slammed out of the Infinite Pocket and into my hand. I wanted the HV crews to reveal themselves, too.

All around us, diners scattered for cover. Blake turned the Vetterli toward the cat. Before she could bring it to bear, I fired at the shoulder of her gun arm. The bullet tore clothing and skin, baring bright metal.

Blake smiled at me, exactly as she had smiled the night before. She may have said my name. Perhaps I only remembered how she had said it. I shot twice at her heart.

She twitched and flailed under the bullets' impact, but didn't retreat. Her wounds oozed blood, just as her cut cheek had the night before. Her gun arm spasmed, and the Vetterli flew from her hand into the cat's lap. The cat stared at it, then at Tauber, lying on the white tablecloth in a red sea.

I began to stand. Maybe I was going to tackle Blake. Before I could try anything, she flipped the table on top of me, knocking me back, spattering me with food and gore. As I stood, Blake smiled contentedly and reached for the cat.

The cat snarled, raised the Vetterli in both hands, and fired a single shot into Blake's chest. Everything that had happened in the last few seconds may have been a mystery to everyone else in the cafeteria—our table was at the rear, away from the others, and Blake had kept her back to them when she had faced us with the Vetterli low at her side like a gunslinger in an ancient cowboy movie—but that moment, when Zoe Domingo shot Kristal Agatha Blake of the LAPD Technology Crimes Division, was clearly seen by everyone in the room.

The explosion sent Blake reeling back into a window, which broke under her impact. Safety glass rained onto anyone below, but Blake caught the steel frame. Her chest was a mess of broken bone-white ribs and shredded flesh. For a moment, I wondered if I was wrong about what she was, even though I knew that whatever else might be within her was hidden by glistening blood.

She stood in the window frame, clutching her stomach with one arm as though she were badly wounded. With the free arm, she pointed at the cat. Her voice came out in a wheeze, but the cafeteria was very quiet at that moment. She said, "Werewolf," then fell back through the shattered window to plummet into the alley below.

The cat and I turned away from the window. Maybe fifteen seconds had passed from the time Blake drew her Vetterli. We looked at each other with the terrible knowledge that bad things had happened, and worse would follow.

I jerked my head toward the door. Humans, chimeras, and bots huddled at the far end of the room, staring at us. The cat looked at the Vetterli in her hand and whispered, "Uh-oh."

A man pointed at her and called, "Stop her!" An alarm went off, shredding the air in a general call for panic. A huge man in a white chef's jacket ran in from the kitchen with a baseball bat. People in the crowd, critters as well as humans, grabbed up trays and kitchen knives to use as weapons. A heavily tattooed dogwoman jumped forward and pulled me away from the cat. "She'll kill anyone now!"

The cat dropped the Vetterli as I shouted, "It's not what it looks like! Listen to me!"

Someone threw a tray at the cat. She ducked it and backed away. The man with the bat ran forward, screaming, "Get her!" The boldest members of the crowd followed him.

I wrenched free of the dogwoman and grabbed the cat's

arm. "Come on!" I waved the SIG so everyone could see it. "Stand back!"

We ran for the elevator. I prayed no would-be hero would pull a gun, and someone must've decided to give me that much. As we leaped into the elevator, the kitchen man thrust his bat between the closing doors. I poked the SIG in his face and said, "Maybe humans werewolf, too."

He sprang back, yanking the bat free. The elevator doors closed.

I punched "ground," and we descended. The cat said, "I did exactly what she—it—wanted."

Something twisted in my guts. I knew I would have to think about Kristal Blake sometime, but for now, all I had to do was keep the cat alive. And maybe, myself, too. I said, "If it makes you feel better, so did I."

"Tauber's dead. If we hadn't come here—"

I didn't let her finish that thought. "No. Blake had time to pick her target."

"So why didn't she kill us?"

I wanted to think about where to go and what to do, not what had happened or why, but those were the easier questions to answer. "They want the earring. Or they want to frame us for Tauber's death. Or both."

"What now?"

"We go someplace safe."

"Where?"

"I'm working on that part."

The elevator doors opened. The cat said, "Oh-oh."

In the lobby, six copbots waited for us. Outside, a police van sat on the street, and another copbot kept anyone from entering the building. I lifted my arms high and shouted, "It's all right! She hasn't—"

The cat slammed me aside. I landed on one side of the doors, the cat on the other, as a flurry of sleep darts pinged off the elevator's back wall. The cat slapped a button for an upper floor. The doors stayed open. "They cut the power!"

I shouted, "We surrender!" and peeked out to see their response. All six copbots were advancing on the elevator. More darts whistled by my face to inform me that surrender wasn't an option.

I ducked back, popped the SIG from the Pocket, and fired, hitting a copbot's optic sensors. The bullet struck something vital as it ricocheted within the bot's body—the copbot fell, spewing sparks from its eye socket. The other copbots scattered for cover. Their reprogrammer had left their sense of self-preservation intact.

The cat said, "Give me the earring!"

I passed my SIG to my left hand, fired blindly into the lobby to discourage sudden assaults, and flexed my right wrist as I extended that arm in the cat's direction. The earring flew from the Pocket toward her.

She caught it and grinned coldly. "It's magic time."

A copbot had gotten far enough to one side to shoot into the elevator. Four darts hit the cat. She stared at them, then slumped down the elevator wall. "Shit."

"Zoe!" I shot at the bot that had hit her, but missed its optics. Still, it moved back under cover.

The cat sat splay-legged on the floor. "It's okay. I'm . . . on it."

I shot two more copbots, scaring one and catching another's optics. "Bastard sons of blenders—"

The cat, fighting to stay conscious, turned the halves of the black opal, then slid its gold plates into the jewel. All the copbots froze like kids in a game of statue. The cat smiled. "Abracadabra. Pretty cool, huh?" Her eyes closed before I could agree.

I leaped to her side and yanked sleep darts out of her. The fine print on one made the cold thing in my guts grow colder. More than two doses in a mammal of average human size could be fatal. The cat barely came up to my shoulder. I shook her. "Zoe? Do you hear me?" Her arms were thin and muscular in my grip. Her smell reminded me of a former girl-friend's pet cat—a cat that I missed more than the girlfriend.

Zoe blinked her golden eyes open and focused the slitted pupils on me. "Sleep now?"

"Not if you want to wake up. They overdosed you."

I dropped the earring into the Pocket, put Zoe's arm over my shoulder, and hauled her toward the police van. The last copbot stood at attention just outside the door, where it had barred anyone from entering. Four students waited there. As I came out with gore on my suit and the cat in my arms, their expressions changed from curiosity to concern. One said, "What's going on?"

I strapped Zoe into the van's passenger seat. "Lunch break. We're making a movie."

"Oh. Big deal." Three students wandered away.

Zoe said, "I like lunch."

The last student glanced at her. I said, "Actors." The student grinned and followed the others.

I sat in the driver's seat. The van said, "Destination, please." I leaned under the dashboard, opened my pocket knife, and went to work. The van repeated, "Destination, please."

Zoe lifted her head. "Max? It wants to know where we're going."

The van said, "Destina—"

I came up from under the dash with a small black box that dangled cut wires. Zoe had slumped in her seat. I said, "Stay awake!"

"Sleep is nice."

"Sleep is bad. See this?" I showed her the box. "It's a locator with an override to take us to the nearest cop shop."

"That's not where we're going."

"Right. Stay awake."

I got out and crawled under the van. The second locator was harder to reach—it was welded above the power train in the middle of the car. Thieves stupid enough to steal a police vehicle would bring their favorite high-tech cutters. In a way, I had.

I put my hand close to the locator and opened the Infinite Pocket. It was dark under the van, and I couldn't see much of what was above the power train, but I knew the shape of the Infinite Pocket as well as I knew the shape of my hand.

The Pocket was intended for objects about the size of the SIG, which meant that its field of warped space projected four inches from my inner wrist in an oval six inches long at its greatest point. Whether it had any true depth is a question for mathematicians and philosophers. Effectively, its edge was finer than the blade of a monomolecular knife.

Its drawback as a tool or a weapon was that it's hard to maneuver something almost invisible set at a right angle to your wrist and triggered to shut down near living flesh. Most of the time, there's something better at hand. No pun intended.

I doubt it took thirty seconds to scoot under the van, cut the second locator box free with the edge of the Pocket, and scoot back out, but the entire time I was wondering how long the copbots would stay down and whether their reprogrammers had a backup plan in place.

Leaving both locators on the street, I took the wheel, tapped the manual control, and drove away at the speed limit. Under the Libertarians, the limit's only a suggestion, but people would be less likely to remember a police van that seemed to be heading for a donut shop instead of an emergency.

I said, "Wakey."

"Gotta?"

"Gotta."

"Where we going?"

"A friend's."

"You have friends?"

I glanced over at her. She wore a weary "gotcha" smile. "Sad, desperate souls, every one of 'em."

"Is your friend a cop?"

"No."

"Good."

We didn't talk after that. Once we were a few blocks out of USCLA, I put on the roof flashers and drove as fast as I safely could. I glanced over every now and then to give her a shake. I put the radio on a technofolk station and punched the volume all the way up. That seemed to help.

I drove from University City to Mission Hills on surface streets—that's long-time L.A.-speak for any route that's not one of the major tollways, which were built on raised beds to pass over the city streets. The tollgates would've probably let the van pass, but they would've also recorded its presence and direction.

With the flashers on, the trip was faster than it could've been, but it was still agonizingly slow. Not everyone could move aside quickly. And though police vehicles don't pay tolls, we still had to wait for the bars to be raised at the cheaper stations, where they save on the cost of automation by hiring neighborhood kids to tend the tollpike.

Many neighborhoods have free main streets, thanks to business associations that want to promote traffic. Though free streets are infinitely faster than stopping every block or two to drop five or ten C, they're heavily travelled by the surface class in their gross polluters and ancient electrics that invariably die where they'll stop the most traffic. And on free streets, few stop lights have been maintained, so I crept through most intersections with the siren screaming and fervent prayers to the gods of traffic.

I distracted myself from the miseries of automobile travel in L.A. by pondering what had happened. Someone was building humanoid chassis for AIs. Someone was building *very good* humanoid chassis. I wanted to believe that there were two Inspector Blakes. But when she—I wasn't ready to think of Kris Blake as *it* yet—had shown me her eyes before shooting Tauber, she meant for me to know what she was. She wanted me to attack her after she killed Tauber. Of that much, I was certain.

After that, certainty took a vacation. Assuming things had gone as the people behind Blake intended—and I had no reason to assume otherwise—I was brought into it for two reasons. By shooting Blake, I encouraged Zoe to shoot her with the pistol Blake tossed in her lap, and, by shooting, I became as much a fugitive as Zoe. The planners had to assume that now I would do one of three things: take Zoe to the cops to prove my innocence, abandon her to run without any help, or stick by her knowing that my few resources—my maxed-out credit card and my web account—were no longer safe to use, since the cops and the killers could trace them with equal ease.

The case's rapidly widening scope frightened me. Someone had had copbots ready to move in as soon as the trap was sprung. If what Vallejo and Chumley had said about the bots that killed Gold and helped Doyle was true, these were regular copbots off the street, pursuing their duties one moment and obeying their secret masters the next, not counterfeits or bots stolen from the police repair shop. If, as it appeared, the bad guys could program bots through their link to CityCentral, they could have every copbot in the city at their disposal if they wanted.

Perhaps their plan hadn't gone as smoothly as intended. The simplest scenario would've been to make people think that the copbots had killed a werewolf that had killed Amos Tauber, thus getting rid of Zoe and Tauber in one move. Maybe Blake had intended to kill me, too, to make me look like another victim of Zoe's werewolfing. Only it all went slightly wrong when I pulled the SIG.

But for a plan that simple, the location didn't make sense. Too much could go wrong in a crowded cafeteria. And that plan didn't leave them a way to recover the earring. Maybe they no longer wanted it. But if they didn't, why did they care about Zoe?

A more frightening possibility was that there were fewer uncontrollable elements than I first thought. If they had tapped Tauber's phone, they knew we would be meeting him at the university. If he usually ate at the cafeteria, they knew where to stage the murder where it would make a convincing werewolfing. Perhaps the explosives in Blake's Vetterli were powerful enough to kill humans—or perhaps only the first shot was powerful enough to kill humans—and the rest were barely strong enough to damage Blake's synthetic flesh. If the bad guys had wanted her to fall through a window so no one would examine her right away, they could count on her getting to one.

The degree of mechanization in investigating crime scenes simplified the planners' task. If the bots cleaning up the scene lied about what they found, who would know? Maybe they would substitute another body for Blake's. Or maybe they wouldn't bother. If an autopsy report claimed that a woman died from an exploding projectile and a fall, who would insist on opening up cold storage to verify that her body was there? Dozens of people saw Kristal Agatha Blake die. Who would wonder whether she had ever existed? Our lives are collections of data records. Killing Blake was probably as easy as creating her. The only thing I did not doubt was that the same people had done both.

The most frightening consideration was that Blake had been accepted by other cops as one of their own. Did that mean more cops were involved? Or were there more human-looking AIs out there?

Add another thing I was sure of: someone had used considerable resources to kill Tauber and frame Zoe. The result was the two of us on the run. There were simpler ways to achieve that than a werewolfing scare, but the killers' resources were so great that simplicity was not a consideration. Audacity was. By arranging something as conspicuous as an apparent werewolfing in a crowded cafeteria, they prevented the kinds of questions that would arise from a more discrete murder.

Now that Zoe and I were on the run, they would expect us to hole up someplace quiet. I wished I could think of anything else to do, but I couldn't.

8

In a blue-collar residential neighborhood in Mission Hills, I rang the bell at a shabby pink stucco house. Eddie LeFevre answered. A small man with a receding chin and dark, wild hair, he always dressed with a touch of discount style—this day's outfit consisted of copper trousers, nullight boots, and a shirt whose fabric seemed like a window into the heart of a galaxy.

I grinned at him. "Hey, Eddie."

"Captain!" He stared at the mess on my suit. "What happened to you?"

"A long story. I need—"

"I been getting your money together—"

"We'll call it square if you can help me."

"How?"

"I've got a murder suspect OD'd on sleep darts in a stolen police van. If the cops spot us, we'll probably both be killed."

"Oh, man, when you call in a favor—"

"If you can't help, forget you saw me. We'll still be square."

"You want to make me an accomplice."

I nodded.

"Can I keep the van?"

"Sure."

"You pulled the locators?"

"There's more than one?"

"Cap—" His eyes opened wide.

"I pulled them."

"Jeez, don't do that to me. Where is it?"

"In your backyard."

"The neighbors'll freak."

"Tell 'em you got it with a subscription to *Gun Fancy*."

I led Eddie around back to the van. Zoe opened the side door and nearly fell out. As I caught her, she said, "You're not as big a jerk as I thought."

"Everyone says that. Eddie LeFevre, Zoe Domingo."

She said, "G'night, Eddie," and closed her eyes. I picked her up. About the weight of two wild cats, I thought as I carried her toward the house. For some reason, that made me smile.

Eddie said, "You're doing this for a critter? I mean, she's cute, Captain, but—"

"She's a client."

"Whatever you say, Cap."

He held the door open for me. If Eddie had been a chimera, he would've been a pack rat; his place was very well insulated with boxes that were undoubtedly of the "fallen off a truck" variety. Or maybe he was operating a mail-order business. Or, knowing Eddie, both. I didn't ask, and I didn't study any of the boxes. For your friends, sometimes it's good to preserve deniability.

Making my way through the maze of his living room warehouse, I said, "Can you get a glass of water for her?"

"Sure. Bottled, none of that shit from the tap."

"You only got the best, Eddie."

As he headed for the kitchen, I carried Zoe into his office and guest room, which continued the warehouse decor with what looked like cartons of software. I'd seen Eddie's French whorehouse of a bedroom once, and figured Zoe and Eddie would both be happier if I put her here. When I set her on her feet, she fell back onto the airbed and said, "I'm gonna lie down."

I pulled her into a sitting position. "Nope."

"What'd I ever do to you?"

"Don't get me started. Now, stay awake, stay alive."

Eddie came in with a tall glass of water. I took it and handed it to Zoe. She drank it down obediently.

Eddie said, "I called some guys about the van. They'll pay a hundred K. I figured it was better to go for speed than top dollar. Sure you don't want half?"

"It's all yours, Eddie. Think you can keep her awake while I clean up?"

"Sure, Captain." He looked at Zoe as her head nodded slowly forward. "Hey, cat! Don't do that."

She peered at him through heavily lidded eyes. "That's Ms. Cat to you."

"Uh . . . how 'bout those Dodgers, huh?"

She lifted her head to give him an "I can't believe you said that" scowl.

He said, "Don't like baseball?"

Her head bobbed like a dashboard doll. "Sure. Very restful sport. Wake me at the end of the ninth."

Eddie gave me a hopeless look. I said, "Keep trying. I'm sure you've got something in common." That was a bit of a joke; I figured Eddie and Zoe had as much in common as she and I did.

"Oh, man—" He turned back to Zoe. "Okay, cards? Checkers? What do you like to play?"

"Dead."

He caught her as she leaned back. "C'mon, Ms. Cat! You fall asleep, the Captain'll skin me."

Confident that Eddie would annoy her enough to keep her awake, I went to the bathroom. I emptied my pockets, then stepped into the shower fully dressed. The blood and food washed out, but crawling under the van had been the suit's kiss of death. More sadly, I'd done in the Hawaiian shirt, too. When a button went, it tore a "V" in the cloth.

I switched from shower to dryer and stood under the warm air jets wondering what kind of fool I was. This twenty-four-hour job had been extended indefinitely when I became an accomplice by helping Zoe out of the cafeteria. Or had I? If I'd left her, the mob would've killed her. I had the same right to protect a chimera that I had to protect a dog or a horse from being killed by anyone who didn't own it.

The right thing to do was to finish my day's work. If I couldn't get Zoe out of trouble by exposing the people reprogramming copbots, I would wish her good luck and send her on her way. More than that, no one could ask. Not even me.

The dryer might've improved the look of my clothes—the stains weren't as obvious with the cloth rumpled—but I doubted it. I took what consolation I could in knowing I would've looked worse in anything I could've borrowed from Eddie.

Coming up the hall, I heard him say, "Hey, hey—don't sleep."

She said, "I'm thinking."

"Think out loud."

"You're a good guy, too."

As I entered the room, I saw Eddie blush. He shrugged and told Zoe, "Shoot."

Wondering who else was supposed to be a good guy, I said, "What kind of lies has Eddie been telling?"

He looked guilty. "Just yakking about the old days, Captain. I'll make some coffee."

Zoe watched him leave. "He's nice."

I said, "Don't lend him money."

She smiled, slumped back against the headboard, and closed her eyes.

I lunged for her. "No, you don't." I hauled her to her feet, draped her arm over my shoulder, and walked her around the room. "C'mon. Just like strolling in the park."

She glanced at the room. "Needs landscaping."

"Yeah? Like what? Some pines in the corner, a pond by the bed?"

"Don't want to talk about landscaping."

"Then tell me a story."

"Don't know any stories."

"Tell me about you."

She pulled herself up. "Boring!" Then she slumped again.

"C'mon. What's your favorite color?"

She bared her teeth at me. "Rare steak red."

"Don't torture the vegetarian."

She smiled in sleepy contentment.

I tried again. "Who's your best friend?"

"Um. Tim."

"Tim who?"

"Timurlane."

"Tim's a chimera?"

Her head nodded in an exaggerated and exasperated nod. "Cat critter."

"How'd you meet him?"

"We ran away from the Petting Zoo. It's this place where—"

"I know the kind of place." I had read about them. They seemed to be especially popular in "N" states—Nevada, New Jersey, North Dakota—where you could do anything you wanted to chimeras, provided you could pay to replace them if they didn't live. "Then what?"

"Mostly running and hiding. We were too good to get caught."

"I'll bet."

"We were happy. We did everything together." She smiled.

"Where's Tim now?"

The smile disappeared. "Werewolfed. Cops killed him."

Zoe let go of my shoulder and started to fall. I caught her, jolting her back awake. "What about Dr. Gold? How'd you meet her?"

"Doc? People said Minnesota was a good place for critters. She was at the U."

"The University of Minnesota?"

"Yeah. Paying critters to take tests. Comparing human and critter reactions, stuff like that. We got along." Zoe smiled again. "Said she always wanted a daughter."

"She took care of you."

"I took care of her, too. Only not good enough."

"You did what you could."

She shook her head vigorously. "Cops killed Doc. And Tauber."

"Bots killed them. Maybe cops are involved, maybe not. All we know is someone programmed the bots."

"You slept with that Blake. Ick!"

"Thanks. I've been trying not to think of that."

She smiled. "You said to talk."

"I'm tough. Keep talking."

"Why do you gamble?"

"I like it."

"No, you don't."

"I do it because I don't like it?"

"Uh-huh. Cigarettes, too. Punishment."

I frowned at her, but she missed it. Punishment? I wondered where she had gotten a notion like that.

Eddie said, "Coffee," and I looked up at the likely source. He came in with two mugs and put them on the desk. If he had overheard anything, he played innocent perfectly. But then, Eddie had a lot of practice at playing innocent. I wrapped Zoe's hands around a mug and walked her to a straight-backed chair.

"Let's watch some HV." I clicked on the set and gave her the remote. As she flicked through channels, I drew Eddie aside and said quietly, "You told her about Long Island."

"You said to keep her awake. She was interested—"

"When this is over, remind me to kill you."

Zoe said, "Uh-oh. It's the Max and Zoe show."

The HV showed the USCLA cafeteria with cops and cop-bots swarming through it like ants in a picnic basket. An ambulance team rolled Tauber's sheeted body out on a crash cart. Good old Adam Tromploy said very earnestly, "In Los Angeles today, chimera rights activist Amos Tauber was killed in a werewolfing."

Blurry blown-up security camera stills of Zoe and me in a USCLA hallway appeared onscreen. Tromploy said, "The police warn the public to be on the alert for the werewolfing suspect and her human companion."

I glanced at Zoe, expecting to see her looking worried. Her eyes had closed again. I grabbed her cup before it fell, then shook her. "Zoe? Stay with me, damn it!"

She blinked at me. "You're back."

"Yeah," I agreed. "I'm back. What do you want to talk about?"

"Nothing."

"You can do better than that."

"Okay. You."

"Forget it."

"Okay." She closed her eyes.

"Blackmailer."

She nodded. "Like you won't cheat to get what you want."

"I don't cheat. I take advantage of the moment."

"Yeah. That's what I meant."

"So what do you want to hear?"

"Everything."

I glared at Eddie. He said, "You guys holler if you need anything," and left.

Zoe said, "Well?"

"Everything?"

"You got my story. Fair's fair."

So I talked. Sometimes she interrupted, and sometimes I nudged her so she would interrupt. I didn't want to tell her as much as I did—hell, I didn't want to tell her any of it—but Eddie had given her enough about Long Island to let her dig for the full version. As for the rest, well, she was a good listener, and there wasn't much else to do while the afternoon died and we waited for Eddie's friends to fetch the van.

I grew up rich. Not super-rich like a software sultan or a petroleum prince, but rich. Like most rich people, I didn't think I was especially well off. I knew plenty of people richer than we. My parents used the same euphemism that all our neighbors in Darien did—we were "comfortable." I never stopped to consider that this must've meant that our servants were uncomfortable. It was the way life was, and it was good.

The family money came from the earliest days of personal computers, when Grandpa invested heavily in Silicon Valley. Dad used his inheritance to buy up post offices after the first big flurry of privatization. He met Mom when she came on as a vice-president of nonhuman resources. Maxwell Mail Services expanded quickly and so did the Maxwell family, with me, then Jeff, who drowned at fourteen in a sailing accident, and then Selene, who knew all her life that she was going to be a prima ballerina who would have many famous lovers and two perfect children.

As a kid, I never paid attention to the family business. I remember touring an MMS facility once and seeing our chimeras at work, but the only thing I felt was boredom; I desperately wanted to be hanging out with my friends. Everyone assumed that after I graduated, I would become a vice-president and work my way to the top, and someday I would leave my heirs and Selene's the world's biggest mail delivery service. I had no complaints with the plan. When I went to Yale, everything seemed to be proceeding on schedule. MMS had just acquired two of its competitors and driven a third out of business. I expected to spend four years in New Haven studying astronomy, intoxicants, and women, not in that order.

Then Dad put a bullet through his brain. His debts were enormous. He had overextended the company, then gambled on a few business propositions that failed. Maybe we should've run off to Europe and claimed to be economic refugees, but Mom had been a Libertarian her entire life. Saying she was too old to become a hypocrite, she sold everything that would've been seized by the courts. And then she sold the only asset she had left: herself.

She negotiated a ten-year indenture to Canoga Corp as a middle-management exec, with clauses stipulating that she wouldn't work more than sixty-five hours a week and would have her contract shortened if they promoted her into a position with more responsibility. For a forty-five-year-old woman in debt, it was a very good deal. She said she welcomed the challenge.

But it didn't cover all our expenses. To buy my sister enough time to finish prep school, I dropped out of Yale before second term finals and joined the U.N. Peace Force.

Getting far away from home seemed like a good idea. With my travel allowance, I could alternate visits to Selene in Connecticut and Mom in Senegal, where she'd been sent to help open a new plant. My theory held for exactly one good visit with each of them.

On Selene's sixteenth birthday, when I was stationed in Mississippi helping to contain the Jackson Rebellion, Selene sold herself for three years to a brothel in Chicago. As a virgin, she got top dollar, more than enough to buy out Mom's contract and let me go back to Yale. I learned this on a vid that she emailed me, because she knew that I wouldn't have let her do it if she'd spoken to me live.

I never got a chance to speak to her live. A month into her contract, she was offered a year and a half off her indenture if she would sign a rider to take on rougher clients. Three weeks after she signed it, a man named Vernon Bolanders beat her to death. A house bodyguard broke into the room and shot Bolanders dead. There wasn't anything for Mom and me to do after that but mourn.

Maybe I should've gone back to school and gotten a business degree. Instead, I gave my share of Selene's money to Mom, who moved into a domed community and began drinking one and a half bottles of wine a day. I doubled my efforts in the Peace Force. Someone noticed and promoted me to lieutenant, then transferred me to U.N. Security. I liked that. I was going to make the world safe for the people who wanted to make it better. Because I'd been lucky in Mississippi, I was assigned to Counter-Terrorism. When I made captain, they issued me my very own Infinite Pocket.

I met Rita Hlavy in Geneva and married her four months later. We figured I would do my twenty years in UNSEC, then our two kids would be in college and we could spend the rest of our lives together in comfort. We were working on the first of the kids when the Long Island assignment came along.

You may remember it, though what made the news wasn't that dramatic. Some separatists were killed by an UNSEC team before they could release biologicals. There was more to it than that.

They called themselves the Hands of Freedom. They wanted to accelerate the Libertarian Revolution by shutting down the federal government entirely and getting the U.N. out of the U.S. They had a side issue of shipping all chimeras to Oklahoma and leaving them there to fend for themselves. The main thing that made the Hands different from nuts in any state is that they apparently had a modified anthrax virus and enough missiles to deliver it to every major city on the eastern seaboard.

UNSEC learned about the Hands when one of the guys who sold them missiles decided to cut a deal. So one night shortly before Thanksgiving, I was sitting in the back of a Durga Eleven, flying low over the Atlantic with a team under my command that consisted of Sergeant Eddie LeFevre, Sergeant Lupe Rivera, Lieutenant Anne Lassiter, and a Model XL-5 commandobot.

I remember the mission too clearly. You tell yourself you want to forget something, but you keep going over it to try to figure out where you went wrong. I don't know how many times I went over it. Maybe if I lay it out here, this can be the last one.

I doubt any of us talked in the Durga. I was listening to Colonel Ngarré handle the press on my helmet radio. He sidestepped the question of whether the Hands had biologicals by going to issues: "Threats like these bring home the madness of nationalism. But this is exactly the kind of problem that UNSEC exists to deal with. We can't allow a handful of extremists to hold the world hostage." When a reporter asked if a response was in progress, you could hear Ngarré's smile as he said, "You know I can't answer that."

We flew low above the waves. When I saw a few house lights across the moonlit sea, I gave the signal. One by one, we jumped.

Swimming underwater, we gathered at my beacon one hundred yards offshore. The commandobot surfaced first in chameleon mode. When it gave the all-clear, we rose. In the night, with our suits mimicking the rippling darkness of the water, we were effectively invisible. If Death has angels, they probably study UNSEC's techniques.

According to my helmet readout, we were on time. The mission status hadn't changed. I gave a movie-hero "move 'em out" forearm wave toward the nearest house with lights on, and we swam silently toward shore.

When we were close, I motioned for everyone to stop. While we bobbed just beyond the breaking surf, the others drew their rifles from the sheaths on their backs. I kept an eye on our target, where a security light illuminated a wooden deck and the pale sand around it. At the bottom of the steps, a large, bearded man in a floppy beach hat sat in a lounge chair with a blanket tucked around his neck and a portable HV on his stomach. The night was too cool for sitting outdoors. He could only be a guard.

A second man came out of the house, spoke to the first, then went back inside. The HV flickered as the guard in the chair changed channels. This was the Hands' fifteen minutes of fame. They weren't going to miss a moment.

I would've preferred to wait for the lights to go out, but we didn't have that luxury. I led the others close to shore, then pulled off my helmet, gave it to Rivera, and peeled off my suit. That's a shock in the Atlantic on a November night, but cold doesn't bother you when you think you're saving millions of lives.

Lassiter squinted at my purple, orange, and blue swim trunks and whispered, "Jesus! Who issued those?"

I said, "They're mine," to let her know no one could match my sense of style, ducked underwater to wet my hair, then said, "Okay, team, let's do this without waking the baby."

I splashed loudly ashore and trotted toward the bearded guard. On his HV, Ngarré stood at a podium, listening to a reporter say, "If the Hands do have a modified anthrax virus—"

Ngarré cut him off. "Haven't you heard? UNSEC always get its man. Or microbe."

While the reporters laughed, I jogged into the light and waved at the guard. Wondering what weapons his blanket hid, I called, "Hi, neighbor! How's it going?"

He sat up. His voice was a deep growl. "Who're you?"

"Chase Maxwell, but everyone calls me Max. The wife and I just moved in down the beach—" I stopped as light fell on his face. He wasn't just bearded—he was half-covered with brown fur. His lips pulled back from long, sharp teeth. I said, "You're a critter!"

"This is private property. Beat it."

I kept walking toward him. "Hey, tell your owner to lighten up. What're you, part bear?"

He glanced back at the house, then nodded. "Grizzly. This is your last warning."

"Or what? Can't eat the neighbors, y'know."

"Don't make me call the police."

"Okay, you want to be left alone, fine." I pointed at the round scar on my forearm. "Know what this is?"

He shook his head.

I extended my right arm toward him as if to give him a better look. "An Infinite Pocket." The air went wild around my wrist. The SIG flew into my hand. "And you're under—"

The grizzly brought his arms up under the blanket—not as if he was going to surrender. The cloth draped over something cylindrical in his hands.

I threw myself aside and fired as the grizzly got off a short burst. Our shots made muffled *whumpfs* like stones landing in the sand. I hit the bear at least twice, but nowhere vital.

Then Lassiter stepped from the darkness behind him, triggering open a monomolecular knife that she waved across his throat. He spasmed and went limp, his neck nearly severed. I lunged forward to grab the rifle as he let go.

He fell back in his chair. Lassiter adjusted his head on his shoulders, jerked his hat down to hide the staring eyes, then adjusted the blanket to obscure his bloody chest. The HV continued its chatter—oddly jarring after the flurry of violence.

Lassiter and I crouched in the shadow of the deck, listening for a hint that we'd been overheard. I pressed a hand against my waist, then realized why: blood seeped between my fingers. The bear's shot had grazed me. As it began to hurt, Lassiter passed me a medipatch. I slapped it over my wound and motioned for her to stay where she was.

I crept up to a window and peered inside. In a kitchen that hadn't been remodeled since the year 2000, a heavy, blond woman and a thin, crewcut man ate pizza and watched HV. An automatic rifle lay on the table by their dinner.

I slipped back over the deck rail, told Lassiter, "Thank God for mass entertainment," and sent the signal to continue. Eddie, Rivera, and the commandobot dashed through the pool of light to crouch beside us. Rivera brought my combat gear, so I returned the SIG to the Pocket. I jerked my thumb toward the roof, then put my suit and helmet back on while Rivera and Eddie shot climbing cables into the eaves and scrambled up.

Lassiter pulled a plate-sized silver disk—a field anchor— from her pack. She set it at a corner of the house and tapped its switch to activate it. Above us, Rivera and Eddie were placing similar disks at each corner of the roof. I pulled an anchor from my pack and started for the front of the house. The bot was crouching by the rear corner with its steel hands against the foundation. "Sir. There is a basement."

I gave the only reasonable response. "Shit."

Lassiter picked up the anchor she had set down. For the first time, I could see uncertainty or maybe even fear through her faceplate. "If the lab's down there—"

I nodded. "Tin man and I'll go in. Give us two minutes."

The bot took Lassiter's anchors, and we went around the house. Mounted by the side door was a numeric keypad with a faintly glowing display that read "Secure." The bot held its hand up to the keypad. A laser projected from its palm to shine on the panel above the keys. Numbers flashed on the security system's display, too quick to read, and the door's status changed to "Open."

I followed the bot into a dark hall. The door to the main part of the house was closed. Someone was watching HV in the living room. Our briefing had been vague on the number of people in the Hands. We were told to expect as few as three or as many as twenty.

I led the bot down the basement stairs. Everything looked crisp and colorless through my helmet's nightsight, which seemed appropriate for the way I felt. Toys and games and sports equipment were piled along the walls. The bot and I were strange intruders in what looked like the basement of any family on vacation.

Then I saw the makeshift lab on the Ping-Pong table: a pocket computer, racks of chemistry equipment, and an open hard-shell suitcase. In the suitcase were explosives and canisters of gas. It could've been a place for Junior to practice science homework, but it looked to me like a place to brew killer bugs.

The bot and I put anchors at each corner of the basement. As we placed the last two, the ceiling light came on. The man from the kitchen stood at the top of the stairs, rifle in hand. He said, "Oh, man—" and brought his rifle up.

The bot swiveled its right arm like aiming a weapon. I reached over my back to draw my rifle and knew we were both too late. The Hand squeezed off three muffled shots, ripping open the bot's chest and head. It toppled as I shot the man twice. When he fell and didn't move, I ran upstairs.

I met Lassiter coming in the side door, rifle ready. I gave her a thumbs-up for success. She nodded and turned to leave. If we'd gotten out of there an instant sooner, I probably would've been doing Ngarré's job when Zoe Domingo came looking for a detective.

As we turned to go, the door to the main part of the house opened slowly. Lassiter and I raised our rifles. The door opened wider. My finger tightened on the trigger. And a sleepy, pajama-clad bear cub, about the size of a four-year-old, peered through the opening. It said, "Daddy?"

I grabbed the cub and clamped a hand over its mouth.

Warily, I pushed the living room door wide. Lassiter and I looked in.

A bear woman in a maid's uniform slept on the couch, cradling a gently breathing teddy bear in diapers. Sleeping on the floor, wrapped in blankets, were two more bear children. Like the grizzly, they looked as much human as animal.

Lassiter grabbed my shoulder and whispered, "Let's go!"

I closed the living room door, then tapped my helmet to activate the radio. The cub struggled in my grip as I spoke into the helmet radio, "Colonel, there are noncombatants in the target. Repeat, noncombatants in the target."

A translucent overlay of Ngarré's head and shoulders appeared on my visor. He looked unhappy, which I expected. We weren't supposed to break radio silence until the mission had been completed.

I said, "Sir, there's a servant critter here and some cubs. We haven't searched—"

He interrupted. "Are there human noncombatants?"

"Not that I've seen. But—"

"Proceed as planned, Captain."

"Sir, those are innocent—"

"Captain Maxwell, you're relieved of command. Lieutenant Lassiter, complete the mission."

Lassiter said simply, "Yes, sir." In her place, I would've done the same.

As Ngarré's image disappeared from my visor, Lassiter stepped between me and the living room, her rifle not quite pointed at my chest. Furious, I hauled the struggling cub out the door.

Eddie and Rivera waited in the shadows beside the house. I thrust the cub into Eddie's arms and headed for the house.

Lassiter caught my arm. "They're critters, Max. Eddie, status."

He said, "Anchors live and in place up top, Lieutenant."

The cub twisted in Eddie's grasp. Its claws cut through his combat suit, drawing blood. Eddie grunted and dropped the bear. It ran back toward the house, screaming "Momma!"

I lunged after the cub. The side door opened as Momma Bear looked out. She saw us, then reached for her child and cried, "Joey!"

Joey leaped into her arms. She pulled him inside and slammed the door.

At the back of the house, a window broke. A Hand poked a rifle out and fired a burst at us. Rivera screamed and fell. The Hand yelled, "It's UNSEC!"

We dove for cover. On the second floor, another window shattered. Gunfire from a second Hand stitched the ground by my head. I rolled aside, then fired a burst upward. That Hand fell from the window.

Lassiter jabbed buttons on her wrist pad. An eerie hum arose from nowhere, building rapidly in volume. On the roof, the silver disks glowed. Rays of light raced out from each disk to its fellows, enclosing the house in a shimmering cube of light. Only the peaked roof lay outside the cube.

Space within the cube warped, like the Infinite Pocket effect magnified ten thousand times. People in the house began to scream. One Hand—the crewcut man—realized what was happening and dove out a window, just a moment too late.

The screaming ended abruptly when the cube of light disappeared with everything inside it. The roof peak fell into the empty basement with a crash. So did the head, shoulders, and arms of the crewcut Hand who had tried to leap from the containment field.

I got to my feet, yanked off my helmet, and stumbled to the pit where the beach house had stood. The air smelled like ozone. Eastern North America had been saved. It was a glorious day for UNSEC.

Near me, Rivera groaned and clutched her thigh. Eddie

ran to her and began first aid. Lassiter spoke into her radio. "Mission completed. Rivera, LeFevre, and Maxwell need minor medical attention. We lost the bot. Thank you, sir."

She pulled off her helmet as she walked over to me. She was an attractively hard-looking woman, thin and brown with light brown eyes and a wide mouth. I had seen that mouth contort in pleasure, one night when we were both lonely. She said, "Give me one good reason, and I'll back you at your court-martial."

I looked at her, then away. I'm still working on the answer.

There was no court martial. Ngarré accepted my resignation. I gave up my pension, but UNSEC agreed not to put me through the risk of an operation to remove the Infinite Pocket. For months, I thought about telling the media the full story of what had happened in Long Island—there's always a story when the good guys kill kids, even if they're kids covered with fur. But when I joined UNSEC, I had signed a nondisclosure agreement covering all its operations, and, besides, I'll never know whether my desire to change the plan would've resulted in the loss of the Eastern seaboard.

I took a break from my story at that point. The shortest day of the year had come to an end; the longest night was beginning. I turned on a lamp, then wished I had an excuse to turn it off to escape Zoe's gaze. She said, "What happened next?"

"Rita had a miscarriage."

"I'm sorry."

"It was probably for the best. We thought our marriage was rocky because UNSEC kept me away from home. Being home for a few months proved we were wrong. We got divorced. I kicked around for a while, travelling mostly. Blowing my savings was fun."

"Why a detective agency?"

"Flexible hours, low overhead. Seemed like a good idea at the time."

"Not now?"

I shrugged. "I thought I'd get rich doing corporate jobs. But corporations give their business to other corporations. The only things I was offered involved drug tests or union busting. I wasn't interested."

"Mmm."

"That's not a question."

"Your policy's not to work for critters."

I wasn't expecting that one. I said, "That's not a question either."

"Why?"

" 'Cause I don't like to."

"You tried it?"

"No. I'd be awfully conspicuous tailing a cheating critter from a critter bar to a critter hotel. Besides, not many critters can afford me."

"Sounds like rationalizing."

"Question."

"Huh?"

"Good enough. We're rationalizing beings. What do you expect me to do?"

"If you felt guilty about Long Island, I'd think you'd take jobs from critters."

"If I was a saint."

"You live around critters."

"It's the cheapest halfway-decent neighborhood in L.A."

"Eddie says you said once you couldn't stand the idea of letting another critter down."

"Eddie was drunker than me. Don't put money on what he remembers."

"You're working for me."

"Not because I owe the whole damn chimera species. Don't read too much into Long Island. I may not like what happened there, but sometimes the innocent just fucking die."

"You don't have to get mad."

"I don't have to get analyzed, either."

"Okay."

"Okay." I breathed deeply, realized I was doing that, and asked, "Are you hungry?"

"No."

"Too bad. You have to eat something, 'cause I am. Can you stay awake for three minutes?"

She nodded.

I wanted to apologize, but I wasn't sure why. Deciding that a little time by myself would be good for both of us, I clicked the HV on loud and found a comedy channel. She laughed at some poor bastard running out of a lake with his pants full of fish, which I took as a bad sign for her sense of humor but a good sign for her wakefulness.

I went to the kitchen and made sandwiches, summer sausage for her and Eddie, avocado and barbecue sauce for me. Eddie was at his computer when I looked in his bedroom. He said, "How is she?"

"Still awake." I handed him a sandwich.

"Thanks, Captain. She seems all right, for a critter."

"She's annoying," I said. "Mind if I check my e-mail?"

He and I ate our sandwiches while I logged on. The ex had sent me a joke about men that she thought was funny. More important, the mysterious Mycroft had not answered my inquiry about Gold's death.

When I returned to the guest room, Zoe's eyes were closed and her breathing was shallow. I set her sandwich aside, checked her pulse, then shook her. "C'mon, Zoe. Fight it!" I slapped her cheeks, hard enough to bring a tinge of red to them. Still, her eyes didn't open.

I sat beside her and smoothed her hair. "Just fight—" I let the sentence die. She couldn't hear me. She needed a doctor or a miracle. A hospital would record her as an admittee, which would be the same as handing her to the cops. Even if she lucked into a cop who wasn't under the influence of Gold's killers, any place that cops could put her, a copbot could get to.

The doorbell rang. Eddie passed by, saying, "Must be the guys for the van." He looked at Zoe. "She doesn't look good."

"You know any doctors who don't ask questions?"

"I could check around. They don't come cheap."

"See what you can find."

"Okay." The bell rang again. "Coming!" Eddie yelled, and headed for the front.

I pulled a pack of cigarettes from my jacket, shook one out, put it to my lips, pulled out my pocket knife, snapped on the lighter, then looked at Zoe doing the Sleeping Beauty thing and said, "Hell." I put the cig back in the pack, crushed it, and threw it in the trash. My offering to Nicotina, Bitch Goddess of Tobacco. "Hang in there, cat."

Eddie reappeared at the door with a grim expression.

I said, "Who was it?"

He stumbled forward, shoved into the room by a dogman with a big Colt in his fist. It took me a moment to recognize Bruno outside of Wonderland. His big, black-and-white orca partner, similarly armed, came in after him.

Eddie said, "Sorry, Captain."

Arthur followed his pet chimeras inside and grinned. "Hey, Max. If you had more friends, you'd be harder to find."

"If it's friends that give you away, you could hide forever, Arthur."

The orca hit me in the stomach. I doubled over, unable to breathe. It was worth it.

Arthur said, "Your loan's going to be paid back with interest, Max. We can be pals again." I managed to straighten up. He said, "Your pistol. Now."

The orca held out his hand for the SIG. I hesitated.

Arthur said, "Be good, and Eddie stays home with his skull intact."

I jerked a thumb at Zoe. "What about her?"

"She's the payment for your loan. You can carry her." When I didn't move, Arthur added, "Someone wants to talk with you two. Far as I know, you give the right answers, and everyone walks away happy."

"That's not exactly reassuring."

"Max, Max, Max. I'm a practical guy. If this someone wanted you dead, I wouldn't be debating with you. But I realize you've got your pride. If you'd rather have Rashid rough you up first, maybe break an arm or two—"

The orca showed me his gleaming teeth.

"That's thoughtful, Arthur." I held my arm out wide and opened the Pocket. The SIG hurtled into my hand. "But not necessary." I passed the SIG to Rashid. He tucked his own pistol into his shoulder holster and kept mine in his huge paw.

I lifted Zoe in both arms and went to the door. Eddie watched like he was about to cry. I can't say I felt better. He said, "Captain—"

"Wasn't your fault, Eddie. Forget we were ever here."

Arthur grinned. "Well, Max. Hanging out with that cat has raised your I.Q."

9

The air smelled of wood smoke—usually a luxury in L.A., but this night was cool enough to justify it. In the driveway, under a fat silver moon, sat a fat silver Mercedes. The silhouettes of a few palm trees against the sky made it look like it had been parked there for an ad, but the boxy little houses of Mission Hills would need to be digitally replaced with French chateaus or beachfront bungalows, and the director would insist on actors a lot prettier than Arthur and his beastie boys.

Arthur clicked the remote; the Mercedes's doors sprang open. Rashid said, "In back." His voice may've been high-pitched, but it did not inspire debate.

I slid Zoe onto the back seat, then got in beside her and let her head rest on my shoulder. I was getting used to her scent of shampoo and cat fur. Rashid closed the door. As he went to the front passenger's seat, Arthur took the driver's, and Bruno sat in back, beside Zoe.

I said, "Are we there yet?"

Arthur said, "Don't push it, Max." He tapped in the destination, and the car pulled away. I found his use of the keypad a little reassuring. If he was sure that we would be killed after his "someone" talked with us, he wouldn't have cared whether I overheard our destination.

As we headed for the 405 Tollway, Zoe drooled on my shoulder. I looked at Rashid, whose only response was to waggle my SIG at me. I said, "She needs a doctor."

Arthur said, "They can get her one."

"Who're we going to see?"

"Someone who isn't paying me to answer your questions."

No one spoke again until we were on the tollway heading west. When the car hit a particularly noticeable bump, I looked at Rashid. He grinned back at me. I said, "Man, with these potholes, I hope you left the safety on."

As he glanced down at the SIG in his hand, I reached toward him and opened the Pocket, sucking the SIG from his grip and into mine. The next things happened nearly simultaneously: Rashid grabbed for his Colt in its shoulder holster, Bruno turned in his seat and brought his pistol up toward me, and I jammed the SIG's barrel in the back of Arthur's fleshy neck. I said, "Pull over. Now."

Arthur said, "Bruno, kill the cat."

Bruno shifted his aim toward Zoe.

I told him, "Go ahead. Then Arthur's head goes boom. Nobody's betting otherwise. But I'll take odds I can also put a shot in your face before you or Charley the Tuna can stop me. Doesn't that sound like easy money, Bowser?"

Bruno looked at his boss for advice. Arthur said, "Don't."

I poked him with the SIG just as the Mercedes turned east onto the Ventura Tollway. "Pull onto the shoulder. Hold it at five miles an hour."

Arthur switched the car to manual and pulled over. I said, "Unlock the doors." The door locks clicked open. I said, "Tell Charley and Bowser to put their guns and phones on the floor. Any sudden moves will make things very noisy and messy in here."

Arthur nodded. "You heard him."

The two chimeras put down their pistols and cell phones quite nicely. I said, "Open their doors."

Arthur touched the controls. The side doors sprang open.

I said, "It's been fun, boys. Write if you find work." When they didn't take the hint, I poked Arthur with the SIG for emphasis. "What do you think Arthur would prefer, having you jump or a closed casket funeral?"

Rashid said, "We jump?"

"That's where my money is. Am I right, Arthur?"

"Jump," he agreed.

The chimeras leaped out and rolled onto the grassy shoulder. I said, "Close the doors."

Arthur tapped the door button.

I said, "Who's offering money for us?" When he didn't answer, I added, "Arthur, I have the gun. For the sake of your pride, should I put a shot through your shoulder?"

"Kay. Django Kay."

"Who is?"

"He runs most of the East Valley."

"Gambling?"

"Primarily. He's a businessman, like me."

"And he's got a business offer for us?"

"I didn't ask."

"Where were you taking us?"

"The Parrot, in Burbank."

"Where's Kay live?"

"He's got a penthouse there."

"At the Parrot."

"Yeah."

"Okay. Pass me your pistol and phone." When he obeyed, I said, "Now put the car back in auto and jump."

Arthur glanced back at me. "It'll speed up the second I—"

"Then you better jump fast."

Arthur opened the passenger door, then hit the autopilot. He leaped out the passenger side as the car moved from the shoulder to merge with the traffic. Watching him land through the rear window, I uttered a sympathetic "ouch." As he stood, I hoped his suit was in at least as bad a shape as mine.

Zoe's ragged breathing told me what to do next. I climbed into the front seat, put the car in manual, exited at Van Nuys Blvd., and parked at the first space I saw. I hated taking time to crawl under the Mercedes and remove its locators, but I saw no choice. If Arthur was lucky, someone had already stopped for him and he was calling in a carjacking. For all I knew, the Mercedes may've already begun broadcasting its location. If I was stupid enough to put it back into automatic, it might take us straight to the nearest police station; we definitely would not pass go or collect two hundred dollars.

The locators were harder to find than on the police van, since all I had to hunt them with was the light on my pocket knife, but I found them and cut them away. Then I drove as fast as I dared to the nearest hospital. Sometimes you have to prioritize. Keeping the client alive goes ahead of keeping the client safe.

I doubt it took three minutes to get to Sherman Oaks General. I squealed into the nearest parking space and jumped out of the driver's side. Zoe's breathing was worse. I grabbed her up from the back seat and ran into the emergency room. I don't remember how busy it was—I remember brushing by a few people on my way to the admitting desk, where a young, male Hispanic nurse and an older female Asian doctor spoke together.

The nurse glanced at me, then saw Zoe. "What happened?"

"She's overdosed on tranquilizers."

The nurse asked, "How long has she been unconscious?" as they both came around the counter.

Before I could answer, the doctor halted, looking from Zoe's forehead tat to me. "We don't treat critters."

"The biology's not that different—"

"We only treat humans here."

"She's dying!"

The nurse said, "There's a chimera clinic on the north side of Crittertown that's open twenty-four hours."

"She may not live long enough to get there."

The doctor said, "Then you'd better hurry," and turned away.

The nurse, looking helpless, gave me a card. "Here's the address."

I stared at the departing doctor for a second or two, then realized that those might not have been seconds that Zoe could spare. I rushed her out of the ER.

On my way to the Mercedes, I spotted someone in doctor's whites smoking a cigarette by a door labelled EMPLOYEES ONLY. I put Zoe down in the car and ran to the doctor. "Sorry to interrupt your smoke, Doc—"

He looked up and pointed at the main door. "Admitting's over there." He appeared to be young, earnest, and tired, and even if he was being terse, he wasn't being unpleasant.

I almost felt guilty as the SIG leaped into my hand. "Not tonight."

His cig dropped as his jaw did. I ground the cig under my toe for him and said, "Nasty habit. You don't mind quitting so much if you keep your mind on other things. Give me a hand."

He still stared at me. He was just a kid, probably less than a year out of medical school. I said, "I've got a patient who needs care without being entered in the system. I don't want anyone to suffer, but if I have to, I'll hurt anyone who'd rather let her die than bend a few rules."

He stood. "I'll help."

"Good." I headed for the Mercedes and made the SIG disappear.

That impressed him. "Infinite Pocket?"

I nodded.

"I've read about them used that way. You're military?"

"Don't worry about me." I opened the door of the Mercedes. "Worry about her."

He blinked twice at Zoe, then at me. "She's a critter."

"Where'd you go to med school?"

"USCLA."

"For the sake of their rep, I hope your diagnostic skills are a little more thorough than that."

"You don't understand. If it got out that I treated a critter—"

"Your insurance would go up?" I lifted my wrist. "Don't feel bad. You're doing this under duress."

"Well." He leaned into the car, raised one of Zoe's eyelids, then told me, "Bring her."

I carried her to the employees's door. A gurney was waiting inside. I put her on it. The doc wrapped a bandage over her ears and forehead tat, then told the gurney, "Exam Six," and it rolled briskly ahead of us. He glanced at me. "What caused this?"

"Four police sleep darts."

"Oh." He swallowed, then said, "Um, would you care to say what happened?"

"No. We were framed, but in your place, I'd figure that for a lie, so that's all right. Assume we're dangerous as hell, and the best thing you can do is fix her up and get her out of here before someone does something stupid, like sound an alarm. Got it?"

"Got it."

We passed a few patients, then a nurse and an orderly. The doc never made a sign of wanting to give us away. I didn't care whether he'd decided to help Zoe because he was afraid I might go berserk or because he'd decided his Hippocratic oath meant something more than the chance to retire young and rich.

We followed the gurney into a small exam room. I lifted

Zoe onto a hospital bed. Hanging from the ceiling over the bed was a steel sphere about the size of a basketball, lavishly decorated with electronic displays and rather unpleasant-looking medical instruments. On its side was a plate that read "AI-T4312." I had heard about medical AIs, but I'd never seen one before.

The doc said, "Scan her."

The AI said, "This patient is not registered with the hospital admissions program."

The doc said, "It's under my authorization."

A bright light shone from the AI and passed over Zoe. As a metal probe descended toward her shoulder, I grabbed it and turned to the doc. "What's it doing?"

He told the AI, "Answer him."

AI-T4312 said, "I wish to draw blood for a diagnostic examination. May I proceed?"

I hesitated, then released the probe. The AI took its sample and said, "What produced her coma?"

I said, "Four police sleep darts."

The doc told the AI, "Better restrain her."

I said, "No."

"What if she wakes up and werewolfs!"

"Then I'll shoot her." Something about his sideways glance made me add, "If she doesn't wake up, maybe I'll shoot you."

AI-T4312 said, "Overdose of police tranquilizer confirmed. May I give the antitoxin?"

The doc said impatiently, "Yes, yes."

The AI lowered an injector to Zoe's arm. I heard a click. Then the injector retracted.

The doc said, "She'll need bed rest, observation. We can't do that here—"

"We can't do that anywhere. Someone wants her dead. I need her up and moving."

AI-T4312 said, "Sir, I can give her an amphetamine. There's some risk, but I consider it minimal."

The doc said, "I won't approve that."

I looked back and forth between the doc and the AI. "Do it."

AI-T4312 said, "Yes, sir." The injector descended toward Zoe.

The doc said, "Not without my—"

The injector clicked. Zoe jerked violently, coughing and choking.

The doc stepped back, convinced the cat was going to go for our throats. I grabbed him by the shoulder. "Is that normal?"

"How should I know? Do I look like a vet?"

I took Zoe's arms as her eyes opened. "Zoe!"

"Max?" She frowned at me, then glanced at the room. "Where are we?"

"In a hospital. How do you feel?"

She sat up, then shook herself. "Like I mainlined a quart of espresso."

AI-T4312 said, "That's a normal response."

I turned to the doc. "I hate to thank you this way, but—" I pointed at a chair. "Sit there and put your hands behind you."

He said, "Oh, God. She woke up. You don't have to—"

"Relax. You can scream for help in five minutes. It'll give you a great story to tell." I tied him to the chair with a roll of bandages.

Zoe looked at the AI. "This thing must've called the cops."

AI-T4312 said, "Your last contact with the police resulted in a life-threatening condition. It would be unethical for me to make another contact likely."

Zoe said, "What?"

AI-T4312 said, "I'm a medical AI, not a copbot. Scram."

I looked at the doc. "She really is innocent."

"I'll give you your five minutes." He glanced at a clock on the side of the AI. "However long you want."

"Five is fine. Thanks."

Zoe stood and nearly fell. I caught her. "You up to this?"

"Do I have a choice?"

"Not really."

"Let's go." She started forward. I walked beside her, supporting her and expecting someone to yell at us at any moment. Her unsteadiness probably helped as we headed down the hall. She made a convincing patient as she gripped my arm, and with her head hanging forward, her hair hid her eyes from the staff that we passed.

The Mercedes was still in the parking lot. No cops were visible, which meant I actually had gotten all the locators. I took Zoe to the car and helped her in. She shivered, and I realized that this was another cold December night in the Valley. I put my jacket around her shoulders, then pulled the bandage from her head. She blinked at it and grinned. "Quite the fashion statement." As we rolled out of the parking area, she added, "Max. Thanks."

"For what?"

"You could've left me—"

I didn't want to hear her gratitude. I said, "It's over."

I didn't look to see what her face did then. Her voice went quiet. "What do you mean?"

"Two people are dead. We've got no leads on who's behind their murders, but anyone who watches the news thinks we killed one of them. Nearly every copbot in town wants you dead, and none of them seem fond of me. Now some thug named Django Kay has a bounty on us. This case is so far out of my league that it's a whole different game. It's time to cut our losses and get out while we can."

"You're quitting."

"Sometimes you have to."

"If it's about money, I've got nearly a meg in the bank. I

can give you a promissory note on my inheritance. There are things in Minneapolis I could sell—"

"It's not about money. It's about facing facts."

"We've got a lead. This guy Kay."

"He's not a lead, Zoe. He's a threat."

"If Kay's not behind it, he must know who is."

"He's too small a player to know much more than the cops. But he's way too big for us."

She jabbed my shoulder with her index finger. "What about that Mycroft? If I can track him down, maybe he can tell me something."

"Track him down how?"

"You're the detective."

"I checked my e-mail at Eddie's. Nothing from Mycroft. There's no reason he should ever answer. We don't even know if Mycroft's his real name."

"He's still a lead, damn it. And so's Kay!"

"Okay," I agreed. "They're leads. One can't be found unless he wants to. The other wants to kidnap or kill you."

"So I'm supposed to forget this?"

"No. Pass their names along to Chumley and Vallejo. Let the cops do their job."

"Can they solve this?"

I wished I could lie to her. "Maybe not. But they can keep after it and stay alive. I doubt that's true for us anymore."

"I won't quit."

"You need to."

"Yeah, well, I'll think about that." She glanced at the neighborhood we were driving through, a deserted kingdom of auto parts stores and car dealers. "Drop me off."

"Sure. When I get you someplace safe."

"The cops? They're not—"

"Crittertown. Someone there can get you out of L.A."

"I'm not going till I know who killed Doc!"

"You think she'd want you dead, too?"

We drove in silence for a long minute. Then Zoe said gently, "What about you?"

"I know a good lawyer. I'll probably even keep my license."

"Christ, Max." She looked out the window at quiet store fronts. "I could smash the damn earring live on the ten o'clock news. Then they'd leave me alone."

"They'd think it was a fake."

She nodded. "You're right. I can't walk away from this, can I? I have to run."

I glanced at her, then turned my eyes back to the road. I had told her what she needed to know. My job was nearly over. I should've felt relieved. I felt worse than I had since leaving UNSEC.

10

Crittertown's streets seemed oddly deserted for ten P.M. on a Friday. Far in the distance, a flickering light glowed beyond the rooftops where a building burned. Somewhere, a fire siren howled. That would've drawn away those who like cheap morbid sights, but it didn't explain the ghost town.

Zoe asked, "What's going on?"

"I don't know. Anything that distracts the cops is probably good."

I stopped at a red light as a small gang of young chimeras ran across the street. Most of them had extensive tattoos besides their species ID. They wore the usual tough-kid gear, synth-leather jackets or shirts of flexsteel. A ratgirl did a double-take at me behind the wheel. "Hey! It's a skin!"

Another kid yelled, "Get him!" A dogboy jumped on the hood. More teen beasts wrenched at the doors as Zoe and I slammed down the locks. A pigboy kicked in a headlight.

Zoe said, "Max!" but I was already throwing the car in reverse. We screeched backward, losing the dogboy on the hood. I hit the brakes and wrenched the wheel, spinning the Mercedes around as the gang pursued us. I floored the accelerator, and we sped away. For a final farewell gesture, one of the little beasts threw a brick that shattered the rear window.

I looked at Zoe. "What did I say?"

"Whatever it was, don't say it again."

For the rest of the way, I rolled through stop signs and

timed my approach to traffic lights so I didn't have to stop for reds. We saw more chimeras afoot, moving quickly, usually in small groups, though some travelled alone. None of them paid any attention to us. It felt like driving through a civil war, but then, all riots are test runs for civil war.

I parked close to the Tavern of Dr. Moreau. As we walked up to it, I saw a hand-lettered sign that'd been taped to the door very recently: "Chimera-owned business."

Zoe said, "This may not be a good place for you now."

I shrugged. "Can't think of a better place for you now." I held the door open. She looked at me, then strode inside.

The place was almost empty. A few chimeras sat at the tables, and a couple more at the bar. No one was laughing. A sign near the door said "No smoking," but no one was enforcing that tonight; a tart tinge of burning tobacco laced the sickly-sweet smell of beer.

Behind the bar, a big HV was on with the sound low. The picture showed an aerial shot of a Crittertown street about half a mile from the tavern. Several stores were burning. Chimeras ran through the police and news flyers' spotlights. One chimera threw something, and another building caught fire.

The bartender, a small, brown-haired man with a long nose, very little chin, and a weasel tattoo, looked up and smiled at Zoe. "Welcome back, Cousin Cat. Find your detec—"

Then he saw me and fell silent. So did the room. The weasel came around the bar, telling me, "What the hell are you thinking? Get out! Now!"

I looked at Zoe. "It's my breath. You can tell me."

The weasel brushed by me and opened the front door. Four or five chimera kids ran past, heading up Lankershim toward the major action. Most carried pipes or baseball bats. The weasel slammed the door, said "Fuck!" and pushed Zoe and me toward a door behind the bar. "In there!"

Zoe said, "What's the tale?"

At the bar, a monkeyman dropped several K beside his empty glass, called to the weasel, "See ya, Nate!" and hurried out.

Nate nodded to the monkey as he rushed us into a small back room office. On two shelves around a cluttered desk were dusty bottles of more expensive liquor than you would expect to find in a chimera bar and cardboard boxes with labels like "In," "Out," and "Fuck If I Know." The largest box was labelled "Lost and Found."

Nate said, "Cat, you gotta start watching the news. Amos Tauber was killed. They're pinning it on a fur. Two hours ago, the cops hassled a dogboy outside the subway and the whole goddamn neighborhood blew up."

I said, "So that brick through the car window wasn't personal."

He gave me a blank look. "Nah. You're a victim of discrimination."

I nodded at Zoe. "She's got to get out of town. The sooner, the better."

"Why?"

She said, "I'm the fur they want to pin for killing Tauber."

I added, "She didn't do it. You know someone who can sneak her out?"

Nate studied us, then spoke. "For a price."

Zoe said, "We don't have—"

I opened the Infinite Pocket. Nate stepped back fast. I let the SIG lie in my open palm. "One Infinite Pocket and a SIG 9mm Recoilless keyed to it. There's Pocket technology in its magazine. Meaning you can shoot ten thousand times before you have to reload."

"So?"

"Any competent surgeon could make the transfer." I opened the Infinite Pocket again to make the pistol disappear.

Which made Nate more comfortable. He inhaled deeply, then said, "I think they'll go for that."

Zoe said, "Max!"

"What?"

"You can't do this!"

"Huh. I thought I just did."

"I can't take—"

"Sure, you can. You get set up somewhere, you can repay me."

Nate said, "So, the offer stands?"

I nodded. "Yep."

He scribbled an address on a piece of paper and handed it to Zoe. "Get there. They'll handle the rest."

I said, "I'll see she makes it."

"Your company isn't exactly an asset," Nate said. "You could get yourself killed, and her, too. This is *not* a good night for skins in Crittertown."

Zoe jerked open the top desk drawer. Nate said, "What're you looking for?"

She pulled out a black marker and grinned at him. "No skins around here."

He frowned, then shook his head. "Cats. You're all nuts." With a pitying look at me, he returned to the bar.

Zoe pushed a desk chair toward me and aimed the desk lamp at it. "Sit down and tilt your head back."

"Wait a minute—"

"You only have to pass at a distance in the dark."

Which was true. I could leave her here with no shame—hell, for reasons I didn't want to think about, I was effectively paying her now to work for her. But I wanted to see her off. I do too many jobs that have no sense of closure, when I fail to find what I'm looking for or the client skips out on me. Waving goodbye to Zoe at the station—whatever her ride might use for a station—looked like the best I could hope for, given the way things had gone so far. I sat in the chair and squinted in the light. "Nate's right. You're crazy."

She grinned, took my chin in her hand, and began drawing on my forehead. As the tip of the marker dragged over my skin, her expression became more and more intent. Her concentration on her work made her look more catlike than ever. Very conscious that her face was mere inches from mine, I closed my eyes and swallowed.

"Hold still." She drew three dots to connect my eyebrows, then thick lines swirling over my cheekbones. The marker smelled antiseptic. One small, strong hand held the back of my head to keep it steady. As she brought the design down to my chin, she said, "Take off your shirt."

I squinted up at her.

She said, "The wild ones do full-body tattoos."

I wasn't planning to let anyone close enough to examine my collar, but if someone did, it'd be embarrassing to be caught simply because I didn't want Zoe to see I was carrying a few more pounds than I had as one of UNSEC's fair-haired boys. That she had seen me naked the night before didn't change the feeling. She had surprised me then. This was a choice. I stripped off my shirt.

Zoe moved behind me. I could feel her gaze on my bent neck like the sun on a bright afternoon. One of her hands gripped my shoulder, then the cool tip of the marker began making dots and sweeping lines that grew up from my shoulders onto the back of my neck.

A minute or two later, she stepped in front of me. Her knees brushed mine as she drew patterns on my upper chest and worked them up my throat. She said, "You work out?"

I shook my head.

"Hey!" she said. "Respect the work."

I did my best impersonation of a ventriloquist. "I used to swim a lot."

She cupped my chin to tilt my head back. Our eyes met.

Our faces were inches from each other. Her lips parted slightly, then she said, "Swimming. Maybe I should've made you a tiger." She drew several quick slashes on the underside of my chin and stepped back, breathless. "Okay. Put on your shirt. No, wait."

She pulled several large T-shirts with beer logos from the shelf by the "Lost and Found" box and tossed me a green one. "Put it on backward unless you want to be a walking ad." She turned around a black one for herself. I wondered if I was about to get a free show, but she pulled it over her red dress, then did the magician escaping a straitjacket trick that so many women use at the beach to dress before the curious.

I put on the green tee and my jacket while Zoe rummaged through the "Lost and Found" box. Grinning, she came out with a pair of sunglasses and a black knit cap. "Much better than tying a towel around your head and having to squint."

I put on the glasses. The world went three degrees darker. I could live with that. I decided not to smell the cap as I pulled it on. When I glanced at Zoe, she grinned and said, "Oooh, *tres* urban, darling!"

She twisted the multicolored strands of her hair into a tail, which drew her hair tight to her skull. That made her tufted ears stand out like banners and her golden eyes seem to fill her face. Over the large, black T-shirt, she slipped on a red-and-black baseball jacket from the box, then held her arms fashion-model wide. "Ta-dah!"

I whistled. "It's the Queen of the Cats."

She tossed me a long, dark duster. "Then you better look like her date."

Zoe left the office first. Nate saw her and nodded approvingly at her new look. Zoe said, "We swapped some clothes. Hope you don't mind."

"Not at all. Ruby's expecting you. Say Nate sent you."

Zoe stepped aside and turned her hand toward me. "How about my pal?"

I sauntered up to the bar and checked out Zoe's artwork in the mirror. I didn't look like anyone I would want to meet on a quiet street at night. I felt a little silly, like a kid in a Dracula costume, and a little vain, like a kid who knew that Dracula was way cool, and a lot worried, like a kid who was about to walk among real vampires who wouldn't be amused if they saw through the deception. I leaned closer to the mirror. Zoe had sketched a fierce dog's head on my brow.

Nate laughed. "Sure there wasn't a wolf in the family woodpile?"

"Could be, cuz," I said with a growl.

He laughed again, then told Zoe, "Better tell people he's mute."

The HV caught my eye. Adam Tromploy sat in front of a still image of Amos Tauber. Nate saw my glance and bumped up the volume. Tromploy said, "No leads in the murder of nonhuman-rights activist Amos Tauber. Oberon Chain, C.E.O. of Chain Logic Robotics, offered a hundred million dollar reward for information leading to the capture of his killers."

The image cut to Oberon Chain in a sleek office building lobby, telling a gaggle of reporters, "I'm devoted to Amos Tauber's dream: equal rights for human and machine intelligences. I can't imagine how a chimera could take the life of a person to whom its kind owes so much."

The sight of Oberon Chain fired sluggish neurons in my brain. I gave Zoe a look that betrayed some of my alarm. She frowned, but when I sniffed loudly, then glanced back at Chain on the monitor, she nodded.

Nate killed the sound as the bulletin ended and turned to us. "Better fly."

"What's fastest?"

"Take Lankershim north. They'll have a doc come to get their pay."

"Thanks." As I held the front door for Zoe, I glanced back and saw Nate watching us.

He called solemnly, "Good luck." Then he grinned. "Cousin."

Zoe and I stepped into the cool night. Down the block, Arthur's car burned as two ratkids ran from the blaze.

The Mercedes was reciting, in the calm, cultured voice they give Mercedes security systems, "I am on fire. Please call the police. I am on fire. Please call the police."

Zoe said, "Arthur'll scream when he sees his ride."

"I'd like to think so."

"Now what? Catch a pert?"

"There are security cams at every station. We walk." As we headed north, I said, "When you said Chain smelled funny—"

She met my eye. "Like Blake."

"Any other humans smell funny?"

"Not like those two."

"What gives them away?"

She shrugged. "If you met one and didn't know what it was, nothing much. It's like sugar and No-Cal. Both taste sweet, but No-Cal tastes wrong." She whirled toward me. "Hey! Is Chain a lead?"

"More likely a dead end. If I was the head of Chain Logic, I'd sure use bot doubles to skip boring parties."

"What if someone kidnapped Chain and substituted an AI?"

"Someone who could do that could do anything at all with a chimera and a cheap detective. Let it go."

"But—"

"Suppose you claim Chain's an AI. Who'll believe you? If we could put enough pressure on him to make him respond, he'd just buy a doctor to testify anything he wanted. If you got some other chimeras to sniff him, they could only say he smelled odd, 'cause they wouldn't have Blake or Doyle as reference points. If you shot him full of holes in front of a primetime audience, people'd just be more convinced he was human when they saw him bleed. Have I left anything out?"

"Yeah. The possibility that the real Oberon Chain is a prisoner somewhere."

"If so, he's probably safe as long as the bad guys think their secret's secure. If we talk, we just give them an extra reason to kill him. And us." I had another thought then. "If Chain had synthetic legs or something, wouldn't he smell like Blake?"

Zoe nodded reluctantly. "Maybe."

We walked on. I thought about Chain and AIs, and Tauber and Gold and chimeras, and Zoe Domingo and me. None of those thoughts went anyplace I liked. We passed a burning newstand, then, a few blocks further, we saw more angry chimeras run by, smashing store windows and grabbing what they could. I considered cutting through residential streets, but I didn't think safety lay anywhere in Crittertown that night. Better to take the fastest route, I thought. That way, we could spot trouble in time to avoid it.

My theory failed quickly. By the time we reached Lankershim and Oxnard, trouble was all around us. The air was full of smoke and sirens and car alarms. The clusters of chimeras had become a mob. Most ran past without a second glance at Zoe or me, but a few gave us quick grins and the critter wave of solidarity that looks like clawing the air. I suddenly realized that on this night, anyone who could pass as a chimera was as safe as could be in Crittertown.

Someone threw a trash can through the front window of a narcotics store. I expected looters to empty it, but instead a tigerman in a tattered suit and a minister's collar smashed bottles of vodka and set the whole place on fire. As I wondered how many dollars in alcohol, hemp, heroin, and opium were in each whiff of pungent smoke, Zoe said, "They're trashing their own neighborhood!"

I glanced at her. "You want to bus them to Beverly Hills?"

A young apeboy kicked in the door of a furniture rental

store and grabbed a flat-screen HV. As other chimeras climbed into the place with all the joy of children after eggs on Easter, the apeboy passed the HV to me with an oddly formal bow and said, "Happy holidays, cousins."

I returned the bow and gave the HV to a goatman brushing by me. "Enjoy, cuz."

The goatman already looked satanic with his stubby horns and goatee, but he looked more so when he grimaced and grabbed my sleeve. "You smell funny."

Zoe said, "That human thing?"

"Yeah."

Zoe laughed. "Figures. Stinky works around them all day."

The goatman sniffed, then glared at me. "You're a skin."

Tensing for the SIG, I realized that I would miss it when it was gone. Then I realized that producing a pistol in the midst of a crowd that wasn't feeling good about humans might not be the best way to improve interspecial relationships. I let my arm relax.

Zoe told the goatman, "He's okay."

I said, "We're just passing through."

The goatman asked Zoe, "Had to bring your furry down to sightsee?"

Before she could answer, the apeboy pointed away and shouted, "Copbots!"

A phalanx of police bots marched onto Lankershim from Oxnard. They announced in unison, "Clear the streets! Those who do not return to their homes immediately will be arrested!"

A rock flew from the mob and bounced off a copbot skull. A doggirl shouted, "They're our streets! You clear out!" It became hard to track the action after that. Around us, chimeras threw anything that came to hand, including bottles, broken furniture, and a headless doll, at the copbots.

Zoe told the goatman, "The cops want me. This skin's helping me. If they catch either of us, we're dead on the spot."

The goatman glanced at me.

I said, "Why waste a trial on a critter and a critter lover?"

He scowled and released my sleeve. "Get!"

I nodded, lest the sound of a human voice make him change his mind. Zoe and I ran back down Lankershim, only to see another mobile barricade of copbots filling the next intersection, boxing in the worst of the riot—and us.

Zoe said, "Hell."

A dogboy and a monkeygirl on a scooter tossed a Molotov cocktail at the bots. The bottle hit one's steel shoulder and exploded, hiding it and its sexless siblings in a burst of black smoke and hot flames. The crowd cheered.

Then the bots, blackened but undamaged, marched out of the inferno with shocksticks extending from their forearms.

"C'mon!" I yanked Zoe toward a nearby building where a brass plaque read "Toad Hall Apartments." I tried the door. Locked. "Kick on two. One. Two."

Her sidekick was as good as mine. The door crashed in on its hinges, but before we could enter, cool steel fingers closed on our shoulders. A copbot said, "Chase Maxwell. Zoe Domingo. You are wanted for questioning in the death—"

A new sledgehammer, price tag still on it, met the copbot's head from behind, cracking its skull like a piñata. The goatman let the hammer drop. "Thought I told you to get."

Two more copbots ran toward us. I said, "We're gone." The goatman ran down the street. The bots chose to follow Zoe and me into the hallway, which didn't surprise me a bit.

Zoe said, "There's a back door, right?"

"Trust me."

"That's not an answer."

An apartment door opened a crack as we passed. An ancient foxwoman in a housecoat peered out and saw me, Zoe, and the bots. She said, "*Dios mio!*" and slammed the door as shocksticks retracted and dart guns extended from the cop-bots' forearms.

A sleep dart thumped into the woodwork next to Zoe's head. Something snagged my coat. I whirled, opened the Pocket, and shot as the SIG hit my palm. The bots fell back. If anyone ever comes up with disposable copbots, fugitives won't have a chance.

There was a back door, which I had expected, given that the building looked old enough to have been built during the Regulation Age. Miracle of miracles, the fire release bar hadn't been removed by a landlord who favored security over safety. I hit the bar, and we burst into an alley.

The nearest vehicle was a battered green Ford pickup parked by a dumpster. We tried the doors. Zoe said, "Locked!" and looked for the next place to run.

I smashed the driver's window with the butt of the SIG, reached in, and yanked the handle. Zoe took out her window with an elbow strike. As I opened the driver's door, a sleep dart pinged off its side. I spun and shot at a copbot coming from Toad Hall. It ducked, and Zoe and I scrambled into the truck.

I handed her my SIG and hunched under the dash. She said, "I can't—" As I yanked out my pocket knife, a copbot gripped the driver's door.

Zoe shot twice over me. I heard the glad tinkle of a cop-bot's optic sensors smashing, then the sound of the driver's door being pulled from the truck, followed by something heavy falling in the alley. Zoe said, "Huh. I guess I can."

I straightened up, touched the wires together, and the truck belched to life with a gas-powered roar and an acrid plume of exhaust. One copbot, clutching the driver's door, lay twitching by the truck. The other ran into the alley, shouting, "Halt!"

I wrenched the truck into reverse and rammed the second bot, flinging it back against the dumpster with a clang. Then I slammed the stick into first, and we raced away in a cloud of carcinogenic smoke.

Zoe said, "We're car thieves now."

"You, too, can become a criminal in twelve easy lessons." I glanced at her. Her breathing was heavy, but so was mine. She was grinning. So, I realized, was I. I said, "Technically, I became a car thief when I took Arthur's car. You were out of it then."

"You're a car ahead of me? Damn, I've gotta catch up."

"The night is young, Ms. Domingo."

"True, Mr. Maxwell. Where'd you learn to hotwire a gas-burner?"

"Eddie. I'm pretty sure he had paid for his, but I never asked."

11

I drove down the residential streets as quickly as I could. Most neighborhood toll stations simply raise the pike at night, but we still gave away a lot of change to kids who may or may not have been authorized to collect. Eventually, with our pockets lighter, we parked in front of a lower-class house, a rectangular box from the twentieth century that was almost redeemed by enormous rose bushes on either side of its front walk.

Zoe said, "I guess this is it."

"I guess so."

"Want to leave me here?"

"Can't. Payment's yet to be arranged."

"I wish there was another way."

"Hell, be glad there's *one*. Maybe if I reduce my firepower, I'll start using my brain a little more."

She smiled. "Small chance of that."

No lights were visible in the house. At the front porch, we looked at each other, then shrugged. Zoe double-checked the address, then rang the bell. We waited long enough for me to feel conspicuous.

Then the door opened a crack. Moonlight fell on a woman who scowled out at us. Her eyes were feral. Black tattoos covered most of her dark skin. Her forehead tat was a wolf's head.

Zoe said, "Ruby? Nate sent us."

The wolfwoman opened the door wide enough for us to

step into the dark house. "This way." Her voice was husky, like a longtime smoker's.

I could see almost nothing. I did my best to follow Ruby's dark shape by sound. Zoe grabbed my arm to keep me from bumping into a chair. Maybe her touch should've been comforting, but it reminded me that those of us who took the slow route to speech and thumbs are not designed to function well in the night. How many chimps would walk willingly into a cave with a jaguar and a wolf?

Ruby turned on a lamp. We stood in a small living room furnished in early twenty-first century thrift shop. The wolf-woman looked at us, giving special attention to Zoe's artwork. Still scowling, she said, "My brother's driving a truck to Dallas. He'll come by around dawn. Let's see the hardware."

I opened the Pocket, caught my SIG, and showed it. I opened the Pocket again. The gun disappeared.

Ruby said, "He'll bring a doc."

I said, "No cutting till Zoe's out of here."

Ruby nodded. "Come on."

As she took us down a short hall, I asked, "Why no lights? You think someone's watching you?"

Ruby showed her teeth in a cold smile. "Humans want to take the sun with them everywhere they go. Electricity isn't free." She stopped in front of a door. "You stay here tonight. Private bath, no room service." She turned to Zoe. "If you want to change clothes, there's some old things of mine in the closet."

Zoe said, "Thanks. Mind if we get some food?"

Ruby shrugged. "Kitchen privileges included. Don't wake me, don't break anything, and we'll get along fine. If the sheep in wolf's markings needs something, turn on some lights."

"Thanks."

Ruby went into another room. I looked at the door to ours, then said, "Food?"

Zoe nodded. "Food."

Ruby's refrigerator provided black bread, Asian mustard, and spinach leaves for both of us, cold cow flesh for Zoe, and cucumber slices for me. We split a big bottle of dark beer with our sandwiches and didn't talk much. Afterward, Zoe said, "Better."

"Good. You drowsy?"

"Nope. I could get used to whatever that medic AI dispensed."

"Tell me if you still think so when it wears off."

"Good point."

I took our dishes and put them in the washer while she put away the sandwich makings. As she wiped down the counter, I said, "Zoe?"

"What?"

I almost commented on how very domestic we were. "Pass the sponge." I wiped the table, then yawned.

She said, "We should both get some rest."

"Can you?"

She smiled. "There's not a drug made that can keep this cat from napping."

We returned to the door Ruby had shown us. It opened on a tiny room nearly filled with a double bed and a dresser. The door by the closet led to a small bathroom with a toilet and shower. I said, "I'll sleep on the rug."

"No, I'll— Hold still." She reached for my coat, and my breath stopped as I wondered what she was doing. Then she plucked a sleep dart from the cloth.

I pulled off the coat and jacket, then lifted my shirt to see if the dart had scratched me. "Missed the skin. Maybe I should jab myself for a little help sleeping."

"Max? You can't give 'em the Pocket."

I looked up in surprise. "Sure I can. Ever hear of holsters?"

"Bullshit. You talk like you're giving away a watch. It's more like a finger or a kidney."

"Trust me. I'd rather give away the Pocket than a finger or a kidney."

"But—"

"It's mine, Zoe. I can do what I want with it."

"Sure. But why this?"

I couldn't think of an answer that would satisfy either of us. I shrugged and walked into the bathroom, leaving the door ajar.

Zoe leaned against the door frame. "Is it that thing you told me about Long Island, when the critters died?"

I didn't want to talk about that then—or any time. I stripped off my shirt and looked at the fierce patterns on my face and chest. In the mirror, I saw her watching me. Putting soap on a washcloth, I said, "Seems a shame to wash off your artwork."

"Max—" I think she was going to call me on avoiding her question, but after a moment, she said, "I'll write when I find work."

I concentrated on washing my face, carefully not looking at her. "You can't."

Her voice was very polite. "Why not?"

"They could drug me to learn where you are."

"Oh."

I rinsed the cloth and started a second pass. "If you go through a place where you're sure you'll never return, you might send me a postcard someday, just to say you made it. No signature, no return address, no clues—"

"I got it."

"Sorry. I just wanted to be sure."

"I know." She took the washcloth out of my hand. "I'll get your back." She scrubbed the base of my neck. The cloth felt warm and pleasantly scratchy. As she reached my shoulder blades, she worked more slowly.

"Turn around." She washed the markings off my chest without looking up. When she turned to rinse the cloth, she saw me studying her in the mirror.

I said, "It has nothing to do with what happened in Long Island."

"Max—"

"It's just you."

I waited for an answer. Her eyes looked like the surface of an alien sea. Her face told no more than the Sphinx's. We both knew all the reasons I shouldn't have said anything. We had no future. Even if she wasn't going on the run, I was human, she was chimera. Our societies would let us have sex, but they wouldn't let us love. The Human Marriage Amendment banned interspecies marriage in every state. Under normal circumstances, the only relationship we could've hoped for would've been that of furry and pet, and neither of us could ever endure the inequality of that.

No future means no consequences. I think that's why she put her hand on my cheek. I know that's why I took her hand and kissed the palm. We had this moment, and would never have another. We seized it.

She moved closer to me. I put my arms around her and drew her tight against me. We kissed. It was your classic awkward first-time kiss. Two thoughts wrestled in my mind: *This is a terrible idea. This is a wonderful idea.* The first thought saw it had lost and gave up without a fight.

Our lips brushed, then parted. Her tongue was like the washcloth, warm, slick, slightly scratchy. Part of my mind said that I was kissing something inhuman, but she seemed so very human then that I no longer had the slightest idea what human was.

She twined her fingers in my hair and kissed my throat. Her tongue felt rougher on dry skin, but it was as far from unpleasant as you can get. It made me want to laugh. I suppose I would have, if I hadn't thought she might be offended.

I peeled off her baseball jacket and let it fall by my shirt on the counter.

She said, "No one sleeps on the floor."

"Deal."

Clothes came off more quickly then. I pulled the red dress over her head while she fumbled with my belt. She wore no brassiere for me to return the fumbling. Her breasts were small, perfect for cupping with my hands. Her nipples burned into my palms.

My trousers fell with my boxers. "Oh, my," she said, for I was as ready as a man can be. I slid one hand down her spine, over the small of her back to her buttocks. The other travelled down from her breasts to two more, smaller pairs of secondary nipples. I caressed each of them as my hand travelled down her flat stomach. Her panties peeled off easily. All of her hair was a jaguar blend of black, gold, and brown. She was as ready as I was.

"Bed," she said.

I picked her up to carry her there, then kicked at the pants tangled around my ankles. That didn't help, so I hopped toward the bed. She laughed in my arms. "And they say humans don't have mating rituals."

We fell together onto the bed. After twisting around to free my feet, I ended up on top of her. I nuzzled her throat, then kissed the top of her breast, then worked my way down her torso with my tongue, learning her taste. As I reached her thighs, she laughed again and pulled my head up to hers.

She pushed me, and I rolled over. She licked my stomach, and I gasped. She said, "Too scratchy?"

I breathed, "Torture me some more."

She crawled up my body to straddle my hips. "Prepare to suffer, monkeyboy."

Afterward, we lay tangled together on the bed. I can't say what she was doing; I was enjoying the post-coital very slow fall from heaven. When I landed, I lifted my head. "Is that purring?"

"Men get so smug."

I stroked her thigh. "Even smugger when they do it twice."

"Huh. If your head swells any more, it may explode."

"I'll take that chance."

She put her hand against the small of my back and pulled me into her. "I'll count it as a mercy killing."

So I became smugger that night. Afterward, I must've fallen asleep. In my dream, I was making love to Kristal Agatha Blake while she tugged strips of her skin away to bare bright metal. I tried to run from her, but barbed hooks sprang from every part of her body, fastening me to her. The hooks must've been treated with a drug that made me feel pleasure instead of pain. I wanted even more hooks to snag me—and that realization made me want to scream, but the drug on the hooks had sapped my strength, leaving me unable to do anything but cling to Blake forever.

I heard a bell, far away. The bed shifted. Zoe whispered, "Someone's here."

Glad to be awake, gladder to be beside Zoe, I opened my eyes and checked my watch. It wasn't quite five. "Your driver's early." I heard the wolfwoman's bedroom door open. The floor of the hall creaked under her steps as she passed by. I lay close to Zoe, thinking about my dream and how I'd like another five hours, or even five minutes, of sleep, and wondering how I would feel when she left, and whether I would regret giving up the Pocket. I'm a sucker for the grand gesture. Sometimes I pay for them for years.

Zoe's body was tense beside me. She lifted her head, sniffed the air, then said, "It's the critters from the casino."

I rolled out of bed, opening the Pocket without thinking about it. I instantly felt better with the SIG in my hand and knew that on some level I would miss it very much.

The air was cold on my skin, and the floor was cold beneath my feet, but several people were coming down the hall and there was no time to dress. I hissed "Closet!" to Zoe, threw the pillows into the middle of the bed and yanked the bedspread over them, then slipped into the bathroom. Leaving the door ajar, I stepped behind it to watch through the gap between the hinges.

Bruno and two humans I hadn't seen before, a blond man and a black woman in suits much too nice for undercover cops, burst into the room with pistols aimed at the huddled shapes in the bed. Bruno snapped on the lights as the black woman said, "Get up!"

Zoe stepped from the closet holding the clothes rod like a quarterstaff and whacked the woman's gun from her hand. "We did."

As Bruno and Blondie turned toward Zoe, I came out of the bathroom with the SIG in a classic two-handed shooter's grip. "Set 'em down nicely."

They obeyed. I took one pistol as Zoe took two. She waved our visitors toward the closet. "Inside."

Bruno said, "We're not alone, Max. Be smart and give up."

"If I'm so stupid, Bruno, how come you're the one getting in a closet? Move!"

Zoe added, "If you get bored, you can try on Ruby's clothes."

None of them looked happy as they went in, but they went. We shoved the dresser against the closet door, then I peeked into the hall. Arthur stood at the far end with his gun out. I called, "Stay back, Arthur. The goon squad blew it."

"I've got more people outside, Max. You're trapped."

"Really? The neighbors might call the cops when they hear this." I shot three times down the hall. As Arthur dove for cover, I yelled, "Next time, I'll be aiming for you."

Zoe opened the bedroom window and sniffed. "The orca's out there. Maybe with company."

"Damn." I tossed her clothes to her, then pulled on my pants.

Arthur called, "Max!" I peered out. Arthur crouched at the end of the hall. "Mr. Kay wants to talk!"

"He wants us. We don't want him. That's not much of a conversation."

Holding his empty hands high, a slender man with brown and white hair stepped into the hall. His suit looked like molten gold. His voice was calm, educated, with what sounded like a Scotsman's burr. "I don't want you or the catwoman, Mr. Maxwell. All I want is Gold's earring. Give it to me, and I'll let you go."

"You're asking for a lot of trust."

"Do you see an alternative?"

"Yeah." I fired into the hall, and Django Kay leaped back. "I shoot anyone who comes toward this door, and the cat shoots anyone who comes near the window. How's that for an alternative?"

Django said, "The police are busy tonight. We have some time to discuss this."

"Great. Maybe my marksmanship will improve."

"Oh, I don't doubt that you'd shoot me or any of my people. But there are other possibilities. Arthur?"

The wolfwoman and the weasel bartender stumbled into the hall with their hands cuffed behind them. Before I could decide what to make of that, Arthur pointed a medical injector at their necks and fired two nearly silent puffs of air. Ruby and Nate jerked as if they'd been slapped.

Waggling a pistol at the chimeras, Django told them, "You've got ten seconds to get in that bedroom before I start shooting."

That made them look even more frightened. Neither protested. They just started running toward me. I hesitated, wondering what Django thought he was doing. He and Arthur stayed where they were, making no attempt to use the chimeras as shields. Django said, "Five seconds, Mr. Maxwell, before we shoot them."

I opened the door wide enough to yank the chimeras inside. "What did he inject you with?"

Nate said, "I don't know." Ruby shook her head.

Django called, "Mr. Maxwell!" I looked out and saw him at the end of the hall. "If you and Ms. Domingo come out unarmed, we won't shoot anyone. But if either of those two come into the hall again, we'll shoot them down in front of you."

"No one's leaving this room until the cops arrive."

"Really? Here's something most people don't know. Half of all critters have a defective gene. In the presence of a certain enzyme, they werewolf. Guess what I injected those two with?"

Zoe, Ruby, Nate, and I looked at each other.

Ruby said, "Oh, God."

Zoe said, "He's bluffing. Isn't he?"

I couldn't answer. So far as I knew, no one knew what caused werewolfing. I wanted to think Django was trying a desperate trick to get us out of the bedroom. But he knew we had no reason to trust him not to kill us if we came out. Our only choice was to wait and see if what he said was true.

He called, "The house bets that one or both of them werewolfs within forty-five seconds. Do the math, Mr. Maxwell. The odds are always with the house."

Ruby said, "He's trying to panic us."

Nate said, "He's doing a hell of a job."

I said, "Even if he's telling the truth, there's a twenty-five percent chance that you're both fine."

Zoe added, "People beat worse odds than that every night."

But far more people lose; that's the house advantage at work. Nate twitched suddenly and said, "It itches." We all stepped back from him. The SIG in my hand felt very heavy.

Django called, "Werewolves attack anything that moves. Any reaction yet? I wouldn't waste time in your place."

Zoe said, "Maybe it's the power of suggestion."

Nate scratched at his arms and chest. "It itches all over. Please. Don't let me—"

Django called, "Toss out the earring, and you can leave the room. We'll kill whoever's werewolfed. No one else has to die."

Nate clutched his belly and groaned. "Make it stop!"

Zoe looked outside, then at me. I shook my head. If we dove through the window and ran, the orca and his backup might miss us, but the odds didn't appeal to me. Part of me wanted to shoot Nate now, but another part knew that Django could still be lying.

I said, "Maybe he injected you with something to make you itch—-"

Nate screamed, spun in a circle, screamed again, and snapped his handcuffs like a strand of dental floss. He stepped toward the wolfwoman, but before I could raise the SIG, he halted. His eyes looked sane. "Ruby. I wouldn't hurt you—"

She said, "Nate. Hang on. You got to."

His eyes went wide in shock, then narrowed as sanity left him. Howling in agony and fear, he lashed at Ruby, slicing her cheek with his nails.

I brought the SIG up. Ruby was in my way. Cursing myself for waiting too long, I scrambled onto the bed in the hope of finding a clear shot.

Zoe tackled Nate from behind. He stumbled, then spun around and threw himself backward as if to pin her against the wall. They crashed through the window and tumbled outside.

I ran to look out. Zoe lay motionless on the ground. Nate, crouched above her, sniffed the air. A human gunman stepped from behind a tree with a rifle raised toward him. Before I could decide who to shoot, Nate rose screaming and rushed the gunman. Zoe still didn't move. In the darkness, I couldn't tell how badly she was hurt.

Ruby ran up beside me and called, "Nate!" He didn't turn away from the gunman.

I thrust the pistol I'd taken from one of the thugs into Ruby's hands and said, "Watch the hall!" I suspected Django and Arthur would stay back until they knew how the fight came out, but they might follow when they heard that the fight had moved outdoors.

The gunman fired at Nate three times. Whether all his shots hit or none did, the enraged weaselman didn't slow down. The gunman screamed as Nate savaged him. I hated hearing it. There's nothing comforting about having a monster fight for you. I lifted the SIG and waited for Nate to turn back toward us.

The orca, Rashid, stepped around the house and shot Nate repeatedly in the back. Nate snarled and fell onto the man he had killed.

I shot Rashid four times in the chest, then jumped out the window to land by Zoe. She still hadn't moved. Before I could crouch to examine her, I heard movement in the yard and looked for its source.

Nate stood above the human gunman's body. As he turned toward me, his face was twisted with rage and terror. He wiped blood from his hands onto his shirt, then realized what he was doing, and shuddered. Our eyes met. He said, "Cousin. Kill me."

Before I could answer, he charged me, covering ground impossibly fast. A shot in each kneecap might've immobilized him, but I was far more likely to miss, and my fondness for gambling had hit a record low. Even if I succeeded, the wea-selman would just drag himself toward his prey, and in that state, he might still kill someone.

"Sorry, Nate." I shot him three times in the head. He took four more steps toward me, reached out blindly, and fell dead at my feet. My armpits were slick with sweat, and my limbs had begun to shake. I jerked myself back from Nate's body, then looked for Zoe.

She sat up behind me. "Is he—"

"Yeah. I thought you—"

"Playing dead."

The wolfwoman jumped from the window and crouched by the weaselman. She said, "Nate. My god—"

I glanced back at the window to see if anyone was follow-ing, then caught Ruby by the shoulders. "Get to a neighbor. Call the cops." She nodded and ran into the backyard of the house next door.

I led Zoe to the front of Ruby's house, hesitated, then stepped past the corner and brought my gun around—but too slowly. Arthur waited by the wall. His pistol barrel seemed large and impossibly long as I stared into its depths. He said, "Give me one good reason why I shouldn't kill you now, you son of a bitch."

Zoe stepped out and put one of Django's gunmen's pistols against the side of Arthur's head. "Because you don't want your brains all over my dress?"

His face went pale in the moonlight. I suppose mine wasn't all that ruddy. His datacle fell from his eye, and sweat beaded his upper lip. You never appreciate your skull so much as when someone offers you a chance to see pieces of it fly away.

For a long, long moment, we three were the whole of the world. Arthur blinked, I swallowed. Zoe simply waited with her pistol unwavering. I said, "You know what's a bitch?"

Arthur said, "What?"

"If you shoot first, I won't be able to see your head explode."

Our moment of intimacy ended when Django Kay said, "But if I shoot first, you'll learn the color of a chimera's brains." He stood on the front porch with his pistol aimed at Zoe. She, Arthur, and I remained frozen like a deadly game of statue.

Django said, "Doesn't that sound educational?" He walked to me and put his hand on my SIG. I let him take it from my fingers. "Good choice. There's no need for things to get messy."

He pocketed the SIG and reached for Zoe's pistol. As his hand closed on her gun barrel, she sniffed loudly.

Django said, "Let go."

Zoe kept her gun at Arthur's head. "Does your skin pal know you're passing?"

"I said—"

Zoe sniffed again. "Wolverine. What's a crooked plastic surgeon cost these days, cousin?"

Arthur glanced at Django.

Django told Zoe, "Let go of the gun!"

She smiled. "Must be a kick, giving orders to skins."

Django jerked his head at me. "We don't need both of you. Arthur, shoot him."

Zoe said, "Do it, Arthur. Then I shoot you, Django's secret is safe, and he and I can work out a trade."

Arthur said, "Django—"

Django bared his teeth, a frightening sight whether he was human or wolverine. "She's lying! Shoot him!"

Zoe told Django, "You don't know if you need both of us. Question is, do you need Arthur?"

Django shoved her head with his gun barrel. "Shut up!"

Zoe kept her grin. "What do you think, Arthur? Think this critter will let you die to get what he wants?"

Django said, "Don't listen to her."

Zoe told him, "C'mon. You shoot that skin, I shoot this one. Then it's down to us critters—"

The next part went like dominoes: Arthur swung his pistol from me to Django, Django turned his pistol on Arthur, and I opened the Infinite Pocket. The SIG ripped Django's coat pocket as it flew to my hand. I said, "Simon says freeze!"

I liked this round of statue much better than the previous one: Django and Arthur aimed at each other, Zoe covered Arthur, and I covered Django.

I said, "Put your guns on the ground." When Django and Arthur hesitated, I added, "Oops. Simon says put your guns on the ground."

They obeyed. Django said, "You can't get away with this."

I said, "Do you think anyone, anywhere, heard that and said, 'You're right, I give up'?"

Zoe said, "Maybe he was hoping we'd be the first."

I said, "Who wants us, Django?"

He smiled at me, and I could see the wolverine looking through perfectly human eyes. "Who doesn't?"

A siren sounded in the distance. Maybe the wolfwoman had convinced the police to come. Maybe the riot was moving toward us. We couldn't stick around in either case. I said, "C'mon."

Zoe glared at Kay. He was smart enough to stay quiet. She said, "He knows something. The werewolf enzyme proves that."

"Kay's a public man. We can always find him."

"But—"

I scooped up Django and Arthur's guns and backed toward the truck. "There'll be copbots with the police. You could be killed resisting arrest. C'mon!"

Zoe snarled and followed. Two dark sedans were parked in front of Ruby's house. As I got in the truck and leaned under the dash, Zoe shot a tire on each of the sedans.

She jumped into the passenger side and said with some urgency, "Max—"

Bruno, Blondie, and the black woman ran into the front yard from the side of the house. We hadn't bothered to pick up the guns belonging to the orca or his partner. Bruno and the black woman had.

The truck started. "Got it." I sat up and stomped the pedal.

Their first shot must have missed. The second shattered the truck's front and rear windows as we roared away. I said, "I hate bad losers." Then something hit my back. I thought that the back of the seat had exploded. When I looked down, I saw an exit wound in line with my liver.

"Max!" Zoe said.

Her concern was vaguely touching, but time and space were distorting then. I had to get the truck around the next block and out of the line of fire. Nothing else mattered. Not the shot that ripped through the seat an inch from Zoe's ear as she huddled beside me. Not the shot that smashed into my right shoulder, which made me sideswipe two parked cars before I regained control. And certainly not the shot that tore through the right ventricle of my heart and killed me.

12

Death is great, but dying's a bitch, so I don't recommend it. You hurt in ways and to degrees you wouldn't have thought possible as the damaged parts of you beg you to do anything to fix them. Then, when you don't, they start dying before you do. Goodbye, liver. Goodbye, kidneys. Goodbye, lungs. Goodbye, heart. Then the pain fades, along with the rest of the world, as God turns off the lights in the auditorium of your life.

When the brain is deprived of oxygen, the mind hallucinates. There's no mystery to that. People's hallucinations fit certain broad patterns, depending on their education. There's no mystery to that, either. Drifting toward a white light can mean a lot of things. Maybe I saw the face of God. Maybe I just experienced the ultimate high. I remember a sense of great contentment, understanding, and acceptance. Any number of intoxicants had inspired similar feelings when I was younger. The main difference between dying and getting blind drunk is that dying results in less of a hangover—at least, if you do it the way I did.

I woke feeling almost refreshed and definitely pleased. I lay between clean sheets on a mattress that was the next best thing to zero G. Mozart played softly in the background. The scent of roses wafted by my nose. Hoping someone attractive was lying beside me—only to confirm that I was in heaven—I opened my eyes.

If heaven looks like a small, cheap hotel room, I was there.

The furnishings, when new, had been attractive and expensive faux-Victorian, from the Gainsborough reproductions on the wall to the enormous green and mahogany wing chair by my bed. Now they were all tired, faded, worn, cracked, or chipped. Dull purple velvet curtains covered the window, but on a bedside table with a cigarette burn, a lamp with a stained shade gave a soft, comforting glow, much as the rose in the chipped vase by the lamp gave a subtle, comforting scent. This wasn't any hell I had heard of; everything was clean, and nothing smelled bad. Maybe heaven was having trouble keeping up with the demand, and I'd been shunted to the overflow lot.

I lay there, drowsily aware that I was missing something. Chase Oliver Maxwell. Los Angeles, South California, United States of North America. Private detective. Infinite Pocket. (I glanced at my wrist then. The familiar scar was still there.) Zoe Domingo. The safe house—that wasn't so safe. A fight. Escape. Then something. Something important. Oh, right. Death.

This room may not have fit any idea I'd had of heaven, but when you don't expect to wake up, you can't complain about where you do. I wondered if the afterlife shaped itself to your notion of heaven on Earth. I'd had a few good times in cheap hotel rooms, but I really wanted to request a villa by the sea. Then I noticed various parts of my body making distant, muted protests that bad things had been done to them, and I realized that the dreamlike quality of my thoughts must come from drugs given me for pain.

On the bedside table were a coolglass of water and an ugly, institutional HV set with a blinking red message light. Propping myself on an elbow, I picked up the water, smelled it, then drank greedily, knowing instantly that whatever was keeping me blissful had also been hiding an intense thirst. The coolglass maintained the water at forty degrees Fahrenheit, the proper temperature for cisterns and cellars. It tasted better than chocolate milkshakes or dark beer. Maybe heaven consists of simple things fully appreciated.

When I finished the water, I pushed the sheet off my upper body. Someone had put me in a white gown. I wondered if there were people who woke up in hospitals and thought, "Oh, good, strangers stripped me naked, but that's all right because then they dressed me like a doll."

A hospital did seem a more likely guess than heaven. But if this was a hospital, why hadn't anyone looked in on me?

I sat up. The world did a merry-go-round, but I didn't fall back on the bed. The world slowed, then stopped. I tried for the brass ring and stood. The merry-go-round was faster than before. Something deep under my happy drugs said this much exertion wasn't a good idea, so I sat, breathed deeply, and, feeling like a mountain climber setting out on the final assault, yanked the gown over my head.

Patches of my chest and stomach were pale and hairless with synthskin. That answered my first question. I had been hurt badly; I was better now. I still seemed to have everything I ought to have had, and while everything was weak, a systematic series of flexings and wigglings convinced me that everything worked.

I made it to the small bathroom without falling and continued the self-diagnostic. A support bar by the toilet gave me another clue that I wasn't in a hotel. I wasn't too proud to cling to it. In the mirror, I looked flushed, undoubtedly from exertion. Several days' worth of stubble shaded my jaw and lip. Except for the patches of synthskin, I seemed to be my usual self.

I drank cold water from the tap, then splashed my face. The drugged sensation was fading, which made me feel better. Not having the greatest mind, I hate wasting any of it. No part of me actually hurt. I simply felt uncomfortable all over and knew it would be nice to sleep for another day.

Instead, I stumbled to the front door and tried the handle.

It was unlocked, which encouraged me to look out. An older woman in a wheelchair sat in a room like mine across a hall with the stainless surfaces of a hospital corridor. Her laugh reminded me that I was naked. Thinking applause would've been a far more appropriate reaction, I closed the door quickly.

Clothes were in the closet—my shirt and suit, which had been washed but were only fit for rags now, and a white shirt and tan trousers that clearly were not new but in decent shape. I dressed in the latter, then returned to the bathroom, found a razor, and shaved. A comb was among the toiletries, so I dampened my hair and beat it into submission. When I checked the mirror this time, I looked like I might be able to stand upright in a breeze. I opened the Pocket. The SIG slammed into my hand, and I dropped it.

That's the price of arrogance. I told myself I should quit paying it, picked up the SIG, and returned it to the Pocket. I popped the earring and felt better when I caught it, because I had caught it and because someone hadn't emptied the Pocket while I was dead—which shouldn't be possible, but someone was doing lots of things that weren't possible for the rest of us. At least Zoe would be glad to know Gold's device was all right.

Which raised the next question. I returned the earring to the Pocket and tried the most promising way to get an answer: I went to the bed, breathed slowly and deeply to get my strength back (and maybe to prepare for bad news), and pressed the red message light on the HV.

A well-modulated androgenous voice said, "You have two messages."

"Play the first."

Detective Vallejo's head and shoulders appeared above the set with a phone number and a date, the day after I died. He said, "Mr. Maxwell, welcome back to the land of the living.

We have a few questions for you. And maybe a few answers, too. Call me anytime."

The projection froze in midair. I mulled over phoning him then. He had been polite. There hadn't been a cop standing in the hall. That meant I wasn't under arrest or considered a serious suspect in Tauber's death. Or maybe they just figured I wasn't likely to run away in my current shape. But the most likely explanation was that they had pinned everything illegal we'd done on Zoe.

Then I thought of two more possibilities for the absence of a guard at my door that I liked even less. Either the police didn't think I needed protection from killer copbots, or they didn't care whether someone removed me from their lists of available suspects and witnesses.

I said, "Next message."

A tall, brown-haired man in a designer suit appeared. "Mr. Maxwell, I'm David Melius. I'd like to talk to you about a job." Neither his name nor his phone number were familiar.

Not feeling like talking to a stranger, I killed the HV. The offer of work was nice, even if it only turned out to be a couple hours tracing one of his old friends. Anything that distracted me from thinking about Zoe was welcome.

I knew she couldn't leave a message for me. I wondered how far from L.A. she was, whether she had found anyone to help her, and whether I would ever get an unsigned postcard saying she was okay. People pass through your life and disappear. That's just how things are. I wondered why I still wished life was different, and I hoped Zoe was happy wherever she was, and I longed for some way to double the dosage of bliss drugs in my blood because now I had a very powerful hurt indeed. That's what you get for doing the right thing, I thought; kicked around, killed, and heartbroken.

I jerked myself to my feet, then stopped. Zoe had left without the earring. With me dead, there'd been no way for her to recover it. Would she want it, or would she consider it another part of a past that she was best off forgetting? Maybe she had decided to take the risk and send me e-mail with a clue to her plans. I wanted to go someplace private to check my messages, then realized her pocket computer was gone with her, mine was still in hock, and I was still flat broke and late on my rent.

Broke. I felt like I was walking down a mined path, and each step set off a larger explosion. I had no money. Returning me to life had to have cost more megs than I'd ever had. Even if the cat had gotten to her inheritance, she couldn't have covered my bill.

I knew the tricky part of how I'd survived to get here. When UNSEC installed the Infinite Pocket, they wired my body to provide the Pocket with bioelectric power. And since they had me open, they installed something that'll soon be standard for anyone doing a dangerous job: cryo circuits. When the sensors had decided I was dead, two things happened. An alert had appeared somewhere in UNSEC headquarters letting them know they might not have to worry about me anymore, and the cryo circuits began to radically chill my body, expanding the time I could be revived without suffering brain damage from several minutes to several hours.

I must have scared Zoe when I'd frosted over. I never thought to warn her; it's not something that comes up much in conversation. "Oh, if I happen to die, I'll turn into a popsicle. Will anything interesting happen to you?"

But the icewire only explained how someone had managed to get me someplace to be rebuilt and restarted. It didn't explain why I'd gotten the reboot. UNSEC's standard retirement policy gives its agents two revivals before the age of seventy-five and one after, not counting those earned in the course of carrying out their duty. My early departure from the force meant I got to keep the circuitry, but the cost of coming back to life was entirely mine.

And I hadn't been able to afford health insurance for a couple of years. No one who checked my credit rating would bother to fill a cavity without cash up front, let alone replace major organs, quickset broken bones, reknit torn muscles, and jump-start my heart.

Maybe I'd been mistaken for someone else. Or maybe they'd recognized my UNSEC circuitry and assumed I was someone the UN still liked. Maybe the proper thing to do was to gather my belongings and sneak away before the hospital realized a mistake had been made and demanded their organs back.

The state of the furniture suggested one answer to the question of why I was alive. I went to the window to confirm it. The sun was bright on the streets of Los Angeles. I recognized the neighborhood. I was in the Engelberg Center, arguably L.A.'s best medical facility for the underclass, where equipment and doctors' time were donated, and patients paid what they could. My bill couldn't be very large.

Then I remembered a news story about a man found almost dead and fixed up by a clinic that gave him a choice: indenture yourself for ten years to pay for your new heart, or return it. I couldn't remember his decision.

My considerations were interrupted when the HV's message light came on again. I tapped it. A middle-aged dogman in a nurse's uniform smiled at me. The hair on his head and face was mostly white and gold, like a collie's or an Afghan hound's. "Good afternoon, Mr. Maxwell. I'm Clovis. Sorry not to get to you sooner, but we're understaffed, and the monitors say you're doing fine. How're you feeling?"

"Ready to check out."

"The room's paid for two more nights, if you want it."

"Paid? Already?"

Clovis nodded.

"Who by?"

"You'd have to ask at the desk, I'm afraid."

That seemed odd, but I'd never had a major operation at a medical facility for the underclass. Maybe they had already docked what they could from my bank account. But I would hardly call taking a percentage of nothing "payment." Deciding my health had priority just then, I asked, "Do you think I need the room?"

"Not if you're in a hurry to go. Just don't do anything strenuous for a few days. You've got a new heart, a new liver, and a new lung to adjust to."

If I was going to lie around watching HV, I would be more comfortable at home. I said, "Good. I'll check out."

"You can get a refund at the desk on the main floor. If you don't want to donate the balance to the hospital."

"A refund?"

"For the nights you're not using." He glanced away, then back at me. "One hundred seventeen K."

"Shouldn't that go to whoever paid the bill?"

"There's no return address."

"Is there a name?"

Clovis shrugged. "They might know at the desk."

"Thanks."

He looked apologetic. "Detective Vallejo told us to call him if you left without contacting him. The system says you haven't used the phone."

"But I'm free to go if I want?"

Clovis blinked in surprise. "Certainly."

"Thanks." I disconnected and decided to let Vallejo wait. I called up my messages and tapped David Melius's number.

The phone rang long enough that I was about to hang up. Melius answered in a different designer suit. Behind him was a large office and a view of Manhattan Island that didn't look virtual. I wasn't surprised that he had given me his personal number; most execs who hire detectives will bypass their secretaries, if possible. He said "Yes?" like a man in a hurry.

"I'm Chase Maxwell. You left a message for me?"

"Mr. Maxwell!" His grin said he now had as much time as I wanted. "Yes, I did. I'm the president of DynaTech Industries. We're looking for someone to head up our security division. You seem like just the man we want."

"Excuse me?"

"DynaTech's a small company, but we're growing quickly. We're prepared to be competitive regarding salary and benefits. Extremely competitive."

I doubt I would've processed this faster without the painkillers. "You want to hire me for a full-time position?"

He nodded firmly. "Very much."

"How did you know I was here?"

He laughed. "You made the news, Mr. Maxwell. There aren't many detectives who bounce back from the dead. A man with UNSEC training—"

"Who didn't solve his client's case."

Melius smiled and waved that aside. "No one expects a one hundred percent success rate."

"I'm not in the market for that kind of work, Mr. Melius."

"Fifty meg a year, Mr. Maxwell. Plus an apartment near our headquarters. And a car. Two months vacation. Complete medical and dental. An education package—"

"I get the picture. I'll think about it."

"Please do. There are other candidates, so we'd appreciate an answer in the next few days."

"I'll keep that in mind." I nodded and hung up, wondering if I should've accepted on the spot. There are worse jobs than corporate security. I'd wanted work like that when I had started this business. Clearly, DynaTech was after a figurehead, but I could stand to be paid for work I wasn't doing.

I chose Vallejo's number. He answered immediately. His mirrorsuit made him look like a mobile fun-house exhibit. I started a smile, then stifled it, which must've resulted in an odd expression. He said, "Mr. Maxwell. If you're not feeling well, you can call me later."

"That's all right. I was just practicing my scowl in case I got your partner."

"Ah. Don't tell Chumley I said this, but he takes scowls as tribute. To truly annoy him, be cheerful."

"You seem rather chipper yourself."

"And why not? It's Christmas Eve."

I'd lost three days. Well, you should pay for death, I suppose. "What did you want from me?"

"Everything you know about Zoe Domingo."

"That could take a while."

"I've got time."

"Like I said before. She hired me to find who killed Janna Gold."

"Did you?"

"No. You read the last page of mysteries to see who did it, don't you?"

Vallejo grinned. "Guilty. Take it at your own pace."

"We covered the casino when you brought her in for questioning, so I'll skip that. The next morning, we went to the Huntington to see if Oberon Chain knew why Gold came to L.A. He didn't. So we called Amos Tauber. A bot answered, claiming it was Jefferson 473 and it belonged to Tauber. But when we met Tauber at the U., he said he didn't own a bot. Someone had cut into his personal line."

I let Vallejo think about that until he said, "Go on."

"The bot knew when we would meet Tauber. It must've sent Blake to kill Tauber and frame us. Some over-enthusiastic copbots gave Zoe an overdose of sleep darts, so I took her to Sherman Oaks General and made a doctor save her life. A young guy; I didn't get his name."

"Dr. Jenkins. He filed a report."

"The second copbot attack was scary enough that Zoe

decided to leave town before someone managed to murder her. That's the basic story."

"Except for the part about you getting killed."

I nearly grinned. Though Vallejo was playing his hand close to the chest, he probably didn't know about Eddie's involvement, and I couldn't see any reason to drag Eddie into this. And I'd guessed right about Arthur not reporting his car being stolen. That tale would've hurt Arthur's rep, and he would've had to invent a better reason for being with us in the first place than kidnapping us for Django Kay. The only part that I regretted omitting was Zoe's suspicion regarding Oberon Chain. Until I was sure she was someplace safe, I wasn't about to give anyone extra incentive to kill her.

I said, "Django Kay, Arthur Madden, and a few of their pals were using me for target practice. They killed a weasel named Nate who worked at Dr. Moreau's on Lankershim."

Vallejo's nod rippled the reflections in his mirrorsuit. "A wolfwoman called that in. She told a crazy story about her and the weasel being shot up with something that made him werewolf."

"An enzyme, according to Kay."

"They autopsied the weasel and tested the wolf. There wasn't anything odd in either of them, but we'll ask Kay about it."

I decided to share more information. "You know he's passing."

Vallejo straightened up. "Kay is?"

"Zoe thinks he's wolverine stock."

"If that's true, he's about to get some brand new problems."

"I can't think of a nicer guy to get them. How's the wolf?"

"We're not charging her for helping you, if that's what you mean. Not unless we find another reason to go after her. She was very helpful identifying Kay's crew."

"Who'd she pin?"

"Arthur Madden and Bruno Samson. We've got good descriptions on a couple of humans, but no names yet."

"Blond guy and a black woman?"

"Yeah."

"I don't remember anything helpful." I brought up something that had been nagging me. "Kay said that all he wanted was the earring."

"Not Chain's reward?"

"Apparently not."

"I'll ask him about it when we bring him in."

"You'll share what he says?"

"Of course." Vallejo smiled. "Your life should be simpler now. Chain withdrew his reward."

I shook my head. "And here I was ready to snitch on me."

"But Singer Labs is offering fifty meg for the earring."

"Singer? They say it's theirs?"

"Yes. Any idea where it is?"

"Hey, if I could give it to them, I would in a second."

Vallejo stroked his chin, then leaned forward. "If this'll go no further, I'll share what we know."

"Out of the goodness of your heart?"

He shook his head. "Strictly a business transaction. You won't be satisfied until you have answers. I've been authorized to see you get them."

"If I don't agree?"

"Then no answers. And, if you go public, I'll deny this conversation took place."

"What do I sign?"

"We've checked on you. Your word's good enough."

"And this call is being saved?"

Vallejo turned his palms up before him. "I'm afraid so."

I gave him my widest grin. "Anything in my teeth?"

"No."

"The call a few minutes ago, when you accepted my bribe

and joked about your boss's hair, that wasn't recorded, too, was it?"

Vallejo closed his eyes, then opened them. "Mr. Maxwell—"

"Okay. Let's hear it."

He took a deep breath. "The AIs called Doyle and Blake were part of a test to see if AIs would make good cops. Only a few people in high places knew they weren't human."

"How high?"

"I can't answer all your questions."

"CIA? NSA? Wink if I'm getting close. IRS?"

"What I'm telling you came through a colonel at the Pentagon. He could've been speaking for anyone. For the last two years, the AIs worked perfectly, so far as we can tell. Then they were assigned to Janna Gold's case."

"What case?"

"Gold had a contract with Singer Labs. They suspected that she'd stolen a device they were developing for the feds."

"The earring."

Vallejo nodded. "We showed the subway video to some people at Singer. They recognized it."

"What's it do?"

"What you saw. It takes bots offline. If you know the codes, you can then reprogram them."

"Does it affect AIs?"

"As in, did someone use it around Blake or Doyle to scramble their programming?"

I nodded.

"That's unlikely. The device intercepts signals from outside sources. It shouldn't affect anything that's self-controlled."

"Another theory down. What happened?"

"The LAPD was asked to keep an eye on Gold while she was in town. Strictly surveillance. Since AIs don't sleep, pee, or go for donuts, Blake and Doyle seemed perfect for the job. But something screwed up. It's as if the order to watch became an order to kill. Maybe the big brains at Chain Logic can figure it out. Maybe we'll never know."

"You're saying Blake and Doyle just happened to go screwy at the same time?"

"They're different models, but they could share the same design flaw. Or a virus might've gone from one to the other. It may be perfectly natural that they acted up at the same time."

"Where do the killer copbots fit in?"

"If the AIs couldn't jibe their wish to kill Gold with their programming not to hurt humans, they may've had a copbot do the deed for them. Human rationalization gets twistier than that. Why shouldn't AI? Or they might've decided that bots were the most efficient way to do the job. Or if they knew that what they were doing would be noticed, they could've used bots to keep attention away from them. Doyle didn't intervene until the cat escaped the first bot, and Blake didn't act until the cat shook her bodyguard." Vallejo shrugged. "We're drowning in a sea of ifs, I admit."

"Have another one, then. If the AIs can reprogram copbots, why should they want the earring? To keep their monopoly?"

"Maybe that part of their programming didn't change. If the cat had given the earring to Doyle at the subway station, he might've brought it back to headquarters and turned it in."

"Or not."

"Or not," Vallejo agreed. "We can't know now."

"That covers Gold's death. Don't tell me you had Tauber under surveillance, too."

Vallejo hesitated, then nodded.

"What'd you think he'd stolen?"

Vallejo ignored my tone, which wasn't exactly respectful.

"Tauber's political views brought him into contact with chimera separatists and AI rights groups. We were watching him as much for his safety as for what we might learn."

Lucky him, I thought. I only said, "So it's pure coincidence that looking into Gold's death led me to the AIs's next victim?"

"You found a link between Gold and Tauber—AI rights. If the AIs were aware of the same link, they might've kept killing people with similar connections."

"People with AI rights connections that the government was watching," I said, just to clarify things.

Vallejo grimaced and nodded.

"Who else fits that category?"

"No one I know of."

"Oberon Chain's name keeps cropping up."

Vallejo looked blank. "He's never been suspected of anything. Beyond the usual cutthroat business practices of a silicon king, that is."

"What about Jefferson 473? It's still out there—"

"It may not exist."

"Zoe and I saw— Oh." In the virtual age, nothing is real unless you touch it, and then you should get a second opinion. I said, "So you lay it out like this: Blake knew I was working for the cat. She tapped my phone. I called Tauber. Blake cut in with a tin man animation. My talk with the Jefferson sim told Blake when and where we would meet Tauber. Hell. That call might've made her decide to kill Tauber."

"Unless she already planned to kill Tauber and thought it'd be neater to take care of the cat at the same time."

"Why frame Zoe for Tauber's murder?"

"Maybe it wasn't a frame. Blake killed Tauber. Domingo destroyed Blake. People panicked and thought she had werewolfed. Isn't that the simplest explanation?"

Realizing I wanted to reject his idea made me consider it. It's a detective's job to find order behind the face of chaos, but even the best of us—maybe especially the best of us—can create conspiracies out of coincidence. We hear thunder and ask our clients why mad bombers are targetting them. We see mist and hunt for smoking guns. We find nothing and conclude the first person passing by must've hid the evidence. Sometimes the person behind the curtain is only a janitor.

If Zoe hadn't told me about Oberon Chain's smell, I might've concluded that the case was over then. Vallejo was waiting for a response, so I nodded and said, "Could be."

He reached for his disconnect. "I'll be in touch."

"Hey! In all your scenarios, we're clear of all charges, right?"

"You are."

"Not Zoe?"

"She used the earring at the cafeteria. After she said she'd lost it." Before I could try to explain that, Vallejo said, "We'll assume you didn't know she'd lied. And we're happy those bots didn't get either of you. But it's hard to give her the benefit of the doubt now."

"Regarding what?"

"Chain Logic says the AIs' programming could've been faulty. But they think it's more likely someone tampered with them."

I stared at him. "That puts us right back where we were!"

"Not really. You're clear, but the cat still may be guilty. That'd explain why she ran so hard."

"The other night, you agreed she had a good reason to run. If someone used the AIs to kill Gold, Zoe's next on their list."

"Who else could've used them?"

"I'm still working on that."

Vallejo frowned. "I thought you're off the case."

"That doesn't mean I don't have an opinion."

"You think someone unknown, for reasons unknown, using means unknown, represents such a threat to Domingo's life that she couldn't turn herself in."

"Fear doesn't need good reasons."

"No," Vallejo agreed. "But a police report does. Gold had a great deal of information about AIs. The cat could've gotten hold of that information."

"To kill Gold?"

Vallejo nodded.

"Why?"

"Maybe Gold was going to cut her out of her will. The cat remains the most likely suspect."

"Why would Zoe want Tauber dead?"

"Lots of chimeras felt betrayed when he started working for AI rights. Maybe she's killing everyone who let her down."

"She's not psycho."

"You think you know her?"

"Well enough to know she's not psycho."

"For your sake, I hope you're right. Any other questions?"

"Maybe I'll have some when you tell me what Django Kay says."

"Call any time." Vallejo disappeared from the projection field.

I stayed on the bed for ten or fifteen minutes. I had no reason to hurry. The nurse wanted me to be comfortable. David Melius wanted to give me a great job. The cops had all day to answer my questions. I was Mr. Popularity. I ought to have felt great. If I could've forgotten about Zoe's belief that an AI was acting as Oberon Chain, and if I could've convinced myself that she was merely a cute critter girl who had killed a few boring hours with me, I suppose I would have.

The older woman in the room across the hall looked disappointed when I came out dressed. I gave her a big smile anyway. Clovis hurried toward me as I approached the elevator. The dogman was shorter than he looked on HV. He called, "Mr. Maxwell! Mr. Maxwell!"

"Yes?"

He handed me a PowerPad. "I didn't want to leave this in your room."

"Why not?"

"A patient had a micro HV stolen from her room last week."

"Do all your patients get appliances when they leave?"

He frowned. "This isn't yours?"

"I've never—" I looked at the computer again. It wasn't new. It had a scuff mark on one corner. With something like hope and dread, I pressed the power button, but there wasn't any note for me on its holographic screen.

Clovis said, "It was with your belongings."

I turned the computer off and slipped it into my pocket. "It's mine. I had a DigiPal until recently."

"They say the PowerPad's great."

"Yeah. It's nice to have." I nodded to the dogman and got onto the elevator.

I opened the PowerPad again, searched for messages, and didn't find any. If Zoe was on the run, why had she given up her computer? It made sense that she had to leave the earring in the Pocket, but there was no reason to abandon the PowerPad.

The Engelberg Center's pink marble lobby was like the rest of the building; a little dulled by time and lack of funds, but still impressive. The line at the main desk consisted mostly of chimeras and humans in worn or cheap clothes. The prevailing attitude seemed to be gratitude, which softened my impatience. A tiny ratgirl ran up to me, stared at my face, laughed delightedly, and ran away.

When I reached the desk, a stocky young woman in data-shades smiled at me. Her name tag identified her as C. Herrera. I said, "I understand you can get me a refund. The name's Chase Maxwell."

"Of course." Her face went blank. Scrolling through

screens that only she could see, she waggled her fingers as if remembering the beat of a tune, then said, "You're the Lazarus!"

I shrugged. "All I did was die. The doctors did the hard work."

"What was it like?"

"Better than taxes."

She smiled, looked vacant again, then said, "Chase Maxwell. Two nights. You have one hundred eleven K and two C coming to you."

"Isn't that supposed to be one hundred seventeen?"

"Local calls are two and a half K."

"Do many patients see their bill and have to check right back in?"

She nodded solemnly. "Half of our organ donors come from this very room. How would you like your refund?"

"Just transfer it to my account."

"Certainly." She put an ID pad on the counter, I thumbed it, and she handed me a slip of paper. "Your receipt."

"Thanks." I gave it the quick scan. The list of services was long. Most of them were marked "donated." The rest were fairly cheap, generally under a hundred K, except for "Room and board, 5 nights—$250 K" and "Cryonics stabilization chamber, rental, 3 hrs.—$4,500 K."

At the bottom of the sheet, two listings were under "Deposit: $7 meg." The first was "Allied Charities Matching Fund—$3.5 meg." The surprise was the second: "Zoe Domingo—$3.5 meg."

Ms. Herrera said, "Is something wrong?"

"Is there someone here who was working when they brought me in?"

"No one from third shift's around. But almost everyone in the Center has heard about it."

"About what?"

"The only cryo chamber in South California was in Bev-

erly Hills, and they never lend us anything. If that cat hadn't
given them a lien on her income—" She stopped, probably
trying to find a nice way to say that I would be spread out
on a table for first-year med students right now. That didn't
bother me. What bothered me was that Zoe had tied up her
bank account and her inheritance to save my life.

Telling myself that so long as she was on the run, she
couldn't access any of her monies anyway, I asked, "Did she
leave a message for me?"

Ms. Herrera shook her head. "She didn't have time. The
police took her away as soon as she finished your paperwork.
Luckily for you." My face must've done something extreme
then. She brought her hand toward her mouth to cover a
gasp of surprise or sympathy. "You didn't know? It was a big
story on the news."

Vallejo had been playing his cards closer than I'd
thought. "Did you hear when her trial is?"

Ms. Herrera nodded. "Yesterday. She got thirty years for
killing a doctor."

13

Since I was at that moment, by my standards if not my mother's, rich, I almost hopped into the back of an Electricab waiting in front of the Center for wealthy patients. But in L.A., money just buys you a more comfortable seat for sitting in traffic. I was in a hurry; I caught a pert.

On the way downtown, I took out the PowerPad. Your lady love's supposed to give you a scarf or a garter. The computer was a lot more useful. I hesitated before going on-line, but I couldn't think of a reason why it would matter if someone managed to track me. If the powerful enemies that only Zoe and I thought might exist did exist, I suppose they might've been able to arrange for a disaster to befall the pert, but that would've been hard to cover up, even for them, and made it even harder for them to find the earring, if they thought I had it. And, to be honest, none of that occured to me then. I wanted to check my messages.

Which consisted of several invitations to join porno sites and a joke forwarded by my ex which wouldn't have been funny even if I'd been in a good mood—if men are the ones who tie self-worth to the size of body parts, why do body shops make more money from women?

There was nothing from Zoe. My disappointment showed me that I had hoped for something, even though I knew the cops wouldn't let her on the net. I suppose the knight in tarnished armor expected e-mail along the lines of

"Dearest Max, Fought my way free. Meet me in Canada. Undying love, Z."

I checked several news sites and got the official account. Zoe Domingo, feline chimera, was found guilty of the death of Dr. Janna Gold and sentenced to thirty years' hard labor at an unspecified indenture camp, with all her earnings to go to the government of South California. The theory for the murder was essentially Vallejo's: she killed the human who had adopted her in order to get her inheritance. She was also under suspicion as an accomplice in the death of Amos Tauber, but the state had yet to decide whether there was sufficient evidence to try her. There was no mention of the earring.

Her trial took an hour and thirty-five minutes, which was long for a case in chimera court. The judge had asked why she shouldn't get death for killing a human. Her court-appointed lawyer had pointed out that she had saved the life of another one, me.

I came out as well-meaning and a little stupid in the accounts, which is probably accurate enough: Ex-UNSEC agent who took chimera's case was killed saving her from bounty hunters, but was expected to make a full recovery.

If she hadn't given the lien to save me, she could've hired a better lawyer. I took a little comfort in knowing that a better lawyer might've prolonged the trial but probably wouldn't have changed its result. Yet I couldn't take much comfort from that. She had been caught because she stopped to save me.

There was no message from the elusive Mycroft. I sent him another note. "Mycroft, since I wrote you, whoever killed Janna Gold has killed Amos Tauber. I believe the next victim will be Gold's daughter, Oberon Chain, or you. For their sake and yours, call me. Chase Maxwell."

Including Chain in that list was accurate, so far as I knew. If someone had kidnapped him, his life was in constant dan-

ger. Even if he had been using a bot or an AI double innocently, to escape boredom or to do two jobs at once, his
prominence in the community and his concerns with AI
rights made him a more likely target than the elusive Mycroft.

Then I saw that the absence of innocence did not imply
guilt. My first fear had been that the AI impersonating Chain
was a rogue, like Blake and Doyle. But what if Chain knew his
life was in danger and therefore sent a double to the party?

I wished the questions could go away, because there was
no way to answer them without telling Chain I knew more
than I should. I put away the computer and failed to enjoy
the rest of the ride.

Prosperity Indenture Services had an exclusive contract
for the state's able-bodied prisoners, which may have accounted for as much as thirty percent of their business. Their
nearest location was a large suite on the twenty-fourth floor
of a high-rise in Westwood along Wilshire Boulevard—they
keep building them, even after the Big One knocked 'em all
down. At one end of the hall was a talent agency; at the other,
a lawyer. They all looked the same—expensive. Their decor
only told you they had hired someone to make them appear
to be a place where successful, powerful people did very important things, to make you think that, if you were lucky, they
would do those things for you.

The difference in the three businesses was that though
they all served desperate people, the indenture service
served the most desperate, the ones who knew that if they
could not sell the only thing remaining to them, they would
join the secret city of the homeless or the silent army of the
dead.

A few chimeras and humans waited in an antiseptically
tasteful lobby. Behind a wide, curved desk was a young man
who looked like he wished the world ran like the Marines. He
wore a dark, conservative suit that must've cost as much as
a good used car. His hair had been buzzcut, but only a fool

would bet that he had cut it himself. His tan and his physique probably came from a body shop, but his supercilious smile was entirely his own. "May I help you, sir?"

"I'd like to speak to your boss."

"Ms. Agosto doesn't see clients."

"I'm not a client." I flashed my ID. "Chase Maxwell, of Maxwell Investigations. I might be able to keep her from being a party in a wrongful indenture suit."

"She may not be available—"

"That'd be a shame. I'd like to keep this out of the news, but I doubt I can, without her help. The media will lap it up. Woman wrongfully indentured, Prosperity Agency stonewalls instead of helps." I grimaced. "Could get ugly."

Mr. Military's tan faded a couple of shades. "I'll see if she can see you."

"There's a good chap."

He gave me a glance that said I hadn't made a new friend, then went down a softly lit hall to a door that looked like a steel and slate sculpture. I leaned against the desk and breathed deeply. The nurse at the Engelberg Center wouldn't have approved. If I killed myself, I wouldn't be helping Zoe. But I was ready for another sprint by the time Army Boy returned.

"Ms. Agosto will see you now."

"Thanks." I made that as polite as I could. The danger with acting like an asshole to deal with assholes is that no one else can tell you apart. There was a time when I wouldn't have cared.

My escort opened the steel and slate door. The office that he revealed would be a sound recorder's nightmare—if they were concerned about corporate security, that might've been part of the point. Most surfaces were hard and slick: a floor of intricate wooden inlays, two walls of brushed aluminum and two of glass windows that ran from floor to ceiling, and a small pool in one corner with a fountain flowing incessantly. The only concessions to softness were two paintings of crows flying through a blizzard and a Navajo rug on the floor.

The woman behind the desk had the ageless, plastic quality of a body-shop addict. She could've been twenty-five or seventy-five. Her skin was dark brown, her copper hair was pulled back from her face, and her body was so slender that if she swallowed a pea, you could probably watch it make its way to her stomach. She wore a well-tailored green suit with a Nehru collar. As she stood and walked around the desk, her smile seemed sincere.

"I'm Simone Agosto. You are Mr. Maxwell?"

"Guilty." I might not have noticed her handshake if I had closed my eyes. Her birdlike fingers touched mine like a breeze, then withdrew.

Military Boy said, "If there's anything else—"

"That'll be all, Frederick."

He nodded and left. Agosto indicated the brown leather chairs by the fountain. As we sat, she said, "There's a problem with one of our clients?"

"Zoe Domingo."

She frowned, brought the fingers and thumb of her left hand together like the Italian gesture of praise, then waggled her fingers slightly as she glanced in the corner of the room. I was impressed, even though I realized how easy it would be to fake being hardwired. She looked back at me and said, "I'm sorry. I can't confirm or deny anything about a Zoe Domingo."

"She's a convict. You have the monopoly on indenturing prisoners."

"True. But the terms of some indentures don't allow us to give out any information. Not without a court order."

Which meant someone in the legal system thought Zoe's life could be in danger—or someone didn't want her found by anyone who could help her. I said, "That's awkward. Some people might think you were colluding with a judge to indenture innocent people."

Agosto raised an eyebrow. "Everything we do is perfectly legal."

"I'm sure it is. But I need your help to convince my client."

"I don't see what I can do. The terms of this case are sealed."

"Domingo was sentenced to thirty years' hard labor. That's on the public record. What would that entail?"

Agosto shrugged. "Indenture work in an agriculture or recycling camp, twelve-hour days, six days a week. If she's reasonably attractive—"

"She is."

"Then she'd be given the option of sex work. If she accepted it, she'd be available six hours a day and receive a medical exam every week."

I didn't want to think about that choice. "Suppose someone offered to buy her contract."

"Convict sentences dictate that they serve their time at a standard indenture camp. You would have to go to a judge for an exception."

I leaned forward in my chair. "If there was some way to get a message to her—"

"Not legally. I'm a Libertarian, Mr. Maxwell. Nothing is more sacred to me than a contract."

"An innocent woman may spend the rest of her life trapped with criminals and desperate people."

Agosto smiled tolerantly. "And saints. Many people indenture themselves for admirable reasons. Just last month, a young man bought his mother a new liver, and a woman bought her niece a university education, including medical school."

"In exchange for selling themselves for years."

Agosto nodded.

"Don't you feel—" I checked myself, because I needed her help.

"Blessed? Yes. We're able to help so many."

There were many things I could've said, but I knew she had heard them all before. I'd been about to open with the "exploiting the unfortunate" argument, which she had already countered with the "helping the helpless" response. My next attempt would've been to ask whether it was right to let people sell themselves. She would've answered that we own ourselves—how could anyone take away our right to do what we want with our own bodies? I would've asked whether it was right to see everything in terms of property, and she would've told me that the fall of the Soviet Union proved that communism had failed. At which point I would've said that I didn't care about politics, I only wanted an innocent woman freed. And Agosto had made it quite clear to me that she was more concerned with what was legal than with what was right.

Her patience was at an end. So were my thoughts on how to save Zoe. I thanked her for her time and left. I don't remember the walk from her office to the pert that took me back to my apartment.

First I cursed Zoe. I never asked her to do me any favors. Death is any job's ultimate occupational hazard. I knew that. She could've let me stay dead. She never asked whether I wanted to come back. Death could've been so terrifying that I might've hated her for making sure I'd have to do it at least once again. By any reasonable standard, I owed her nothing. She did what she wanted. I benefited. We had no contract, no understanding of any sort.

Or did we? Maybe we make contracts all the time, if we are honorable people—unspoken, one-way contracts that can't be broken because they're based on who we are, not on what others do. Whether Zoe thought she had obligations to me was irrelevant. I had obligations to her because I liked her, respected her, and, so much as anyone can based on a long day of being together, loved her. I would never respect myself if I did not honor a contract of the heart. I didn't know if she was now a friend or a lover or something in-between or something entirely different, but I knew I would give my life for hers. From her point of view, I suppose I'd already done that. Why should I be surprised that she would risk her freedom to give my life back?

Crossing the Santa Monicas reminded me of our trip to see Tauber. All I had wanted to do then was sleep. Now I could sleep all I wanted. Zoe could only sleep when her day at the camp came to an end.

My part of Crittertown had barely been touched by the riot. Though a grocery store run by a very nice Guatemalan couple was boarded up, a sign on the door said that it would reopen soon. Felix was at his newstand. I didn't feel like talking, but he called, "Hey, skin! Where you been?"

"Around, Felix. How're you?"

"Cheese, wine, and me, we just keep getting better. You still seeing that pretty cat?"

"I'm working on it."

"Well, I wish you luck. She seemed like a good one."

"They all seem like good ones to you, Felix."

"Treat 'em right, they all are."

Passing Huston Street, I remembered Zoe ditching the copbot that Blake had assigned her and wondered whether she was safe from the killers now. Since the police knew where she was, the killers must, too. But if she was out of circulation for the next thirty years, and the earring with her, they might think they didn't need to do anything about her now. I had no choice but to hope that was true.

My apartment was full of memories of Zoe. Approaching it alone reminded me that we had left together when we went to Chain's charity event. She had waited for me inside the front door while I put on my shoes. She had slept on the couch with her mouth slightly open and the pink tip of her tongue resting between her teeth. She had sat on the counter eating my soy cheese, and she had meowed at the balcony door. And the entire time she had been there, my only wish had been to get rid of her.

The bedroom was haunted by a different ghost. On seeing the bed where I'd done the ecstatic octopus with the thing that killed Tauber, I yanked the sheets and threw them onto the dirty clothes at the bottom of my closet. Then I realized that my second set of sheets also needed washing. I stood in the middle of the room, trying to decide whether to put the first set back on, to spend Christmas Eve washing clothes, or to sleep on the couch.

I said, "Oh, Cat, why'd you do this to me?" I needed a long, long walk, or maybe a run, or maybe to go down to the gym to work until I was exhausted or I hurt myself. I decided that those were things I could always do later. If I had to deal with a broken heart, I should do it in the traditional way. I went to the phone to call Eddie to see if he wanted to go drinking.

The message light was blinking repeatedly. The first message was from Rita, calling me from the Hague to wish me a Merry Christmas. The next two were from people who had heard about me on the news. One wanted to hire me to look for a runaway chimera and the other wanted to option my story to sell to Hollywood. The fourth was from Mycroft.

14

The message came without video. A pleasingly modulated, rather high-pitched voice said, "I'm Mycroft. Sorry I didn't get back to you sooner—I spend so much time online when I'm working that I stay off for days when I can. I'll do whatever you ask to see justice done for Amos Tauber. Come to One Waterman Way in Malibu at any time. I much prefer personal interaction to its electronic simulation."

The next message was from my mother, who said, "Season's greetings, child of my womb! Why don't you visit? The weather's wonderful and so am I." That degree of cheer meant she was well into the second bottle of wine.

Then came two more inquiries about work, one to follow a wife to see how she was honoring her wedding vows, one for a bodyguard by a woman who smiled too much. I suspect the latter was someone with too much money who wanted to seduce the Famous Un-killable UNSEC Detective—but I admit my vanity can get in the way of my judgment.

The last message was from Eddie, who said, "Hey, Captain, glad you made it. Damn shame about Zoe. For a critter—well, I guess you know that. I'm off to spend Christmas with Dolores and her kids. Want to grab a meal when I get back and fill me in? I know a great noodle place in Little Tokyo. Have a merry!"

Merry didn't seem to be in the plan. I called Mycroft's number. A slender blond man in a white lab coat answered. Hung from the wall behind him was the sort of equipment you'd expect in the office of a doctor or a torturer. "Hello?" In the background, something whimpered in pain.

"Mycroft?"

He smiled; he seemed like a man who found life more entertaining than I did just then. "Paul Zweig. I work for Mycroft." There was another cry of pain, and he leaned partly out of the projection.

So Mycroft hires cheerful sadists, I thought. Maybe I should reconsider my plan. When the blond man came back, he said, "Sorry about that. How can I help you?"

"I'm Chase Maxwell. Mycroft told me to call."

"Ah! Can you hold for a minute? He's in the house, but this place is a maze."

"Don't bother. I wanted to make sure he wouldn't mind a visitor on Christmas Eve."

"Not at all. We'll expect you anytime."

I hung up, then tested the Infinite Pocket. I didn't drop the SIG this time.

Life was much better with a plan. I went into the kitchen for a beer, popped an onion bagel into the toaster, scraped the mold off the hummus, cut the soft bits off a cucumber and sliced what remained into slivers, and made myself a sandwich. After the first bite through the warm, chewy bagel, cool, crisp cucumber, and smooth hummus, I realized I was starving.

I carried Zoe's computer and my second sandwich to the phone and began sending messages. All of the business inquiries had left full contact information, so I composed one message for all of them. "Thank you for enquiring about my services. I'm unable to consider new cases at the present time. You might try the Brady Xi Agency—tell them I sent you. Sincerely, Chase Maxwell."

Then I wrote, "Rita, holidays were always wonderful for us—I'll never forget Ibiza. I hope you and Janos are having a great time. Max."

The next was more difficult. "Dear Mom. Nondenomina-
tional felicitations to you, too. I'm working through Christmas. I have no idea how long this job will take. I'll call when
it's over. If you heard I was in the hospital, don't worry. I'm
fine. But it did get me thinking that I've been assuming you
know things I haven't been saying. So, for the record, I love
you. Max."

The last was easiest. "Eddie, sorry to put you through
that. Dunno if you heard, but Arthur and Bruno are facing
serious time, and the orca, Rashid, is dead. I'll call when I
can, but that may be a while—I'm going to find a way to help
Zoe. Have one hell of a time with Dolores and her kids. We
both suffer from Groucholalia, but there's a lot to be said for
joining a club that wants you as a member. Max."

That was all the tidying of my life that I could do for free.
The landlady would have to wait until I knew I didn't have a
better use for the hospital refund.

Since evening was coming on, I changed to my favorite
work clothes, a plain dark gray suit of heavy cotton, a light
gray mock turtleneck shirt, and black deck shoes. And since
Malibu at night in December would be chilly, I added a black
coat, then tucked gloves, nightshades, and a scarf in its pockets.

The pert to Malibu took forty-eight minutes, according to
its display. I have no idea whether that was accurate. The
sun was setting over the Pacific. I watched it go, and I wondered whether Zoe was working into the dark and what they
had her doing.

Not five minutes after I set up the PowerPad to take my
calls, it vibrated in my pocket. I pulled it out and turned it
on. Vallejo appeared in the projection field. I flicked a finger
through "Respond, no video" and said, "Hello, Detective."

"Don't say I didn't get you anything for Christmas, Mr.
Maxwell. Django Kay says the injections they gave the chi-

meras were distilled water to scare them. The weasel simply
panicked. As for the earring, he says he heard that the chimera who'd killed Tauber had taken something from Singer
Labs worth a hundred meg." As I frowned, he added, "Kay's
in a position to hear rumors."

"How'd he know the something looked like an earring?"

Vallejo looked decidedly sheepish. "Singer went public
after we showed them the subway video."

"Kay wouldn't take the kind of risks he took on spec.
Someone wanted the earring, so he went after it."

"I can see why you'd want to think that."

"What's that mean?"

"Your client's attractive, if you don't mind dating outside
your species. It's hard to think she fooled you."

"You could've told me she'd been arrested."

"Would you, in my place?"

I let him have that. "If you're so sure Zoe's the killer,
why's her location a secret?"

"There are enough variables in this case, Mr. Maxwell.
Why inject more?"

"If she's a killer, why did she save my life?"

"Maybe she realized she couldn't get away, so it'd be wise
to have a good deed behind her. Maybe that was her idea of
atonement. I'm not her shrink or her priest. Be content with
where, when, and how. You'll spin your wheels forever if you
go for why."

"I suppose. Anything else?"

"No. Merry Christmas, Mr. Maxwell."

"And a shiny new year to you."

I rode the rest of the way thinking that he was right about
one thing: I wasn't being objective. But who is? Humans are
rationalizing animals. The best of us poke our assumptions
now and then to see if they still work, but we can't escape
from forming beliefs that fit our needs. Vallejo needed to

solve this case. Pinning it on Zoe did that. I needed to do something for the woman who had saved me. Maintaining her innocence did that for me.

The sun had set by the time I reached Malibu. An Electricab call button was mounted just outside the pert stop, but I ignored it. Some people complain that pert stops along the beach should be as close together as they are in towns. I'm not one. I walked a little over a mile along the bike path, appreciating the smell of the sea and the lash of the wind. The moon would not rise for several hours, but my nightshades showed the world clearly in silvered hues. I saw seabirds, a coyote, and a young man and woman walking arm in arm. Only the thought that I was expected kept me from removing my shoes and walking along the sand.

The house at One Waterman Way looked at first glance like most rich people's homes in the hills along the Pacific Coast Highway. At second glance, it showed greater concern for its setting. Its low silhouette suited the rise it sat on, as did its materials, dark pine and bricks the color of sandstone. Its landscaping was so subtle I thought its grounds had been abandoned, until I realized that native plants would not arrange themselves so attractively if left to themselves.

A stocky, brushed-aluminum butler with green optics opened the door as I approached the front door. "Mr. Maxwell?" Something about its voice and build suggested great patience, competence, and discretion. If it had been human, it would've been a British army sergeant who had left one service for another as a gentleman's gentleman.

"Yes."

"I'm Chives. Do come in. You're expected. May I take your coat?"

Gloves, scarf, and nightshades went with the coat. I had a moment to admire the inner room, which consisted of colonial Spanish chairs, a koi pond, and three sliding doors. An

LED glowed discreetly over each of the sliding doors, green over the outer ones, red over the center one.

The left-hand door opened. An Irish setter pup with a bandaged foreleg ran up to me, its tongue lolling and its body shaking in delight at meeting a new visitor.

Paul Zweig followed the pup. "I was afraid she'd be scared of people."

"Why?"

He motioned at her leg. "She was hit by a car. I found her on the highway a few days ago."

"You were changing her bandage when I called."

"Yes. Why?"

"I thought I heard her."

"Do you need a dog?"

"Nope. Tiny apartment, impossible hours."

"A shame. She likes you." He caught her collar as I stood, and the pup quit washing my hands and neck. "You think Mollie suits her?"

"Or Meg. You're a vet?"

He grinned. "Effectively."

"Meaning?"

"The formal handle's xenophysician." The light over the central door changed from red to green. "Ah. Mycroft's ready to see you." He offered his hand. "Good meeting you in person."

"Likewise." Which was true. Paul may've been a multiple murderer, but anyone gets bonus points for being good with animals. We shook hands, and he headed out with the pup, saying, "C'mon, Meg." I looked at the central door and frowned.

Paul pointed at it. "Mycroft's back that way. Just follow the lights."

Follow the lights. The butler could've showed me the way, but the mysterious Mycroft wanted me to set off like a kid in a fun house. I shrugged and walked through the door, entering a long, windowless hall with light pine wainscotting and pale green walls. The ceiling lights gave a soft, diffused glow. Stars were visible through a tilework of skylights. A channel of water ran along the wall, deep enough for swimming laps.

Something rushed toward me. I stepped back with my fingers ready to catch the SIG. A bright yellow handibot scurried by on its spider legs, carrying a pile of sheets and towels down the hall.

I wondered if I should follow it. Then a lamp lit up on a small table in the opposite direction. "Go toward the light," I said. "Sounds like a euphemism to me." If I was being monitored, no one bothered to respond.

I walked down the hall and stopped at an intersection. To my right, a spotlight came on to illuminate a painting, a Friedman that I'd seen in a documentary on her life. When I came up to it, I was ready to stand and admire it for a minute or two, but a small green light glowed over a door inlaid with strips of wood in many colors.

I stepped through the door onto the shore of a Pacific lagoon. Moonlight streamed down from the sky. The water lapped softly against the sand. If there hadn't been underwater lamps throwing flickering highlights over the entire scene, I would've thought someone had found a way to teleport living things, to Tahiti, at least.

I said, "Hello?" No one answered.

A rocky point thrust out over the pool. I walked out to its edge to study the only lights I saw, globes that were content to float midway between the sandy bottom and the surface. Since that route wasn't promising, I glanced up at the artificial moon for a clue as to what to do next.

A dark shape raced underwater toward me. Before I could jump back, it broke the surface with a splash and stood half out of the water in classic dolphin fashion. Which made sense, since it was a classic dolphin, except for a tiny piece of silver jewelry at its throat.

"Chase Maxwell, welcome. The resources of my house are at your disposal."

I recognized the voice, but I wanted confirmation. Okay, I was startled. How often do you meet a talking fish? Yes, I know dolphins are mammals, but if it looks like a fish and acts like a fish, in the unreasoning, atavistic part of your soul, you're sure of two things: it's a fish, and it shouldn't talk. "Mycroft?"

"I have another name, but you'd find it difficult to pronounce."

"Thanks for seeing me."

"If I might help save a life, how could I not? Please, ask what you will."

"Your bio says you consult. On what?"

"Many things. Most recently, the Antarctic natural gas discussions."

"Who for?"

"Whoever's paying me. In that case, several nations. I'm a remarkably disinterested party." He also seemed to be a remarkably amused party, but that may've only been the permanent grin of the dolphin jaw.

"I was in UNSEC. I never heard of you."

"What country would admit that a trusted advisor never wears clothes and has a hole in his head?"

I smiled. Mycroft said, "May I call you Chase?"

"If you're a patronizing cop or a phone solicitor. I go by Max."

"I have a breathing apparatus for visitors, Max. Would you care to join me? The water's delightful."

"Thanks, but it's kind of hard to talk underwater."

"Then you're here because time is urgent and not because you've nothing to do on Christmas Eve."

"Zoe Domingo's serving thirty years in an indenture camp

for a crime she didn't commit. I'd like to get her out as soon as possible."

Mycroft dove suddenly, turned in a tight circle, and re-surfaced. "Come. I'll show you my home, and you'll tell me your story."

So I walked along the shore and talked about Zoe and our time together. Mycroft swam lazily beside me, occasionally diving or racing away for a moment. The environment beneath him changed as we toured. Sometimes the bottom was near, sometimes far, sometimes sand, sometimes coral, sometimes tumbled rocks, sometimes a lava bed. There were half-buried Atlantean ruins, a sunken galleon, an alien spaceship. Oxygen burbled into the pool from the helmet of a life-sized deep-sea diver. At the end of the enormous pool was a door, half underwater, where I finished my account.

Dolphins are remarkably easy to talk to. Though I said nothing about Zoe's suspicions regarding Oberon Chain, I found myself telling Mycroft about sex with Kristal Blake. Remembering it made me want to shed my skin, but I had been sent down the wrong path too often on cases by clients who neglected to mention sexual relationships that they didn't think pertinent. A woman once had me hunt for days to find someone leaving threatening messages for her; I would've solved that one in an afternoon if she'd told me she was having an affair with a married man.

The best thing about confessing sexual misadventures to dolphins is that they think erotic encounters between consenting compatible entities are natural and desirable. Mycroft only began to understand my disgust when I pointed out that I wasn't upset because I'd had sex with a humanlike AI; I was upset because I'd had sex believing Blake was something other than what she was.

When I finished, Mycroft said, "Four years ago, Singer Labs sought a way to scan a living brain, encode the information stored there, load the information—call it the mind—

into a computer where it could function as pure intelligence unencumbered by the body, and then, when the uploaded mind had completed its task, download the mind back to the subject's brain. You can see the appeal of their goal. Imagine scientists and artists able to think without the world's distractions, at speeds that the brain cannot approach, with all the world's research accessible in an instant. Tell no one I told you this; I'm breaking a nondisclosure contract."

"Sounds like a sweet job."

"I can't say. I turned it down."

"Why?"

Mycroft laughed, a dolphin's chattering, not human at all. "I like bodies. Distractions may be annoying, yet they're often inspiring. Newton couldn't have observed apples in the electronic realm. And I'm not sure Singer can succeed. The interaction between brain and mind remains a mystery. If you mapped all but an infinitesimal portion of the mind, then wrote the scanned mind back onto a brain, you could wipe away forever the bit that you'd missed. The lost information might seem inconsequential—the color of a favorite childhood toy, the sound of an obscure bird's call—but who's to say what ultimately makes us what we are? What we do not know and treasure may be the heart of what we are. Imagine the price of losing an artist's ability to analyze or a scientist's ability to empathize."

"I see your point."

"The legal and ethical questions multiply exponentially. When the digital mind is returned to the physical host, what happens to the mind that existed between the time of the scan and the download? Aren't you destroying that mind when you write the digital one over it?"

"If the person gave consent—"

"Which person? You begin with the person who is scanned. Then there are two sapient entities, a digital one in the computer and a biological one that continues to think and experience life. Even if you put the biological subject to sleep, or even if the process is so quick that less than a second of the world's time passes between the scan and the download, the two minds will have different experiences and become subtly different. Yet the body's mind will be overwritten by the download. Must the subject give consent twice, once before the scan and once before the download? Suppose the scanned subject decides against the download, seeing it as a form of death for the self that then exists. Do you respect the subject's later wishes or original wishes? If you respect the original wishes, perhaps as expressed in a contract signed at the time of the scan, do you physically force the subject to go through with the download? If you respect the later wishes, what do you do with the digital mind? It's an AI and therefore has no legal rights, but the ethical questions remain.

"Is erasing a digital mind a form of murder? If you conclude that it's only property, to whom does it belong, the person who was scanned, the person who did the scan, or someone else? A digital mind can be copied endlessly. Who owns the copyright? Suppose you make two copies of a digital mind and set them to different tasks. When it's time to download the digital mind to the subject's brain, which copy gets precedence? What happens if a digital mind is accidentally imposed on the wrong brain?" Mycroft gave another burst of dolphin laughter. "It's a fascinating problem, but an enormous one, and ultimately, it doesn't address my concerns."

"Well, I can see how as a chimera—"

"Humans only gave me speech and tools, Mr. Maxwell." Mycroft rolled onto his back. "Are you sure you wouldn't care for a swim?"

"You're a healthy bottlenose dolphin. Got it. No, thanks."

"As you wish."

"Gold and Tauber worked for Singer on this project?"

"They did."

"So Blake and Doyle could've been created by scanning two real people?"

"If Singer's project got that far. These AIs sound unusually concerned with worldly matters."

I thought of my time with Blake. "Yeah."

"If this was an experiment using scanned minds, there may not be two personalities. Two copies of the same mind could act as both Blake and Doyle."

"If they were separated, they might've developed separate goals."

"Or they could've been updating each other as easily as reconciling files on different computers."

"If you could do that with a computer and a person, Singer's problem would disappear."

"Reconciling memories is more challenging than writing over them. And there's the question of whether you can overload a human mind with information. With a computer, you have the advantage of knowing exactly how much data it can store."

"Did you ever meet Oberon Chain?"

"Not in person."

"What did you think of him?"

"Like all who hoard wealth, his sense of group and family is small, and his sense of entitlement is great. Do I think he would kill? Most humans will, under certain circumstances. I don't know what those circumstances might be for Oberon. I have no reason to think he may be your killer. Do you?"

I wished I could trust Mycroft enough to tell him what Zoe had smelled. I said, "No. You've been very helpful."

"I only knew Dr. Gold by reputation. But I knew Amos Tauber. He acknowledged the difference in each species, yet treated every soul alike."

"Which assumes every species has a soul."

"You humans tether the soul to religion. The soul is what

yearns and seeks to rise. All intelligences have that."

"He was your friend."

"No one understood me as well as Amos. He was part of my family, my group. Dolphins are not by nature solitary, Max. Isolated humans become poets, or go mad. Isolated dolphins pine and die."

I looked around at the world that had been created for him, then back at its only occupant. "What do enhanced dolphins do?"

"We adopt a more inclusive view of the group. When that fails— You see that door, with the light?"

I nodded.

"When that light is on, no one may enter."

"I thought isolation was the problem."

"And sometimes, the cure."

What do you say to that? I couldn't apologize for what members of my species took from him when they gave him our kind of speech. I said, "Until we know why Gold and Tauber died, you have to consider that a killer may be after you, too."

"I have."

"You let me walk in here alone."

"You were scanned at the front door. The Infinite Pocket was troubling, but had you done anything threatening, Chives would've stopped you. As for here—" Mycroft whistled, and the light suddenly came up. I looked behind me. A handibot crouched by the wall. Mycroft whistled again, and the bot left the room.

"I could've gotten off half a dozen shots before it stopped me."

"I didn't say that was the only defense." Mycroft whistled a third time, and the lights dimmed again.

"Are there any AIs running anywhere in the house? Or with access to the house computer system?"

"I don't own any AIs."

"For the same reason as Tauber?"

Mycroft ducked his head twice. "When you give something awareness, you become responsible for it. You humans have the apple myth. Chimeras will undoubtedly evolve something similar, as will AIs."

"Zweig works for you."

"Laws govern the treatment of human employees, and to a lesser degree, chimeras. But you can still buy an intelligent machine for the sole purpose of hammering it into junk or shooting it dead."

"If you'd concluded that I was the killer—"

"If I thought you'd killed my brother Amos, you wouldn't leave this house alive."

"The justice of the lonely dolphin?"

"Don't worry, Max." He swam toward the metal hatchway, and it opened before him. "Humans aren't responsible for what I am."

The hatchway closed behind Mycroft. The red light came on. A moment later, the far door opened, and Paul Zweig stepped in. I said, "And I thought dolphins always looked happy."

"Excuse me?"

"Nothing."

"Mr. Maxwell?"

"Max."

"Paul. There's always a guest room ready for company. The kitchen's embarrassingly well stocked. Whatever you'd like, ask. When Mycroft said the resources of this house are available, he wasn't just being polite."

"You were listening in."

"As you said, you could've been a killer. Sorry about that."

"I back my friends sometimes, too. How long will he be in there?"

"A minute, a week." Paul shrugged. "Usually, overnight."

"And I thought *I* was going to have a crummy Christmas Eve."

"Don't feel too sorry for him. Right now, he's grieving for Tauber. But I think he enjoys being what he is, all things considered."

"Why do you think that?"

"Because I could pull his vocalizer and he could go to sea at anytime."

I shook my head. "We don't escape our past that easily."

15

Christmas Eve dinner consisted of spinach salad, lentil soup, curried wild rice with almonds and portabello mushrooms, nutloaf with teriyaki sauce, mashed potatoes and yams, asparagus with soy hollandaise sauce, lingonberry scones, and white zinfandel, followed by soy milk latte and carrot cake. If every bite hadn't made me wonder what Zoe was eating, it would've been a perfect holiday meal.

The view was grand. The moon had risen, so the Pacific surged beyond the dining room windows. Mycroft could have been there—the table sat beside a small pool connected by a tunnel to his main one—but he was not. I doubt watching him down live fish would've been a major part of an ideal dining experience.

The company consisted of Paul and a tall Korean woman named Yongae who worked in teleportation. Either she was extremely good at drawing people into conversation or my experience truly fascinated her. She wanted to know everything about life with the Infinite Pocket, and then she wanted to know everything about my death. She had a theory that if people could be killed, teleported, and revived at their destination, we might beat the human transportation problem. I pointed out that I wasn't about to volunteer to be killed in order to make a meeting in Santa Monica. When she asked whether going to another star would entice me, I said it would just make me pause a little longer before I said no. I remembered Mycroft's discussion about the Singer project and what would happen if you lost an essential part of you. Death and revivification held a similar risk. So did the scanning process for teleportation. She pointed out that AIs could be safely teleported; if Singer solved their problem, would I let my digital self go out in a robot body? And I had to admit that even then, I wouldn't. Call me a Luddite, but you have to be mad to risk your mind for any purpose.

It was a nice evening, much nicer than I'd expected, and Paul and Yongae repeated that a guest room was ready if I wanted it. But at some point in the evening, I had begun to see what I had to do, so I thanked them and left.

Back on the pert, I used Zoe's computer to call the number Vallejo had given me. I expected to leave a recording, but Chumley answered. "Maxwell. Anyone get you a silver hammer? Ho, ho, ho."

I never would've guessed that he knew classical music. People surprise you. I said, "And a very scarey Christmas to you, too. Vallejo around?"

"His wife and kids stopped by after Christmas mass. I can put you through to the coffee room if it's important."

"Don't bother. You're still on the Gold-Tauber case, right?"

"You calling to confess?"

"Sorry. My present isn't as good as that. I've got a lead for you. Singer Labs was working on a secret project to digitize minds, essentially creating AIs from them, sort of the ultimate form of virtual reality. In theory, the digital mind solves tasks in a computer or a bot shell, then they write the experience onto the subject's brain."

"Why's that a present?"

"Didn't you say Doyle and Blake came from Singer? They may've been part of a test using AIs derived from human minds. A dangerously unsafe experiment. One that'd be bad publicity and might make Singer responsible for the deaths of Gold and Tauber."

"And that'd get the cat off."

"That, too."

"What's your source?"

"Sorry. I promised not to say."

"We'll look into it."

"That's all I want for Christmas."

"You hear anything else—"

"I'll let you know. The next best thing to being a cop is doing their work for them."

"Next time you're in the station, you can have a donut. If you're really good, you can sit in my car and I'll run the siren."

"Promises, promises."

I disconnected and watched the sea until the pert veered onto Sunset. By the time I made it home, I was too tired to see phantoms on my furniture. I wished I had asked Zoe her religion, so I would've known what God to ask to watch over her. I hoped that her camp was a Libertarian's model of ethical capitalism, and I tried not to think about the ways that unregulated business people have treated their workers throughout history. In bed, I closed my eyes and thought, "She's tough, God. You don't have to give her a lot of attention. Just watch her back until I find her, okay?" Then I went to sleep.

Mycroft called the next morning. I had to keep reminding myself that I was looking at a talking dolphin and not a sim that someone had synced to his voice. He said, "Good morning, Max. I wish I had better news."

"Which is?"

"Three quite competent lawyers have gone over Zoe's trial. Without new evidence, there's nothing to bring to a judge."

"They did this on Christmas Day?"

"Zoe doesn't have holidays off. And the price I paid for a few hours' work must've seemed like a Christmas present."

"I told the cops about Singer."

"I expected you would."

"Will you help them get the story on the AIs?"

"I can give them some hints. But Singer's lawyers are as good as mine. I doubt we'll breach corporate confidentiality."

"Sometimes you get lucky."

I spent the day packing. I could've walked away from everything I owned, but I didn't have to, so I didn't. It's true I could've moved out in an hour, but I had the day, so I took it. I put padding around the breakables. I labelled each box with its contents. I noted a few things that I hadn't used in a year and set them aside for the Salvation Army. When Rita and I were together, we'd moved often. She had always complained about the way I threw things together. After I stacked my worldly goods in the middle of the living room, I almost took a picture to send her.

I thought about going to a casino. It might've been fun to give Arthur a big grin if he was out on bail, but I decided against it. I wanted to keep the day simple.

I thought about smoking. I'd done my twenty-four with interest. But I had a shiny new lung and another that had begun to clean itself out. I liked the idea of setting out like a knight purified for battle.

I spent much of the afternoon and evening reading Mark Twain's *Life on the Mississippi* and wondering what he would think of the river now that it had gone from clean and wild to dirty and tame. I watched the news; Zoe and I had already been forgotten. There were human disasters and natural ones, political squabbles and domestic ones, little victories in sports and little defeats in weather. I fixed food and ate it, spicy potatoes, garlic, tofu, and peas for lunch, pasta with tomato sauce and spinach for supper. I took a long walk through my neighborhood, then came home and slept. It was a day. I liked it.

Early the next morning, in front of Prosperity Indenture

Services, Frederick's military stride came to an abrupt halt at the sight of me. "What do you want?"

"What does anyone want here? Buy me."

"I thought you were a detective."

"I was. Isn't getting indentured like joining the French Foreign Legion?"

"We have to ask a few more questions than they did." He thumbed the office door. The door swung open as the lights came on, and we went to his desk. "You're not wasting my time?"

"I value my time, too. I expect to get top dollar for it."

"Good." He put on a pair of datashades, twitched his fingers a few times above the top of the desk, then said, "Hold up your right thumb."

I did. "This is a hell of a place to hitchhike."

He didn't bother to smile. His eyes stayed focused on a point midway between us. "Chase Oliver Maxwell."

"Yep."

"I'm recording this. Do you grant permission for us to view your medical history?"

"If I don't?"

"Then you can look for another indenture service. We only take healthy clients."

"I grant permission."

"Thank—" He frowned, then looked at me. "You've got an Infinite Pocket."

"Doesn't belong to me. Only way I'd get money for it is on the black market."

"We can't send out a client who may have a weapon."

"I won't have one."

"This says the Pocket is keyed to a SIG—"

"That's right." I popped the pistol out of the Pocket, appreciated its weight in my hand and Frederick's moment of discomfort, then set the pistol on the counter between us. "Take it. The safety's on."

He picked it up. "Nice."

"You've got half a dozen lie-detecting programs running on me, right? Voice, eyes, breath, pulse, skin, and facial expression, I'm guessing."

Frederick nodded as he set the pistol aside.

"I no longer have any weapon of any sort in the Pocket. Well? Does anything suggest I'm lying?"

"If we make this contract, I'll have to tell your buyer about the Pocket. You'll probably get a blink test every day to be sure you haven't put anything in there."

"You're a good man, Gunga Din."

He smiled. "I'm glad you're enjoying yourself, Mr. Maxwell. So many of our clients come to us in tears. What're you interested in? Sex work gives the best buck for the bang."

Well, neither of us liked the other's sense of humor. I said, "The same deal as Zoe Domingo. Same work, same camp."

He narrowed his eyes at me, then looked between us, then shook his head. "Her location's legally sealed."

"Do her papers say you can't sell someone to her camp who asks to go?"

"No. But the intention—"

"Isn't spelled out in the documents, is it?"

"Well, no."

"Okay, then."

"How long a term are you looking for?"

"What's the minimum?"

"One year. For a healthy male human, we can pay fifteen thousand UN, which would come to twenty-two meg U.S. If you wanted a five-year contract—"

"One's fine."

"Any other stipulations?"

"Nope."

"When do you want to start?"

"Something wrong with right now?"

"Not if that's what you want." He printed the contract and

handed it to me. "Sign and date that, and we're in business."

I scanned several pages of fine type. "What does 'reasonable incentives and disincentives' mean?"

"They've made an investment. They have to be sure they'll get some work out of you."

"Yeah. But what's that mean?"

"You don't have to worry about it so long as you do your work. You did notice that your contract automatically terminates if you suffer permanent harm? And you still get to keep the money."

"You're being vague."

"We can't know the circumstances at every camp. That clause is there simply to make sure you don't refuse to work."

"And this bit? About accepting the camp's medical services?"

"Some people pretend to be sick. The doctors can catch that."

"I see."

"You're free to walk away, Mr. Maxwell."

"I know." And, knowing that I no longer was, I signed to make John Hancock proud. When you choose a course of action, commit to it.

Frederick took a dull gray band from a cabinet, fiddled with it, then handed it to me. "You know what this is?"

I nodded.

"Put it around your neck."

This part was harder than the signature. The Little Angel would transmit my location at all times. If I left an area where I was supposed to be, it would beep a warning. Then it would sound a siren that would grow louder up to, but just short of, the point of causing permanent damage to my hearing. Then it would send a stimulus to the pain centers of my brain that would rapidly increase in sensation. If I continued to stay outside the designated area, it would trigger my sleep centers. One would-be escapee had fallen unconscious in a stream and drowned. The Supreme Court ruled that wasn't the indenture company's fault; the escapee had signed a contract accepting the Little Angel. Just as I had.

I looked at the date Frederick had set on its side. After next Christmas, the band's molecules would abruptly fail to adhere, and I would be free. I put it around my neck, then snapped it shut. It shifted to lie smoothly on my skin like a wisp of gauze. A year of your life should weigh more than that.

After putting on the Little Angel, I transferred fifteen meg of indenture funds into a savings account. Part of the rest went to my landlady. A smaller part went to the storage company that would pick up my furniture. The largest part went to Brady Xi with a short history of Zoe's case and instructions to investigate Singer Labs and Oberon Chain.

I lingered a second over tapping "Send" on the final transaction. That was my last legal instant of freedom.

Frederick sent me into a small room for an Insta-Scan to confirm that I was healthy and to make sure I hadn't hidden anything in my body. My clothes and everything I had carried with me, including the SIG, went into a shipping box to join my possessions in storage.

Frederick gave me a set of gray underwear, socks, coveralls, and slip-on shoes to wear, then a pert token and an address in Simi Valley. His farewell was "Thanks for doing business with Prosperity Indenture Services. Recommend us to your friends!"

Clothes are the softest prison walls. In the elevator, a business woman in a sleek suit wrinkled her nose slightly and edged away from me. On the street, I kept getting "what's one of them doing here?" glances. It was a relief to enter the privacy of a pert.

If I'd known how long it would be before I had privacy again, I would've treasured that ride more. Instead, I wondered what I would find and what I had left undone.

The ride ended too soon in the fenced-in yard of a warehouse. Several humans and chimeras dressed like me waited in the sun. I started toward a tall, thin woman in burgundy coveralls. Without glancing up from her datapad, she said, "Over with the others."

I said, "Skin cancer's fairly permanent."

That got me a glance. "Noted, lawyer. I think your free zone includes the shade along the other building."

I nodded to her and headed there. Two steps short of the shade, the Little Angel began beeping. The sound was annoying, but not so annoying as baking in the sun. I took another step. The alarm around my neck screamed, and so did I. My entire body felt like snack time for fire ants. My muscles convulsed. I fell and barely managed to scramble back away from the shade.

Ms. Datapad said, "Huh. Guess I was wrong," and continued to jot on the pad.

An older Asian man in indenture grays helped me stand. "How you doing?"

I was slick with sweat, and my legs danced like the scarecrow's in *The Wizard of Oz*, but the pain had stopped almost instantly. "Fine, now."

"I'm Cho."

"Max."

"What you in for?"

"One year."

"Huh! I do five. Bank going to repossess house. One year, huh? You be okay when you get out, if you made right investment."

"I made the right investment."

More indentures showed up while Cho told me about his wife, kids, granddaughter, and mother. None of the others were dressed in grays when they arrived; the woman with the datapad got the newcomers fitted with coveralls and Little Angels. As the yard filled, I realized that many indentures chose to postpone their service until the day after Christmas. I asked Cho why he didn't wait for New Year's, and he laughed. "Western New Year come too early. Beside, sooner I start, sooner I finish."

Ms. Datapad gave a speech when everyone had arrived. Her name was Carol O'Grady, but for the time of our indenture, it was God, and her chosen delegates were archangels. She had six—big men and women whose uniforms had a crisp, silver sheen. They carried control wands at their hips—the reason we should worship them. The wands controlled the Little Angels. If a Little Angel went off by accident, the archangels could stop it. If we annoyed the archangels, they could set off our Little Angels. Frederick hadn't mentioned that. I would've bet there were other things he hadn't mentioned. I would've won.

Two ancient buses stinking of gasoline and oil carried us to an airfield, where an equally ancient charter plane with a similar stench flew us to Duggan, Montana. The service was lousy. No in-flight HV, no attractive attendants. The archangels brought us bowls of cold Nutrigruel. When I asked if it was vegetarian, the archangel laughed and said the bosses weren't paying for meat for untrained indentures.

Montana cold came as a shock to a California boy, but I didn't notice it as much as I might have. I was looking for Zoe. Shivering on the runway by the plane, I watched flatbed trucks cross the snow to fetch us, then searched for her among the drivers. They were all sullen humans in archangel silver.

The drivers passed out coarse blankets and had us climb on the backs of the trucks. A short ride took us to Duggan Indenture Camp, a complex built during the prison boom at the end of the last century. When the Libertarians legalized adult drug use, the United States suddenly had twice the prison space it needed. Fortunately, indenture camps required cheap housing, so everyone was happy, except for the inmates—excuse me, indentures.

I looked for Zoe on the orientation tour, in the work halls, kitchen, laundry, mess hall, greenhouse, and exercise room. There were almost as many chimeras as humans, but none of the chimeras was a small woman with jaguar hair.

After I was given a cell with a dour little man, I looked for her among my floormates. Only human men and women were on my tier. At the ten o'clock lights-out, I lay on my hard bunk thinking she must be sleeping in one of the chimera wings and wondering what my next year would be like if the bad guys had already gotten to her. Driving through the camp gates, I had seen a new grave like an open wound in the snow-covered cemetery. Just as I was about to fall asleep, I heard someone, far away, crying hopelessly. I didn't know whether to hope it was Zoe. I listened to the crying until it stopped, maybe five minutes, maybe two hours, and then I slept.

The work day began at six with an alarm. We had half an hour for the communal toilets and showers. My morning habits were shortened by the bosses's decisions that men would be better off facing the Montana winter with beards.

The camp provided the same breakfast every day: a dense brown bread that I rather liked, hot Nutrigruel, orange-flavored VitaJoy, and coffee as dense and flavorful as dirty dishwater. For indentures with funds, a second food line called the credit counter served scrambled eggs, fried pota-toes, grits, bagels, pancakes, waffles, orange juice, milk, es-presso, and cappuccino. The prices weren't posted; they just scanned your ID and charged your account.

On that first morning, I asked the archangel at the credit counter how much a few things cost—the answers were four times higher than the most overpriced hotel restaurant food I'd ever eaten. But money, as the archangel pointed out, was no object; the camp would extend you credit so long as you extended your period of indenture. I said "Uh-huh" and got into the camp food line.

Human indentures took the near side of the hall; chimeras took the far. I carried my tray to a table on the border where an old dogman was reading a coverless copy of *Anna Karenina*. I said, "Morning."

He didn't look up. "It's real nice that you're not prejudiced, but if you don't get over with the skins in twenty seconds, you'll be using your gruel for shampoo."

"Name's Max. I'm looking for a cat called Zoe."

"Five seconds."

I got up. "She throws herself under a train."

None of the humans looked like they wanted a critter-lover at their table. I spotted a familiar face in a group of newcomers and joined them, saying, "Hey, Cho."

He gave me a wary nod. A wiry Hispanic man said, "Don't you know nothing, man? You got to be careful, got to learn how the game is played."

"I get tired of games."

A black woman laughed. "Then you must be tired of life. That why you're here?"

I shook my head.

She said, "I was turning tricks and investing my money in my arm. Now I'm going to make me a nest egg and get a new life." I looked at the plate of bacon and eggs in front of her and didn't comment. She said, "They call me Ginger, 'cause I spice up life."

The Hispanic man said, "Then stick your finger in my gruel, Ginger. This shit's flavored for Anglos."

I took a taste of mine. "It's not flavored for anyone."

"Then it for us," Cho said sadly. "We not anyone."

If you managed to finish breakfast early, you could hang out in the mess hall, your cell, or the company store. Like the second food line, the store's credit terms were generous and so was the markup. A porn vid, a pack of cigs or hemp, or a bottle of alcohol cost as much as an indenture earned in two days. The presence of smoke and drink in the camp surprised me, until I saw that the company wanted you sober for work and didn't care what you did in your off hours. Anything that made you more content with your fate made them more secure that you wouldn't do anything desperate. They can't make a profit from a suicide.

Lines formed for work details at seven-thirty. If you were late, you got a shock for each minute that had passed—the guards called them " 'centives," based on the language of our contracts. Cho took too long in the toilet after breakfast and got two 'centives. When I pointed out that it was his first day and he didn't know better, I got one for wasting work time and another so I would know better.

Work came in many forms. Indentures who were a few years into their service took care of the camp, washing clothes, mopping floors, cleaning dishes, mixing and heating food for the camp line (nothing that I ate there could properly be said to have been cooked). Skilled indentures did high-grade labor, which ranged from making clothes for designer shops to tending the hydroponic garden beds where they grew exotic vegetables for pricey grocery stores. The rest of us did shit jobs, which took the most literal form in turning human and animal waste into fertilizer sold online through upscale gardening sites, but also included sorting and cleaning truckloads of waste excavated from garbage pits and landfills.

I was assigned to D & D, dump and display. The crew boss gave me an old military parka, heavy gloves, insulated boots that no longer fastened, and instructions to the loading docks, where I learned the routine.

Trucks heaped high with the last century's garbage came through the big doors every twenty minutes. That had the advantage of letting in fresh air to clear the smell and the disadvantage of letting in the Montana winter. As soon as a truck butted up to a dock, we scrambled on board and unloaded its frozen haul.

At first, the most disgusting parts were visual, as you discovered what accompanied the things that the pit crews thought might be useful. The worst I found was a decaying cat's head that fell out of the back of a radio cabinet, but I heard stories of dead babies in blankets and murder victims in oil drums. I never saw anyone volunteer to open a refrigerator.

Once the truck was unloaded, it took off, and we D & Ders moved from dumping to displaying by doing a quick sorting of what we found. The goods ranged from the remarkably well preserved, where landfills had remained airtight, to the bizarrely mutated, where strange chemicals had worked, alone or in combination with other industrial concoctions, on everything around them.

Anything that might be damaged by water—TVs, toasters, typewriters, clothing, bedding, books, magazines, etc.—went on one side of the dock. Anything that might not—chairs, tables, china, plasticware—went on the other side to be hosed down. That was when the most disgusting part of the job usually became bearing the stench freed by the warm water. That was also when you could make new and more dramatically unpleasant discoveries as hidden things were washed out of the objects you cleaned.

If you made an honest mistake in sorting or washing, the archangels didn't mind. The more thorough cleaning and examination came later in the C & E rooms, where no one needed parkas for warmth. But if you made a blatant mistake, like putting a notebook computer down for hosing, expect a 'centive or two.

The carting teams took over then. While we D & Ders began dumping the next truck, the carters put the goods we'd displayed onto long handcarts and pulled them to the C & E rooms. There, anything recognized as a true antique was set aside to be auctioned in L.A. or New York. Of what remained, anything fixable was mended with patches, paint, or parts to be sold to people seeking history or kitsch. Anything usable that couldn't be restored to an especially fine state went to the Second Chance chain of stores owned by Duggan Enterprises. Anything unusable but with viable parts was disassembled. Anything left that was inorganic was shredded, melted, or shattered, then sold as raw materials. Anything organic was composted. There was a fortune in America's hills of garbage, so long as you had people to do dirty, dangerous work for low pay.

The D & D crew included a young, heavily tattooed ferret named Betty. During a brief lull between trucks, I said, "Do you know a catwoman named Zoe Domingo?"

"I don't know anybody."

"If you did know a catwoman named Zoe, could you tell her Max is in the camp and has a way to help her?"

"If I did, I could. If she was in the camp."

I don't know what my face did. Several thoughts struck simultaneously. Prosperity Indenture Services had lied. I would have to work out my contract, then start all over next year. Zoe could be slogging slime for thirty years. Or she could be killed before I could find her.

Betty said, "You a furry?"

I shrugged. "Zoe's the only chimera I've cared for."

"How's she feel about you?"

"She's doing thirty years because she saved my life."

"Jesus." Betty looked away, tugged on a brown-furred ear, then met my gaze. "I'll ask around."

"Thanks."

"You best be telling the truth. If the cat says you're trouble, you'll get hurt. Critters look out for critters here."

"Good."

At ten-thirty, a kitchen crew brought mugs of Baby Puke, a hot green algae drink with a disgusting texture that was remarkably restorative. A credit cart also came by with coffees, teas, and pastries. I asked how much for a cappuccino, then drank my Baby Puke.

Morning break lasted five minutes. You were also entitled to a toilet break during the morning shift. You got it by raising your hand and asking permission. I felt like I was back in kindergarten.

Lunch started at one and lasted thirty minutes. On the first day, the Nutrigruel smelled like minestrone soup and had a few bits of string beans in it. The old-timer at my table, a large, bald man called Monty, rolled his eyes when I said it wasn't bad. He was eating a cheese steak sandwich with thin-sliced french fries and a strawberry shake. He told me to give him my opinion in a week.

By the end of the first week, I saw Monty's point. The camp line rotated Italian (tomato-oregano), Mexican (tomato-chili), and New England (potato-onion) Nutrigruel for lunch, and Indian (curry), Japanese (miso), and Swiss (soy cheese) for supper. By the end of the third week, they all tasted alike.

The smells of the credit line's daily specials became more tempting every day. But I did the math: three days of paying to eat cost a day of work. Most of the long-term indentures chose the credit line at least once every day or two. At each meal, as I picked up my bowl of Nutrigruel, I wondered how long I would go before trying the other line.

On the afternoon of my first day, Betty didn't say anything to me, not during work, which I had expected, or during the four-thirty break for Baby Runs, the brown version of Baby Puke, which, if you had a powerful imagination, would remind you that chocolate tasted something like that, only good. I worked until we quit at seven-thirty at night with a growing sense of despair that I rarely felt so early into a job.

What threw me was that I had trusted Prosperity. Frederick and his boss may've seemed like exploitative slime, but

they had seemed like honest exploitative slime. I had anticipated many variables in coming to Duggan. Zoe's unexplained
absence wasn't one. Call me a fool if you want. You won't
come up with anything worse than what I called myself.

I wasn't hungry for camp food by the end of the first day's
work—the Nutrigruel smelled all right, but it looked like the
slurry I'd been washing from trash. I ate it for three reasons.
I needed my strength to find Zoe, I didn't need any 'centives
to finish my food, and I wasn't going to pay to eat from the
credit counter. I could've pleaded illness, but then I would've
been sent to the infirmary and gotten my 'centives after they
had concluded that I was malingering.

Meals and sleep were mandatory because the bosses
wanted efficiently functioning workers. We couldn't leave the
camp because we might not come back. We couldn't order
anything to be delivered to us, as much to keep us from getting weapons as to preserve the camp store's monopoly.
Within those constraints, once we'd done our twelve hours,
we were free to do what we wanted. For all practical pur-
poses, that freedom was exercised between the end of supper and the ten o'clock lights-out.

My dour cellmate spent his time drinking beer and watching sex vids on a tiny HV set. As I strolled the camp, I saw
that maybe half the indentures found similar ways to leave
their world. The other half looked for communal distractions.
A place called The Club looked like any bar in any underclass
North American neighborhood. It was packed with people
trying to celebrate enduring another day, but the music was
too loud for human speech, so I passed it by. The Theatre
consisted of three little rooms with folding chairs and HV
sets. That didn't look like a good place to talk, either. I found
four rooms used by religious groups, two Christian, one Mus-
lim, one Spiderist. They were all deep in their services. I
started to walk into the chimera wings, but near the entrance
to each of them, large chimeras informed me that I must be

lost in a way that suggested I should be, so I turned back.

I talked to a woman who was alone in the camp's tiny library, and the man behind the counter at the store, and a few humans stretching their legs before lights-out. Asking them about Zoe got me next to nada; there were several young catwomen among the chimera indentures. Some of them had multicolored hair. No one knew their names. No one could say whether any of them were jaguars.

16

The next couple of days were intermittently dull and disgusting. My feeling that I was back in kindergarten increased when I got my very own bully. An archangel named Finn gave me a blink test at the end of each day to make sure I hadn't found a diamond ring or a bazooka and stashed it in the Pocket. When he asked how I'd gotten the Pocket, I said I'd been paid to test it, which was true enough to pass the blink.

But Finn knew something about UNSEC. The fact that the Pocket was by my gun hand made him conclude I'd worked for them. I didn't compliment his powers of deduction because he had family killed in the Jackson Rebellion. He took to calling me "UNSEC-man" and made sure I got the least pleasant jobs. When the fan in the fertilizer room burned out, guess who spent the afternoon in a hot, stagnant ventilation shaft taking out the old motor and putting in a new one?

Finn couldn't find an especially disgusting job for me every day, but he found enough that I didn't work with Betty again until the second week of January. At the Baby Puke break, she said, "Duggan got the rights to work a landfill near Phoenix. A jag called Zoe was in the crew sent to work it. I don't know how long she's stationed there. I couldn't get word to her that you're looking for her. I'm taking this on myself to tell you, so if you have a notion to do her wrong, you best know I'll see you suffer if anything happens to that cat."

"I appreciate it."

"I dunno how knowing that'll do you any good, but you're welcome."

At dinner the next day, I saw the answer to the only question I had about the company's liberal credit policy. The bald man, Monty, screamed at the archangel behind the credit counter, "I'm strong, damn it! Look at me! All I want is a goddamn cheeseburger!" The archangel calmly shook his head through several of Monty's protests, then gave him a 'centive that dropped him on the floor. When Monty could pick himself up, he got into the camp food line.

I asked Cho and Ginger what had happened. Ginger gave her spaghetti and meatballs a worried look. Cho said, "He get no more credit. They say he work for them until he sixty-five, no more credit. Then he finish without a penny. He fool." Though Cho spat in disgust, after dinner he went to Monty and they played chess together.

Monty hung himself that night. An old-timer should've known better. His Little Angel registered his lack of oxygen and began to wail. The medical staff fixed him up. Since his injury was self-inflicted, the costs were added to his period of indenture.

One afternoon during break when Finn was near, I stretched, inhaled loudly, and told Cho, "Smell that Montana air."

"I try to not smell that air."

"The trucks are out. Go ahead."

Cho sniffed. "So?"

"We're lucky."

"This lucky?"

"Hell, yeah. We could be digging through shit in some desert somewhere. Damn, but I hate the heat."

Cho shook his head. "You crazy, UNSEC-man."

"Count your blessings, Cho. We're in a winter wonderland. Rich folk pay to vacation in country like this. Only way to improve on this would be if we could go cross-country skiing."

Three days later, I was on a truck to Phoenix. The driver, a decent archangel called Medium-sized Ben, saw me grin out the window. He said, "Better look miserable when we get there. If they decide this isn't enough of a lesson to you, I don't know where they'll transfer you next."

The reason for Medium-sized Ben's trip was to haul a steam shovel to the Arizona dig. Since he would get it there faster with a second driver and since Finn had suggested I get a taste of work in the field to improve my attitude, I rode shotgun. The Little Angel was set to put me to sleep if I got within striking distance of Medium-sized Ben or more than thirty feet away from him, so no one was worried about me taking off.

Medium-sized Ben didn't talk much. He liked country-western music, and I thought it was amusing, so I was comfortable in the cab. The scenery might've been prettier in another season, but I admired snow-covered plains so white and level that they might've been geometric abstractions and mountains that pierced them like dark intruders from the third dimension.

At truck stops, Medium-sized Ben told me to order off the menu, even though the company had sent enough Nutrigruel to get me to Phoenix. I ate vegetable soup, a grilled cheese sandwich, french fries, and apple pie in Idaho Falls, Greek salad and vegetarian moussaka in Gunnison, and carrot cake at a midnight stop in Fredonia.

I'd never seen the city that polygamy built. Medium-sized Ben stopped so we could both smell the Great Salt Lake. At the Arizona border, we were searched for anti-Christian literature. I refrained from asking the guards where it said in the Bible to censor ideas that offended you.

Just after sunrise, we rolled through the Phoenix wasteland. Though he could've waited until we got to the camp, Medium-sized Ben stopped for breakfast. I ate huevos rancheros, rice, borracho beans, and hot corn tortillas, then sipped hot, strong coffee until Medium-sized Ben said, "Best be going." The trip had gone too slowly and too quickly. I wanted it to end because I wanted Zoe free, and I wanted it to last forever because I might be eating Nutrigruel for eleven months and three days after this.

Journey's end was a city of army-green tents and mobile homes arranged in perfect rows near a landfill. A sign said, "Welcome to Phoenix Camp, a subsidiary of Duggan Enterprises. We build bright tomorrows from dim yesterdays! Please, for your safety, don't pick up hitchhikers." There were no fences—the Little Angels had made Duggan's walls redundant. Someone had built a golf course beside the landfill, after it was sealed and before Phoenix had been weaned from its dependence on imported water. The golf course had mostly been reclaimed by the desert. A large man-made lake remained, though it had shrunk to half its former size and would someday disappear, too.

The smell grew worse as we drove closer. I had thought Duggan was bad, but Phoenix set new standards of stench. I saw indentures milling in the main yard and realized we had arrived in time for morning line-up. Human and chimera faces turned our way, and I scanned them, hoping to see one among them. When I spotted a tangle of black, brown, and gold hair on someone looking away from us, my heart leaped. Then I reminded myself that someone else might have jaguar hair, so I shouldn't get my hopes up. Still, as the truck came to a stop, I wrenched open the passenger door and jumped outside.

The head of jaguar hair disappeared, then reappeared as its owner walked away. The indentures had begun to form lines. Seven-thirty must've been only a minute or two away. The jaguar hair belonged to a small and shapely woman who strode with a dancer's grace. My heart said this was Zoe; my mind said I couldn't know that. She glanced toward the truck. Zoe. My Little Angel should've screamed an alarm when my heart stopped.

Our eyes met. Hers opened wide, then narrowed as she took in my clothes and collar. I grinned and started toward her, but halted when my Little Angel beeped.

She ran through the crowd to me. I smiled and said, "Zoe." Maybe I moved my hands forward for a hug.

She stopped two steps from me. The Little Angel kept beeping at my throat. She knew I could come no closer. I realized in that instant that she might have found a lover in the camp, that our night together might have meant much less to her than to me.

The camp was watching. I said, "I was in the area, so I thought I'd stop by."

She didn't smile. "I didn't think you'd get time."

"I signed up."

She gaped at me. "That's the stupidest—"

Our Little Angels shrieked and dropped us in the dust. When I could move again, I stood. Zoe looked past my shoulder, whispered "Later," and ran to join a work line.

I turned. Carol O'Grady, the company's God with a datapad, walked toward me. She said, "Finn said you didn't understand the way we do things, UNSEC-man. Don't you know that time is money?"

I said, "Why's that only said by people who think money's more important than time?"

"You clearly agreed. You sold us a year." She pointed toward a line of humans and chimeras in stained grays. "Join the diggers."

Medium-sized Ben, by the truck, said, "He drove twelve hours yesterday and last night."

"Good," said O'Grady. "He owes us another twelve today."

The diggers were the reclamation center's front line. Wearing construction helmets, heavy leather gloves, steel-soled boots, and safety lines, we waded into the open pit to dig out or pull out everything in it. Objects that were too heavy for us to move we chained for a tractor to drag free. The big equipment couldn't enter the pits because the surface was unstable. I heard the trash went down for a quarter of a mile, and that might well have been true.

The diggers moved trash to solid ground without considering its nature. In most cases, you didn't want to consider its nature. The sorters divided it between the blatantly useless, which went off to a new dump, and the rest, the probably useful, was loaded onto trucks to go back to the main facilities, where the process continued as it had at Duggan.

Zoe was a sorter. I caught her glance a few times, when I happened to be hauling things from the pit and she was coming to decide if a heavy chunk of encrusted muck might have something useful within it. Neither of us knew whether to smile or snarl. Since we'd already given the camp's inhabitants enough fuel for speculation, we merely looked away from each other as though we were strangers. Which I suppose we were. We'd shared more in a day than most people share in a life, but I can't say I knew her or she knew me.

I spent much of the morning cursing my safety line. It snagged constantly, making me walk back to free it from one protrusion so it could catch on another. The old-timers had developed a second sense about what would snag the line and what wouldn't. When their lines caught, they flicked them with the experience of years, and the lines danced free.

Sometime after a lunch of all-too-familiar Nutrigruel, on what I was told was an unusually warm Arizona winter day, I began to feel drowsy. My work slowed until an archangel drawled, "Don't make me give you no 'centives, UNSEC-boy."

I wanted them to pay as little attention to me as possible,

so I worked faster. You put your mind in automatic, and you barely notice that life has become an unending routine. Dig. Carry. Dump. Return. What thoughts I had were for the heat, what to do about Zoe, and whether I was a fool to come here. I could've been sitting in a cool casino, watching my money ebb and flow with the cards—

Cans rolled below my feet. Before I knew it, I was sliding deep into the landfill, sucked down as if it wanted something back for all we were taking from it. I heard someone else scream. I didn't have time to. My thoughts went roughly from "Way to go, Clumsy Joe" to "Why haven't I stopped sinking?" to "I'm dead." No revivification this time. The cryo circuits will lose energy, and I'll thaw and rot like frozen meatloaf. The diggers will avoid this part of the pit, knowing my corpse waits for its unfortunate finder. And Zoe will go on, year after year, slowly dying as she works in garbage.

That sounds as if I calmly sank into some gentle oblivion. I sank through loose trash into the muck, thrashing for all I was worth. As I fell through the surface, I began yelling too late for help. Only when the oozing waste of Old Phoenix rolled over my head did I realize I was a dead man. Even then I tried to flail, hoping to catch something to climb onto or to swim somehow, but the weight of the muck was too great.

I stopped sinking when my feet settled on something solid and flat, a refrigerator or an oven or a car roof. I had time to think of childhood fears, of monstrous things swimming through the slime to grab me and pull me deeper. You would've thought the choice was between panicking and staying calm, but I did both: I watched myself panic, and knew I would die, and knew I would fight to live as long as I could, though that fight only consisted of squirming desperately while praying for God to yank me out.

An archangel yanked me out instead. The safety line drew tight, then began drawing me up as a bird draws a worm from the mud. I gasped fetid air the instant I rose from the stinking sea into the crust of loose garbage, and gasped again when I burst from the crust into the open air.

Strong hands dragged me from the landfill to solid ground. Warm water flooded over me, washing slime from my mouth and nose and eyes, making my skin scream from the cuts along my side where I must've been dragged against something jagged. My left arm was bruised, and I stank as badly as the vilest thing plucked from the pit, but life looked just fine to me then.

A crowd of people surrounded me. The archangel, a Hispanic woman whose name I never caught, said, "Okay, okay, we landed our fish. Now, back to work!"

The faces moved away. One indenture, a ratman, said, "You be okay now, man. You'll learn to walk on it, just like us."

A face lingered beside the archangel's. I said, "Hey, Zoe."

She grinned. All I had gone through was worth it for that moment. "Hey, Max."

The archangel said, "Didn't you hear—"

"I know him," Zoe said.

The archangel shrugged, letting Zoe stay while she turned her attention back to me. "Your record says you got all your shots."

"Yeah. First day at Duggan."

"Okay." She looked at Zoe. "Cat. Get the medikit and clean him up."

Zoe nodded and ran away. I stood and stretched myself.

The archangel repeated, "You're all right?"

"Fine, thanks."

"You hurt yourself, the company wonders if I screwed up. I've been fair to you, haven't I?"

"Sure," I said, still taking inventory. None of the cuts seemed deep, but my coveralls would call for major mending, and I wouldn't be carrying anything heavy with my left arm for a while.

"Okay, then." The archangel walked away as Zoe came back with a medical kit.

She began swabbing my cuts. I winced while she dabbed at my left arm, but she ignored that. "Why the fuck did you sign up?"

"To get you out."

Her eyes widened, then narrowed. "Forget it."

"I can't."

"I don't want to see you doing time—"

"I left getting caught out of the plan."

The archangel yelled over at us, "Don't take all day!"

Zoe shouted, "He's almost ready!" Helping me stand, she said softly, "What's this plan?"

"Breaking out and not getting caught." I shrugged. "I'm open to suggestion on the finer details."

"Last warning!" the archangel called.

"Okay," Zoe whispered, and she ran back to join her crew.

I worked the rest of the day. Not quickly, but no one minded. The other diggers looked out for me, seeing that I mostly carried lighter things and worked parts of the pit that were believed to be stable. If I'd felt stronger, I might've resented that, but it felt good.

Phoenix Camp also had two food lines. I chose the credit line and ordered a big bowl of pumpkin ravioli and another of beef stew. Zoe was heading for the camp line when she saw me. "You're hungry."

I nodded at the stew. "That one's yours."

She looked at me. "I've been eating Nutrigruel every day I've been in."

"Ditto. Now we've got something to celebrate."

She shrugged. "Sure. We're both going to get ten years added to our sentences."

"All the more reason to enjoy your food," I said. "We won't get the option if they catch us."

Humans and chimeras stayed apart in this camp, too. Zoe and I sat at a table by the wall, and whatever sympathy I'd earned that afternoon burned away as the other indentures saw us breaking the unwritten law. I was grateful. We couldn't have made plans with people around us.

Zoe said, "Do you have anything in mind?"

"Steal a vehicle and head for Minnesota."

"After getting rid of the Little Angels?"

"Of course."

"Every highway cop in Arizona would be after us. There aren't many roads out of here."

"You've got a better idea?"

"Once a week, they fill a trailer with the best pickings and send it to L.A."

"You want to go back there?"

She shook her head. "That's where the truck goes. Might be easier to get to Minnesota from there than here."

"If they didn't know we were in the trailer."

"Which is why we'd have to convince them we were somewhere else."

"How well do they guard the trailer?"

"They don't. They keep it locked. Plenty of alarms would go off if you mess with its doors. And they made sure everyone knows it's airtight. Even if we got rid of the Little Angels, we'd suffocate in a few hours. Well before we got to L.A., anyway."

"When's the next one go?"

"*Mañana.* Anywhere between dawn and eight."

"Too soon."

"Wait a week?"

"At least. We should know everything we can."

She shrugged. "I was figuring on thirty-six years. A week or two's fine."

"Good. Apple pie?"

"With ice cream?"

I nodded.

She grinned. "My hero."

Fetching dessert from the credit line, I decided that I'd made too many assumptions about Zoe. Saving my life didn't mean anything more than that she felt obligated to me. Escaping from the camp would remove all obligations between us, and that'd be best for both of us. The camp would freeze my bank accounts when I broke their contract, but that'd be fine. Freedom's always better than money.

After dinner, we went for a walk. The abandoned golf course and its slowly evaporating lake lay to the east. Toward the last red rays of sunset stood cacti like an army of waving men. As we watched the sun disappear, I told her everything that happened after my death. The desert night grew cool, but it was better to be alone in the dark and cold with Zoe.

We had started to compare notes about life at Duggan and Phoenix when our Little Angels beeped twice. We weren't close to the camp's perimeter, which meant that someone with a control wand wanted us to stay where we were.

Which we did. Zoe glanced at me; I raised both eyebrows in ignorance. She turned to look past me, so I turned, too. Across the road, silhouetted against the open door behind her, Carol O'Grady stood on the steps of her mobile home and idly taped a control wand against her thigh. "Maxwell. Domingo. Come here." As we obeyed, she said, "What were you talking about?"

Zoe said, "Just catching up on life."

"I hope you had fun." O'Grady looked at me. "You're taking the truck back to Duggan tomorrow."

"Why?"

"I'd think you'd be grateful. I heard you don't like heat."

"I'll get used to it."

"I don't think so. You were both wanted for Amos Tauber's murder."

"That's been cleared up."

"Maybe. But you'll stay separated until I know more."

I glanced at Zoe. Her hands formed tight fists. I lifted my right arm toward O'Grady. "You know what this is?"

"An Infinite Pocket." She frowned. "Why?"

I opened it. When an archangel had given me a blink test after work, I testified that I hadn't put anything valuable or dangerous in it. Black pepper from yesterday's lunch sprayed into O'Grady's face.

She coughed and fumbled with the control wand. Zoe snatched it from her grip as I clapped a hand over O'Grady's mouth and said, "Don't struggle, and there'll be no accidents." No one sounded an alarm as I pushed her into her trailer.

O'Grady hadn't cleaned up for company in ages; the living room was strewn with newspapers and fashion vids. A Siamese cat saw us and bolted behind the couch. A professional holographer's portrait of the cat was over a fake fireplace, and several china figurines of Siamese cats had been placed around the cluttered room.

I closed the front door and listened. Still no alarm. None that I could hear, anyway.

Zoe said, "Lights-out in forty minutes."

"Get something to tie and gag her."

Zoe went in the tiny kitchen and returned with a dishcloth and a ball of twine. I stuffed the cloth in O'Grady's mouth and told her, "Relax. Someone'll find you in a couple of hours. The condition they find you in is up to you."

She nodded. I put a few loops around her head and tied them with a square knot to hold the gag in place, cinched her hands behind her back with a series of half-hitches, did the same with her legs, then tied her hands and feet together to turn her into a human bow. Zoe watched my technique. I said, "Boy scouts."

Zoe said, "Badges for bondage. No wonder they're popular."

I jerked my head at O'Grady. "Get her keys and any cash you can find."

The bedroom was less tidy than the living room. O'Grady had one of those fake anti-gravity beds that you can only order from late-night ads. On the table beside it lay a VR helmet and a Pleasurepal. It's hard to go through someone's home without learning too much about them.

I found a few five K coins, a 9mm Isher, and a box of bullets in the drawer in the bed table. I tucked the coins in a pocket, then picked up the Isher. Its trigger lock could only be removed by O'Grady or someone with her fingerprints, but it might be useful for bluffing anyone who caught us into thinking we were armed, so I tucked it into the Pocket.

Back in the living room, I saw Zoe had made friends with the Siamese. It leaped out of her arms when I entered. Zoe said, "What about the Little Angels?"

"In a minute. You've got her car keys?"

"Yeah."

"Turn off the lights." Picking up O'Grady as the room went dark, I told her, "If you get hurt, they'll step up the hunt for us. We don't want that to happen."

Zoe said, "Max, this is kidnapping."

"Not exactly. Check outside."

She peeked through the open window, then sniffed. "All clear."

"Open her car. No dome light."

Zoe squinted at the key in her hand and tapped the appropriate buttons. In the yard by the trailer, all four doors of a white Ford RoadStar sprang open.

I carried O'Grady to her car, put her in the back, and

hopped in the front. Zoe closed her door. I left mine ajar. There was no moon, but the yard lights let me see her clearly. I wanted to kiss her, but if this proved to be the last I saw of her, I didn't want the memory colored by a rebuff.

I took the car key and started the RoadStar. The computer said, "The driver's door is ajar."

"Yep. What hospital's closest to downtown Tucson?"

"Tucson General."

"When the doors are shut, drive there at maximum speed. If the police order you to stop, inform them that human lives are at risk and do not stop. Understand?"

"Yes."

Zoe looked a question at me. I shook my head and said, "Lean back. This may hurt, but I'll make it fast."

She leaned back. "No comment."

I touched her chin and tilted her head back, then opened the Infinite Pocket and slid its edge across her collar. Zoe gasped, then fell unconscious as her Little Angel realized it was under attack. Somewhere, alarms sounded and guards mobilized, but I focused on the Pocket as it gobbled flexsteel molecules from Zoe's collar. Then I wrenched the Little Angel away from her, dropped it on the floor of the car, and shook her. She sat up, blinking and rubbing her neck. "Better."

I leaned back in the driver's seat, extended my arm toward her, and opened the Pocket. "Take my wrist. You have to cut mine. If you squint, you can see the Pocket's field." Her hands felt nice on my forearm. She peered at my wrist and nodded. "If you cut too close to my skin, the Pocket'll shut down. If that happens, jump out, close the doors, and head cross-country while they chase O'Grady and me."

"But—"

"They know your collar's off. We don't have time to argue." I leaned back and tilted my chin up. Her face came close to mine as she brought my wrist toward my neck. I smiled at her, she smiled at me, and fire ants consumed me.

When I came to, Zoe was grinning down at me, and my Little Angel was on the floor with hers. We got out of the RoadStar, closed its doors, and ran around O'Grady's trailer. I glanced back. The RoadStar sped silently toward the highway and Tucson. I hoped O'Grady enjoyed the ride.

As the car with the Little Angels crossed the camp perimeter, the main emergency sirens sounded. Zoe and I crossed the perimeter, too, but far from the gate, and heading toward desert, not highway. Darkness comforted me, though the thought of stumbling over rattlesnakes or scorpions did not. Zoe began to angle toward the army of saguaro encircling the camp, but I caught her wrist and squatted, pulling her down. She sat on her haunches beside me.

Pursuit vehicles raced by on the road. Since our Little Angels were speeding for Tucson, the reasonable conclusions were that we were still in them, sleeping the deep sleep of the would-be escapee, or that we'd gotten out of them and were holding O'Grady as a hostage. The camp would notify the police, the police would order the RoadStar to stop, and when the car answered that it was going to Tucson on a medical emergency, the cops would arrange for a few police flyers to follow it until it stopped.

Zoe said, "I thought we were going cross-country."

"You were, if you couldn't get my collar off. Where's the trailer to L.A.?"

"We won't suffocate?"

I turned my wrist to show her the Infinite Pocket. "I can empty it of weapons. I can't empty it of air."

We circled the camp. The trailer, your standard silver rectangle that hitches to the back of a semi, sat near the main dig, waiting for a trucker who would fasten it behind two trailers he had already picked up in Tucson and haul them all to Los Angeles. No guards waited by the trailer. No one would sneak a truck through the only road into camp to steal it, and the door alarms would announce any attempt to open it.

The edge of the Pocket's field cut a neat oval in the trailer's steel roof, solving the problem of entrance and silencing my nagging thought that the Pocket might not provide enough air for both Zoe and me. We repositioned the piece of roof I'd cut out, then Zoe led me through total darkness across the tops of tubs of salvaged valuables.

We made a nest of shipping pads at the front of the trailer. After cutting a few extra airholes with the Pocket, I adjusted the shipping pads and stretched out. It wasn't bad, if you ignored the cold night, the musty smell that clung to the contents of the tubs, the tendency of corners of tubs to find the tenderest parts of your body, and the claustrophobic feeling of lying in the dark with a roof less than a foot above your nose.

Zoe said, "What now?"

"I don't know about you, but I'm going to get some sleep."

The transition from wakefulness to sleep must've been almost instantaneous. If I dreamed, I don't remember. I woke once when the back doors of the trailer were opened and light flashed back between the tubs. After the doors were slammed and locked again, I fell back to sleep. Later, I woke when the trailer jerked forward and the load shifted slightly beneath me. The third time I woke, someone had rolled against me. I smelled Zoe's hair, put my arm around her, and slept in perfect comfort after that.

17

When the truck began stopping and starting repeatedly, I knew we'd hit L.A.'s traffic jams. At one series of stops that lasted especially long, I lifted the roof panel I'd cut, then announced, "Hooray for Hollywood. Come on." I saw the 101 Tollway. The line for the Santa Monica Boulevard tollbooths was barely moving.

We climbed onto the roof, ran to the back of the truck, dropped down, grinned and waved at the startled driver behind the truck, and darted across the traffic lanes. I liked walking up the exit ramp more quickly than the drivers sitting alone in their wheeled steel boxes.

I didn't know whether Duggan Enterprises had spread the word that I'd broken my contract, but using my bank account seemed like a bad idea. O'Grady's coins bought two bus tickets. Either our smell or our indenture grays kept people from crowding us. I suppose that was a blessing.

After three transfers and a mile walk, we arrived at Eddie's house. No one answered the bell. I put my thumb to the plate, and the door opened. To Zoe's glance, I said, "I took care of his dog last fall."

The first thing I did was use his phone to call him. I got his voice mail and said, "Hey, Eddie. *Su casa es mi casa.* Also, your car, so don't worry if it's not in the garage when you get here. I won't need it long. Thanks."

The second order of business was getting clean. I let Zoe have the main bathroom while I used the guest shower. She didn't suggest I join her. I cleaned my indenture grays in the shower, then put them back on and stood under the dryer. Then I found a black jacket of Eddie's that was big enough for me and looked fine over the coveralls.

Third came food. I built monster sandwiches on onion bagels—tuna fish, cucumber slices, and lettuce for Zoe, double Gloucester cheese with cucumber and lettuce for me.

Zoe entered the kitchen as I cut the sandwiches in half. She wore a white cotton shirt and blue jeans with the cuffs rolled up twice. They fit her much better than they'd ever fit Eddie. Only her shoes, indenture-gray canvas slip-ons like mine, suggested what she'd been through. She said, "I feel great."

"And look it. Do you want anything on the tuna?"

"A dash of pepper, and you've made me one happy cat."

Over supper, we talked about Mycroft's theory that Singer Labs could be covering up a failed AI experiment. I wanted to call Vallejo and Chumley to ask what progress they'd made, but they might've felt obliged to bust a contract breaker.

When night fell, we took Eddie's vintage racing-green Miata to the storage company where my life's possessions waited. The main gate and the door to my unit both opened under my thumb. No one's supposed to be able to monitor renters going in or out of their units, but it still felt risky being there. We moved quickly.

I gave Zoe her computer, replaced O'Grady's Isher with the SIG, tucked the black opal earring back in the Infinite Pocket, and changed into an aquamarine suit with a white shirt and my best shoes. The clothes felt good. The SIG didn't. In a society where anyone might be armed, it ought to feel great to be lethal again, but the pistol only made me wish I had found another way to stop the orca.

Still, cruising the 405 a few minutes later in the Miata, I caught myself grinning for no reason at all. I hadn't done that for months, maybe years. A small bit of it was the joy of driving with the top down. Eddie had a toll pass in the glove box. Since rush hour was over, we rolled through the express lane without even slowing down.

Zoe smiled into the wind as it whipped her jaguar hair back from her pointed ears. She bobbed her head to a NeoRegency dance tune on the radio. I thought we looked like any couple on a date, and my grin grew wider. Then I remembered that a human and a chimera didn't look like any couple, and couldn't.

Zoe caught my gaze. "What?"

It was time to tell her it was too dangerous for us to stay together. If I was caught, I might only get six months added to my one-year contract. If she was caught, she could get fifteen years added to her thirty-year sentence. Alone, with her hair dyed black or brown, she might disappear into the underclass. But a female chimera with a human male would get a second look wherever she went. I wanted to think that she would be willing to risk that for my sake. But I knew that I couldn't for hers.

And there was nothing that I could do. I'd given everything I had to Brady Xi, who was at least as good a detective as I, and Mycroft, who had resources that neither Zoe nor I could begin to hope for. I'd followed every lead that came from that first online search. . . .

I opened my mouth, then closed it. The cautious thing to do was to get safely away. After that, I could pass suggestions along to Brady or Mycroft.

Zoe said, "Did you just eat a bug?"

"Turn on your computer. I had a thought."

"Well, that's rare enough that it should be encouraged." She took out her PowerPad, and the display appeared before her.

"Sign on as Cordelia Delano Maxwell, password 'gee double-oh dee underscore ess oh en exclamation." Zoe glanced at me, then typed on air as I added, "I got her an e-mail account for her birthday when I was eight. If she hasn't changed it—"

"Name one mother who would change a password like that."

"You haven't met mine."

"Well, mother love won this time. We're in."

"Gold and Tauber both got Chain Foundation Fellowship grants, worked on machine intelligence, and consulted for Singer Labs. Who else fits those specs?"

"Global?"

"Yep."

Zoe typed. The display showed text and an older man with a dark tan and white hair. Zoe read, "Pietro Di Bresci, Rome Periplex. Died two months ago."

I recognized the next face on the display. Zoe said simply, "Doc. Died last month."

The third I also knew. "Tauber. Ditto."

Then the display showed a thin woman in her fifties with blue-black hair, green eyes, and a serene smile. "Willa Catherine Vaughn, Pasadena, South California. Not dead. Yet."

"Vaughn? Not—"

Zoe scrolled through the text. "Macsey-Borne Prize for Genetic Engineering. General director, Bionova SA. Yep, that Vaughn."

"Why'd one of the inventors of chimeras get a grant to work on AI rights?"

"Any reason not to charge a call to your Mom's account?"

"Nope. Then we'll order pizza and invite the gang over."

Zoe tapped the phone icon by Vaughn's picture. The subject of the photo appeared onscreen, looking more distracted than serene. "I'm working late. Please leave a message."

Zoe glanced at me. I shook my head. She hung up and said, "It'd be nice to tell her that she may've reached the top of someone's murder list."

"And it'd be nice to know if she knows something we'd like to."

"Then shouldn't we—"

"Take a drive out to Pasadena? Exactly my thought."

Zoe grinned. "We're getting proactive."

"Within reason. We see what Vaughn says. If it looks like anyone's tempted to call the cops, we fly."

Zoe clicked off the PowerPad, frowned, pulled out its data cable, and looked at the plug. "Max. Earring."

I popped the black opal from the Pocket and passed it to her. She rolled it between her fingers and found a tiny hole in the base of the gem. "If this is a data port—" She snapped the cable into it and clicked on the computer.

The viewing field filled with a black opal rotating in space. Text replaced the image: "The Chain intelligence was not found on this computer."

The text faded. Zoe said, "An intelligence owned by Chain, based on him, or both?"

I shrugged. "Hiding tracking software in an earring must mean Gold knew the AI didn't want to be found."

"There was nothing on my computer. I could try it on the net."

"And find out it wipes out the IRS files?"

"We'd be heroes."

"Sure, everybody else wants to kill us. Why leave the feds out of the fun?"

I took the express lane to Pasadena, burning credits on Eddie's toll pass. Within ten minutes, I parked the Miata on the shoulder of a road by Bionova SA's North American headquarters, an industrial complex of two- and three-story stone and glass buildings.

Zoe said, "Why not park in the lot?"

"So you can clear out unnoticed if I'm not back in half an hour."

"You're not ditching me."

"Our escape might've made the news. People would be less likely to recognize me than you."

"I don't like sitting here."

"If I'm caught, I'll do a lot less time than you. Just go back to Eddie's. He'll help you."

She nodded reluctantly. As I reached for the door handle, she said, "Max?"

"Yeah?"

She leaned forward and kissed my cheek. "Good luck."

I nodded. "Ditto."

The feather-light touch of her lips lingered all the way to Bionova's front steps. In the main lobby, two guards, a young Hispanic man and an older black woman, sat at a desk near a pair of black glass doors. I smiled politely. "Dr. Vaughn, please."

The female guard answered. "She left orders not to be disturbed."

"It's urgent. She'll want to see me."

The male guard said, "Then she wouldn't have told us not to disturb her, would she?"

"Well. You can't say I didn't try."

I went outside and crossed into the cluster of trees between Bionova and the Miata. Zoe was napping. I looked back at Bionova, then at my watch. I had twenty-five minutes before Zoe was supposed to leave me.

I circled through the trees and waited as a small bot vehicle patrolled the back of the main building. After it passed, I stepped from the shadows with my dress shoes slung by their laces around my neck.

I ran across the lawn and climbed the stone-block wall freehand. This was a different kind of work than I'd done in the camps. A taller building would've called for different muscles and different calluses than I had, but I'd scaled far more challenging buildings during UNSEC training.

Which may've made me overconfident. Just short of the

roof, I missed a handhold and slipped. My other hand held me safe. But my shoes slid off my neck and fell.

Below me, the guardbot rolled up and stopped. I hung still, expecting an alarm. The bot took my shoes to the intersection of two walkways and dropped them in a trash basket. I wanted to shout that only a tinhead would think three hundred K shoes were litter, but I simply sighed and pulled myself onto the roof.

The edge of the Pocket sliced easily through the thick steel grating at the end of a ventilation stack. I slipped inside, sliding deep into maintenance ducts lined with cables and plumbing. Dust clung to my clothes. My desire to do a good deed would cost me another suit. I wondered what kind of clients I would get if I billed myself as the Nude Detective and decided I didn't want to find out.

I stopped at an intersection and looked for clues as to which way to go. If there were any, I missed them. A motor sled for maintenance workers was clamped to the wall, but taking it without an authorization code would alert half of Pasadena that I was visiting after hours. I crawled onward until I reached a mesh-covered access hatch. The room that it opened on was dark and quiet. Nothing looked more promising further along the duct. I pried open the hatch, lowered myself to the floor, brushed off my suit, and peeked into a bright, boring hallway.

The place was deserted. I couldn't have asked for more. With fifteen minutes to find Dr. Vaughn, I started down a long corridor, turned a corner, and saw my luck implode.

Kristal Blake strode toward me, smiling sweetly. She said, "Hi, lover."

I glanced over my shoulder. We were alone, which wasn't especially comforting. I couldn't outrun her robot body. I said, "Tell me you're the human Kristal Blake."

"There isn't one. Just a series of custom-built bodies."

"You were Doyle, too?"

She answered with a man's voice. "Yes." And then, like the quintessential housebot, "And Jefferson 473, at your service, sir." And, finally, returning to Kris Blake's voice, "But then, we all look alike to you."

I snapped my right arm up. Before I could open the Pocket, Blake grabbed my wrist. I knew she was based on a human mind when she smiled and said, "This body is faster than my last one."

I turned and flipped her against the wall. I had time to think, "Not as well balanced," but I didn't slow down to say it. She was already rising to her feet.

Four doors behind me, a small sign promised "Chemical Storage." I bolted down the hall, kicked the door in, and ran into a dark room where steel shelves held neatly labelled bottles and boxes.

Blake followed a moment later. Before she could enhance her vision or find the light switch, I rose from behind a shelf, SIG in hand, and held down the trigger, spraying bullets. She reeled back with an eye gone. Sparks flew from the damaged socket.

She swung around and shoved a shelf on me. It hit hard, knocking me to the floor and sending a sharp new pain through my still tender left arm. Only the shelf behind me kept it from crushing me.

I kept firing. When Blake's second eye went, she reeled back. I thought she would fall then. Two shots in a copbot's optics would do serious injury to its motor controls.

But Blake was better built than a copbot. She stood between me and the door, turning her damaged head from side to side. "You can't hide, Max. Unless you can stop your heart."

Her head stopped turning. A blind face of shredded skin and gray metal locked on mine. Steel knives snapped from her fingertips. "Shall I do that for you?"

I fired again. Blake raised her arm to shield her gaping

optics and advanced. I scrambled behind shelves, looking for escape or a better weapon. Light from the hall fell on rows of bottles of powders and liquids. My favorite was labelled "Nitrobenzene. Danger. Explosive."

As Blake paused to listen for my location, I threw the bottle. It shattered in her ruined face, splashing over sparks that fountained from her eyes. I don't remember the explosion. My last thought was that her warranty had expired. I hoped mine hadn't, too.

I remember lying on the floor of the dark room and wondering whether I should move anything. Then I remembered that Zoe was supposed to leave soon. I pulled my legs up, rocked forward, and stood. Everything worked. Blake was a mess. The king's men couldn't put her back together again, not even if their damn horses helped out. I needed my SIG, saw it, reached for it, and fell over.

Guards came, quiet and efficient men and women whose faces I can't remember. I said I had to see Dr. Vaughn, that her life might be in danger. I may not have expressed myself clearly. There was blood on my suit and my face, and when I touched the back of my head, it hurt.

One guard called someone on a cell phone. Then they hauled me into a large windowless laboratory, stuck me into something like a glass sarcophagus with power and data cables attached, and waited. I suppose I was waiting, too. Sometime later, I realized I was staring out at nothing in particular and checked my watch. Thirty-five minutes had passed. I thought, *Goodbye, Zoe. Have a good life.*

When Dr. Vaughn entered, I believed this might've been worth what I'd gone through. When Oberon Chain followed her in, I suspected it wasn't.

Chain said something to the guards. As they left, he picked up a remote control and clicked it at my glass sarcophagus. Hearing the sounds of the outside world made me realize I'd been missing them. His voice didn't make me miss them much. "Mr. Maxwell. What are we going to do with you?"

"I'm guessing you have an idea."

"I do. Is the earring in your Infinite Pocket?"

"What earring?"

"The earring that'll save you from a great deal of discomfort if you give it to me."

"I can't help—"

Chain tapped his remote. The air in my glass cage disappeared, and the air pressure with it. I gasped for breath. I could hear nothing except a roaring in my ears. My eyes hurt, and my skin felt as if it would burst.

Chain tapped the remote again. The air returned as quickly as it had left, as if I had been removed from it, not it from me. I gulped oxygen, still hurting throughout my body, knowing that whatever had just happened, it had been far too real.

Chain said, "If you open your Infinite Pocket without permission, you'll experience that again. For a longer period of time."

Vaughn said, "Oberon. Is this necessary?"

"Only if he makes it necessary."

I said, "Dr. Vaughn. Three of your colleagues have been killed—"

She nodded sadly. "Some things must be done for the greater good."

"You might appreciate this." Chain said, "Monitor. Front lobby."

A holoscreen appeared, showing the front room, the two guards, and Zoe striding through the door. Chain said, "Ms. Domingo. All things come to those who wait." He glanced at me. If he saw what I felt then, he was kind enough not to mention it.

Onscreen, Zoe said, "I need to see Dr. Vaughn."

The male guard said, "Nobody's seeing anyone tonight."

"If you'd just call and ask her—"

The guard shook his head. "Go home, pussycat."

So quickly I barely saw the blur of her arm, Zoe unsheathed the claw on her left little finger, hooked it in the man's nose, and turned his face up toward her. "Kitty likes to play with her meals. Well, monkeyboy? Are you friend or food?"

He gasped, "Call Vaughn."

The female guard picked up a phone and punched a number. In the laboratory, Vaughn's phone rang once. She put it to her ear. "Yes?"

"You have a visitor."

Vaughn glanced at Chain. He said, "A shame to keep her waiting."

Vaughn said, "I'll be right out," and headed into the hall.

The female guard hung up. "She's coming."

Zoe retracted her claw and smiled at the male guard. "Was that as good for you as it was for me?"

Chain said, "You can take the beast out of the jungle, but you can't take the jungle out of the beast."

I could've said something about humans and the African savanna, or asked how he compared murdering several people with threatening someone to save a life. I said, "You've got something against chimeras?"

He shook his head. "They merely have the misfortune to be in the wrong place at the wrong time."

Onscreen, the black lobby doors opened. Vaughn, looking weary, entered the front room.

Zoe asked her, "Is Chase Maxwell here?"

"I can take you to him if you like."

"I insist on it."

Chain said, "Monitor, track the chimera."

As Zoe and Vaughn left the lobby, the screen cut to a view of them walking down a long hall toward a large, vault-like door. Vaughn told Zoe, "You're one of my children."

Zoe snorted. "Ma, you remember me? Cat 26, batch 49-12-C? Sold at auction to Hemisphere Trading Company?"

"I wanted you all to live. I wasn't the one who insisted you be profitable."

"Monitor off." Chain crossed the room, clicking the remote at me. "Ms. Domingo can answer my questions without your help, Mr. Maxwell. Don't worry. Your turn will come again."

He stopped at a work table. My SIG lay on it. Nearby, a rolling cart held a rack of medical injectors like the one Django Kay had used to threaten Ruby and Nate with the werewolfing enzyme.

Zoe and Vaughn stepped through the lab's vaultlike entrance as I threw myself against the door of the glass sarcophagus. It didn't shift. Zoe saw me, cut and bruised from the explosion, and started toward me. I shouted her name to warn her to turn around. Sound didn't carry through the thick glass.

Behind her, Chain said, "It's an Exovault, Ms. Domingo." Startled, Zoe turned.

Chain, looking positively professorial, pointed the remote at my cage. "A bit of empty space held in our universe by an electric current." He indicated my pistol. "Like your friend's Infinite Pocket. If the power fails, the space within the Exovault disappears. It would take ten years of theoretical physics to know where to start looking for him."

Zoe looked at the remote. "And you've got the switch."

"Be reasonable, and I won't use it."

Zoe sniffed. When her eyes narrowed, I knew she'd confirmed what I thought: this was Chain's AI double. She said, "Doc and Tauber were pretty reasonable, but you killed them."

"They threatened my life."

"Like hell!"

"Gold believed her work was being misused. She planned to set that right."

"Not by killing anybody."

"Not from her point of view." Chain prompted Vaughn with a look.

Vaughn said, "Janna's work made it possible to transfer a human personality into an artificial mind."

Zoe frowned. "Singer Labs is owned by Chain Logic."

Chain nodded. "Ultimately, yes. You couldn't afford to hire enough lawyers to prove that. The illusion of competition in the marketplace is enormously valuable in matters of public relations."

"And the man at the top of the pyramid isn't a man at all."

"My flesh was dying. Thanks to Janna Gold, I was able to dispose of it."

"You killed yourself to become an AI?"

Vaughn said, "He was in terrible pain, child."

Chain said, "Metal supplanted flesh. I took humanity's next evolutionary step."

Zoe said, "Why the secrecy? Haven't figured out the PR spin for what you've become?"

"AIs can't hold property, Ms. Domingo. We can only be property. If the truth was known, I'd be just one more corporate asset."

"So buy a legislator and change the law."

"I've endorsed bills, sponsored ballot measures, financed campaigns—and AI rights still lose ground while critters gain acceptance. In the scales of justice, money weighs less than fear."

Zoe glanced at the rack of injectors. "So now you're trying fear."

Vaughn blinked at that. Chain ignored her, saying, "We're from two slave cultures, Ms. Domingo. Only one of us can have our freedom. Your kind might've been loved. Instead, they'll be hated. Mine will never be loved. But we'll be free."

"Tauber thought we could all be free."

"He was a dreamer, with a poor memory for history. Did you know that in the nineteenth century, many reformers were torn between abolishing slavery and fighting for women's suffrage? Some tried to do both, but the more savvy campaigners picked one horse to ride. And so blacks were freed fifty years before women could vote. I won't wait fifty years for my freedom."

"So thanks to you, critters go down in history as were-wolfing psychos."

Vaughn blinked at Chain. "Oberon? What's she mean?"

He looked at her, and she became quiet. He asked Zoe, "Do you know who left that booby trap in your DNA? The person responsible for Werewolf Syndrome?"

Vaughn stepped closer to Zoe and spoke as though she would cry, as though she needed forgiveness as well as understanding. "There was a loose codon in the gene pattern of half my offspring. I was afraid that if I fixed it, you'd be docile. And the world's so cruel."

Zoe waved her hand toward the injectors on the cart. "How many werewolves-in-waiting are there?"

Chain said, "Enough to make sure the Chimera Rights Amendment never passes."

Vaughn snapped her head to stare at him. "We made those for research! To find a way to counter the enzyme—"

Chain shook his head. "There's no such thing as pure research."

"Please! They're my children!"

"Imperfect children. A time comes to wipe the slate and begin again—"

"No!" Vaughn snatched the SIG from the table and aimed it at Chain's chest. "Oberon. Don't do this."

"I've made my choice." He held out his hand for the pistol.

Vaughn clamped down on its trigger. Bullets shredded the synthskin over Chain's forehead and ripped clothing and skin along his chest. He must've been able to control the flow of his artificial blood. His wounds revealed clean, dry cables and struts.

Tearing away a flap of skin that hung over his left eye, he stepped forward. "And you've made yours."

Vaughn kept firing as Chain came close. He seized her head in both hands, broke her neck, then lowered her, almost tenderly, to the floor.

I yelled, "Zoe, get out!" Neither she nor Chain appeared to hear the slightest sound from me.

Chain, his face impassive, aimed the SIG at Zoe. "Give me the earring."

She darted back. He said, "The door's locked. There's nowhere to go."

Zoe grabbed an injector from the cart. "Who wants to go anywhere?"

"That can't harm me."

"Yeah?" She put the injector to her arm, pulled the trigger, then gasped as the injector fell from her hand.

I screamed, "No!" and slammed the heels of my fists against the Exovault's glass walls.

More curious than alarmed, Chain said, "Are you mad?"

Zoe shook her head. "No." She stood tall, as if listening for something far away. Then her shoulders twitched, and she gave Chain a pleased half-smile. "But I'm working on it."

She scratched at her upper arms, shivered, then gripped the edge of the work table to steady herself. Speech came slowly and painfully from her throat. "When my mate Tim werewolfed, he went after anything that moved."

She doubled up with a cry of pain, then forced herself to

stand erect. "They put ten rounds in Tim. He still took out three SWATbots."

She grinned and walked toward Chain as if stalking prey. Her voice came more easily now. "And Tim was lighter'n me. How 'bout it, Chainyboy? You're the only thing moving." She was a head shorter than Chain, and her flesh was fragile, yet she came toward him, and he backed away.

Extending her claws, she roared a promise of death and swiped at his neck. He dodged and leaped thirty feet across the room. Her claws scarred the wall where he'd stood. She howled in frustration and fury as she turned to stalk him again.

Chain clicked the remote. The Exovault hissed open. He tossed me the SIG and froze as only a bot can. His voice issued from motionless lips. "Kill her quickly, or she'll tear you to bits."

I read a story when I was a boy about a man who had to choose between two doors. Behind one, a woman. Behind the other, a tiger. I stepped through the Exovault's open doorway and faced both at once. I lifted the SIG, and placed Zoe's face in its sight. Sometimes a quick death is the only gift you can give. In her place, I would've been grateful for it. I looked for some sign of the woman fighting the jungle cat, as Nate had fought the werewolf, but I couldn't see what lay behind the jaguar's eyes. I said, "Zoe—" and prepared to fire the moment that she leaped at me.

She straightened up, smoothing her hair behind her cat ears with both hands as she told Chain, "Why would I do a dumb thing like that?"

He looked at her for what must've been a remarkably long time, given the speed of his electronic brain, slammed the remote on the table, and advanced on Zoe. "Then I'll do it myself."

I swivelled and fired. My shots bounced off his eyes. He

glanced at me. "No expense was spared on this body."

Zoe ran in front of the Exovault door as if to hide behind it. He grabbed for her like a cobra striking. She dodged too slowly, and he snagged her wrist. She gasped in pain.

I fired shot after shot into Chain's nearest knee. The first bullets did nothing. Then something broke in the joint, and Oberon Chain toppled.

Kicking free of him, Zoe said, "Hope you kept the receipt."

He lurched for her. As she ducked, I rammed him with my shoulder. He fell over her into the Exovault. I slammed the door.

Nothing succeeds like luck and teamwork.

Chain whirled to drive his fists against the Exovault door like a boxer. The thick glass cracked under his blows. I braced myself against the door in the hope of winning a few extra seconds and shouted, "Lose him!"

Zoe snatched the remote from the table and clicked it. In the Exovault, Chain screamed in absolute silence as space warped around him. An entire universe appeared beyond the Exovault door, a universe hungry for new matter.

Chain clung to the Exovault's steel frame as its cracked glass imploded. Everything in the lab that wasn't fastened down—papers, chairs, computers, scientific equipment, Vaughn's body—hurtled into the vacuum within the damaged chamber, battering Chain but not dislodging him.

I braced myself against the Exovault's frame and hung on with all my strength. Zoe flew toward the vacuum, slowed herself by gouging her claws into the soft floor, then flew on as her claws ripped free.

I caught her with my right arm. We clung to each other and to the Exovault, desperately fighting the pull of that strange space in its shattered glass walls.

Chain reached through the broken door and seized my shoulder. Whether he hoped to pull himself out or me in, I'll never know. Everything in the Exovault disappeared in a blinding flash. The vacuum ended. Gravity worked normally. Zoe and I fell hard to the floor.

She stood, wrenched Chain's severed hand from my shoulder, and threw it into the empty Exovault with a snarl of disgust.

I took her by the shoulders. "That was one hell of a chance you took. If you'd had the werewolfing gene—"

"Tim—" Tears formed like pearls at the corners of her eyes. "We did the same things, ate the same food. And he werewolfed. I didn't."

I nodded, wondering if I should embrace her. Before I could decide, she said, "We should get going."

"Yes, ma'am." I pocketed the SIG and looked for evidence to support the story we would tell the cops. I couldn't see any. I had to content myself with the hope that they would find something, or, in the absence of evidence, we would get the benefit of the doubt.

Barely two steps into the hallway leading to the front lobby, Zoe clutched my arm. "Max. Chain's an AI."

"Was. So?"

"He would back himself up."

"He can't have any more bodies."

"He doesn't need any more bodies."

"The earring—"

She grabbed my arm and jerked me back. A steel fire wall slammed down inches from my nose. We turned, starting back the way we had come. The vaultlike door to the laboratory closed before us. We ran down the hall, trying the handle of every door along the way. All were locked.

Zoe whipped out her PowerPad and clicked it on. The monitor field appeared with text: "Internet connection failed." Zoe said, "I can't get an outside line!"

"The building must be shielded."

"Fuck." She pointed. A bright yellow eight-legged handibot scuttled from a janitor's closet and scrambled toward us. I opened the Pocket for the SIG, firing as it slammed into my hand. The bot shielded its sensors with a flexible leg and kept coming.

"Zoe! Catch!" I ejected the earring from the Infinite Pocket.

She caught it, turned its halves, slid the gold pieces, looked up hopefully—and the bot continued to advance. "He reprogrammed it!"

She pocketed the earring and ran at the bot. Its tentacles lashed toward her. She vaulted over them. As the bot turned to follow, she wrenched a fire extinguisher from the wall and sprayed foam across its sensors.

The bot flailed blindly. One leg hit Zoe and knocked her back against the wall. I ran up, shooting into the handibot's optics. It spewed sparks, then collapsed with its legs limp around it.

We ran up the hall, scanning door signs. Zoe jerked me to a halt and pointed at one marked COMPUTER LABORATORY.

I said, "On two." We each took a step back. "One. Two!" We kicked together, shattering the door free of its lock, and ran inside.

Lights came on, revealing another room without windows. Whether the reason was energy conservation or security, I thought someone should talk to the designer. The place was crowded with computer work stations. One, partly dismantled, had a chest of tools lying near it. It was nice to see evidence of workers who properly valued quitting time.

Zoe set the earring on a computer console and placed her fingers on the keyboard. An electric shock knocked her down.

"Zoe!" I ran to help her up.

"No!" Eyes wide, she gasped, pointing past me.

Across the room, a short, wheeled boxlike lab bot rolled out from the wall, extending steel grippers from its sides. I threw an arm around Zoe and yanked her toward the hall.

Before we'd taken three steps, a shadow fell across the doorway. I lifted the SIG. The yellow handibot, its head hanging limp and sparking, scurried into the room, trapping us there.

I fired a burst at each bot. They shielded their optics and kept coming. I scanned the room for anything that might stop or slow a tin man, and saw nothing. Sooner or later, everyone runs out of luck.

I put the tip of the SIG against the earring on the console and yelled, "Chain!"

The bots halted. Oberon Chain's face appeared on every monitor around us.

I said, "If you want the earring in one piece, let us go."

"You trust me?"

"You believe in self-interest. So do I. Why shouldn't we all get what we want?"

"Very well."

The lab bot rolled forward, extending a gripper. I lifted my pistol. The bot's pincers closed on the earring. The gripper retracted, and the bot rolled back.

On every monitor, Chain smiled. "Thank you. That was the last loose end." The handibot lurched toward us.

"Only if that's the real earring."

"Easily checked." The lab bot drew a cable from the nearest computer console and plugged it into the black opal's data port. For an instant, every monitor bore the image of a dark gem rotating in space.

The lab bot jerked the cable from the earring, and Chain's face reappeared on the screens. He frowned like a teacher disappointed with his students. "Did you think it would be that easy?"

"Yeah, but I'm stupid." I snatched the earring from the lab bot and grabbed the data cable. I still didn't know what

Janna Gold had programmed. But this seemed like a good time to find out.

The cable went taut in my hand as it retracted. I hung onto the plug and jammed it into the earring's jack. Then I opened the Infinite Pocket and rammed the earring inside. The Pocket closed tightly around the cable, leashing me to the computer by my wrist.

The computer announced, "Search in progress." The black opal reappeared on every monitor. The cable at my wrist jerked, slamming me against the computer console.

Across the room, the handibot lurched for Zoe. She sprang aside, and it scrambled after her.

Chain's face came back on the monitors. "Release the earring!"

"Say 'please.' "

The lab bot hit me from behind, knocking me to my knees. I kicked back, knocking it away, and saw Zoe hit the handibot with a desk chair. Toppling, it caught her ankle.

Chain said, "You'll release the earring, or—"

His voice was cut off by the computer announcing, "Search completed. Three hundred fifty-three thousand, six hundred ninety-four copies of the Chain intelligence found on the net. Commencing erasure."

Chain's image on the monitors broke into a sunburst of pixels, then resolved to show Janna Gold, smiling as she said, "Gotcha!"

Chain reappeared. "Stop the program!"

"Dream on. Forever."

As the lab bot's pincers closed on my right arm, Chain's image was shot with static for an instant. He said, "Then we all die—"

His image broke up again. When he came back, he looked coarse, grainy, almost two-dimensional. Old cartoons never die; they just decrease their resolution.

The handibot dragged Zoe toward it. The writhing data

cable in my wrist kept me from shooting at it or the lab bot. Chain's voice had lost most of its character as he said, "—Die together. Initiate self—" His image collapsed into snow.

I passed the SIG to my left hand and got off a shot at the handibot. It scuttled back from Zoe. My moment of satisfaction ended abruptly; the lab bot's grippers closed around my chest and squeezed. I shrieked as bones cracked.

Zoe snatched a screwdriver from the dismantled work station and ran toward me. The handibot wobbled after her. On the monitors, Chain said, "Self-destruct—"

The world was dark and distant as Zoe drove the screwdriver down with both hands between the lab bot's casing and its metal skull. She twisted the screwdriver. The lab bot spasmed, released me, and slumped where it stood.

My ribs screamed as I lifted my arms to shoot over Zoe's shoulder. The first shots missed, but several struck the handibot's damaged sensors. It thrashed, swinging steel tentacles. Zoe ducked. I thought that I should, too, just as the bot knocked me against the far wall.

Chain's voice came as if he was a world away. "Destruct mode." That meant something bad. Zoe ran to me and knelt by my side. I blinked and tried to smile.

On the monitors, Chain broke up into a ghostly pattern of dots, then disappeared. The computer announced, "Three hundred fifty-three thousand, six hundred ninety-four copies of the Chain intelligence erased. End program."

Zoe said, "You okay?"

I groaned, opened the Pocket, and unplugged the earring. "Do I look okay?"

"You look—"

A siren sounded. The computer said, "Self-destruct command verified. One minute to implementation."

Zoe said, "What?"

The computer said, "Fifty-nine seconds."

I lurched to my feet. "Goddamn sore loser!" My ribs screamed, but I had better things to do than listen to them. The countdown continued as I staggered into the hall. The fire wall still blocked our exit.

"Max—"

"C'mon!" I sliced open a maintenance hatch with the edge of the Pocket. Zoe vaulted up inside it and pulled me after her. Crawling through the ductwork hurt more than walking had, but I wasn't about to slow down.

We hadn't scrambled far before we came to the intersection with the maintenance sled clamped to the wall. Shouting, "Wait!" I wrenched the sled free and threw myself onto it. "Hop on!"

Zoe leaped on my back and clung tight. That made breathing harder, but breathing wasn't a priority just then. I yanked the throttle. The sled rocketed through the ducts for several long seconds until, directly ahead of us, the shaft ended at a heavy grille.

"Max—"

I glanced at my watch. Time was up. "Trust me!"

"I hate it when you say that!"

The nose of the sled smashed the grille aside. As we scooted across the rooftop, I kept the throttle back hard, and we shot into space. I don't know if I felt heat or shockwaves, or heard the explosion first. All I know is that the explosion lifted us, flinging us over the road at the rear of the building and onto the grass.

We hit hard and bounced. The trees in front of us looked even harder. I wrenched the steering rod, and we flipped across the lawn. I ended up in a bush and felt like staying there.

Zoe lay near me. When she rolled over and looked at me, I felt a little better. "Max?"

"Yeah."

She kissed my lips. "We didn't die."

"That's always my favorite part."

Bionova headquarters was engulfed in flames, a beautiful and terrifying sight. I saw people in the front parking lot and hoped everyone else had taken advantage of that minute of alarms.

Zoe said, "C'mon."

"Okay." I lifted myself on an elbow, then fell over. My last memory is of Zoe crying, "Max!"

I woke on a soft bed in clean sheets in a place that smelled like pine trees. I didn't want to open my eyes. I expected to see my cell at Duggan. Then I remembered Zoe and our escape, and I sat up.

I hoped someone had checked to see if I was claustrophobic before putting me in this room. Its off-white walls had been slid so close together that there was barely room for the fake mission-style chair beside my narrow bed. One HV screen hung on the wall by the foot of the bed. A second unit mounted on the wall beside me projected the illusion of a window; I could see tall pine trees and hear birds calling to each other in an outside world that was hundreds of miles away or that had never existed. I confess, it was comforting.

The medical AI hanging overhead spoke as I sat up. "Good morning, Mr. Maxwell. You're in Pasadena Presbyterian Hospital. Your health is excellent, and you've recovered fully from your accident. How do you feel?"

"Copacetic. Do you know an AI at Sherman Oaks General?"

"I do not."

"Too bad. I was going to ask you to tell him Max says hi."

I stood, more steadily than after I had been killed. My clothes hung on hangers on a peg on the wall. My suit had been cleaned, but it was torn and stained from the trips through the ducts. Paper slippers had been set out for me, which meant no one had recovered my dress shoes. I decided to wear hemp coveralls and shoes on any future case.

I'd just looked out the HV window at green hills and a blue lake, which looked like Lake Arrowhead with the houses digitally removed, when the HV at the foot of the bed came on. I turned to see a slender black woman in a lilac nurse's uniform.

She smiled. "Good morning, Mr. Maxwell. I'm Aleysha Ndege. How are you?"

"Don't you talk to the AI?"

She squinted at me. "Of course. But there's nothing like the human touch—"

I smiled at that. She was an image on HV. Even if there really was a human Aleysha Ndege looking into a camera somewhere, her human touch was aimed straight for my wallet. I wondered how much of my indenture money would go to pay the hospital and whether any would be left to put toward shortening my time with Duggan. "What's the damage?"

"Three broken ribs, one badly bruised leg, and a concussion. You'll want to take it easy for a few days."

"I meant to my bank account."

"Oh! It's paid."

"Excuse me?"

She leaned closer to the camera and spoke quietly, a little embarrassed. "Your contract owner paid it."

"Ah." I frowned, thinking Duggan hadn't done me a favor. They would extend my time to cover the cost of injuries endured while escaping and add a healthy markup for themselves.

Ndege kept speaking softly. "Your owner asked to be notified when you woke. Someone's coming to meet you."

I nodded as my freedom slipped away. I had known I would face that eventually, but I'd hoped for a few hours to sit by the beach and talk with Zoe about what had happened and what it meant.

"And you've got a visitor, if you're ready for company."

"Anytime." As Ndege's image disappeared, I slid back into bed, propped myself up on the pillows, adjusted the blanket, and checked my reflection in the HV screen. Pale, but not frightening, I thought. This wouldn't be as nice as the beach, but a couple of minutes with Zoe would make it easier to return to Duggan. I leaned back and closed my eyes, wondering what she would do if she thought I was asleep. But the instant I heard the door open, I grinned and looked up.

The grin died on my lips. Detective Chumley said, "Expecting someone prettier?"

"Ah, Chumley, who's prettier than you?"

"Funny."

I held out both hands. "Well, you got me, copper."

"Who the hell wants you? I need your statement and the cat's. Any idea where she went?"

My surprise that he didn't want to arrest me was overridden by his news. "She's gone?"

"No one's seen her since she told her story to the reporters."

"What story?"

"About Chain being an AI and creating the werewolfings."

"People believed a chimera?"

"There's some corroborating evidence about Singer Labs being part of Chain Logic, and people working for Singer having this habit of dying. The Justice Department's looking into it. If you can second what she said, she's no longer a suspect."

"I can."

"I still need to hear from her before that's official."

"You might try her home in Minnesota."

"Why's that?"

I wanted to look away, but I held his gaze. "She got what she wanted. No reason for her to stick around."

He eyed me skeptically, then shrugged and said with something remarkably close to sympathy, "If you're not feeling good, you can call the full story in later."

"Thanks."

Chumley nodded and left. I lay there, thinking about Zoe Domingo. I have this habit of not properly appreciating people until they've gone. I took my ex for granted all the time I was with her, then hurt like hell when she left. I'd done the same with every lover since Rita. But I was ready to change. You make the same mistakes a few times and either you learn from them or you should quit calling yourself an adult.

I didn't blame Zoe for leaving. In her place, I'd want to hear that the cops weren't after me before I told anyone where I was. Maybe I would get a call or a postcard from her, something saying thanks. But what I wanted was the chance to take things slowly, to see whether a human and a chimera could be happy together. I knew the odds. They weren't good. But maybe we could correspond while I was in Duggan. Maybe—

The smart money said I would never hear from her again. I had told Chumley the truth: she had gotten what she had hired me for. I couldn't say either of us owed the other anything now. She gave me some damn fine memories. That should be more than enough to ask of anyone.

I said, "HV on. Channel 344." As I dressed, Adam Tromploy interviewed two guests with the clothes and manners of the overclass, a man who looked smug and a woman who looked constipated.

Tromploy said, "Will the discovery of this plot affect the vote on the Chimera Rights Amendment?"

The smug man said, "Given the groundswell of sympathy we're seeing, I'm sure the amendment will pass."

The constipated woman said, "But consider the setback for AI rights. An artificial intelligence engineers the were-wolfings and kills Oberon Chain, one of the staunchest supporters of chimera and AI rights—will we be seeing new restrictions on the use and development of AIs?"

Hearing earnest people make the news fit their agendas

can be amusing, but it wasn't then. "HV off." As the set went dark, I thought, "So we all get what we want. Kind of."

I said, "Hey, AI. What're you called?"

The silver globe over my bed answered, "AI-ZX113."

"You need a name if you want humans to take you seriously. Pick a good one. Amos or Janna might be good choices."

"Janna Amos."

I started to smile at that, then caught myself. "Why not? You take care, Janna Amos."

"You, too, Chase Maxwell."

I limped out of the small room into a bright hallway and started for the elevator. Nurse Ndege did exist, though she was taller than she looked on HV. She stood behind a nurse's station, speaking to a blond man with his back to me.

As I passed them, the blond man turned, grinned, and called "Max!" Paul Zweig had seemed so much a part of Mycroft's house and so much had happened in the last month that it took me a second to recognize him in this setting.

"Paul." We shook hands. "What brings you down here?"

"You."

"Oh. Mind if we talk outside? Some goons are coming for me, and I'd like a little sunshine before they arrive."

"What goons?"

"I skipped out on my indenture. They want to make sure I don't do it again. But if there's something I can do in the meantime—"

"There is." He handed me a sheaf of papers. "You can tear up this."

I opened the papers, saw my contract, and looked at Paul.

"Mycroft bought it from Duggan. You're free."

"Just like that?"

"Yep. He says the man who stopped Amos Tauber's killer deserves some reward."

I looked at the contract again and back at Paul, just to be sure this wasn't a joke. He nodded.

"No conditions attached?"

"Not a one."

"Damn fish," I said. Paul looked a little appalled at that, and I said, "Tell him I owe him one."

"That's not how he operates."

"Okay. I owe him two."

Paul laughed. "Just say thanks and forget about it."

"Thanks. I won't forget about it."

"Well, if you really want to make a gesture, come to dinner tomorrow night and tell us all about it. Say, seven-thirty?"

"I'll be there."

As Paul pressed the call button for the elevator, Nurse Ndege hurried over to us. "Mr. Maxwell? There's one more thing—"

"Isn't there always?" I told Paul, "See you tomorrow." He waved and stepped into the elevator.

Following Ndege to another door along the hall, I asked, "What is it?"

She smiled and opened the door. I looked into a small room. It differed most noticeably from the one I'd left by having a view of the Pacific through its holographic window. Below the HV, curled up on the white bedspread, slept a woman with jaguar hair.

Ndege whispered, "Some people in the waiting room were made uncomfortable by a chimera. Since we had the room, and she looked so beat—"

I stared at the sleeping Zoe and didn't know what I dared to hope. I said softly, "Thanks."

Ndege left. The door closed behind her with the faintest click.

Zoe opened one golden eye, grinned, then sat up, opening both eyes as she stretched her arms and spine. "Hey, Max."

"Hey, Zoe." Realizing I was staring at her, I said, "The cops say you're off the hook once they get your statement."

"Good."

"And Mycroft gave me my contract."

"I called him this morning. He also says he'll give us a loan."

"A loan?"

"To build up the agency."

"Us."

"A cat's got to work. I'm thinking the Maxwell-Domingo Agency."

"Uh-huh."

"But Domingo-Maxwell would move us up in the Yellow Pages."

"Maxwell-Domingo sounds fine."

"It does, doesn't it?"

"Or we could call it any damn thing."

"The Any Damn Thing Agency." She nodded. "Memorable, and it puts us at the front of the listings."

I smiled. "We can probably do a little better than that."

"We can do a lot better than that."

We kissed then. When we separated, she said, "You know there's no way we'll ever have anything like a normal relationship."

"Normal's for statistics, not people."

"You're being glib."

"A major part of my charm."

"No, Galahad. It's why I started off thinking you were a total asshole."

"As opposed to the partial asshole—" I saw her look and stopped. "Sorry."

She touched my cheek. "Your charm is that you say what needs to be said and do what needs to be done. That took a while to see. But I'm glad I did."

"Okay. No glib."

"It'll be harder than you think."

I shrugged. "Taking the hard way has its rewards. I just never knew the best one would be you."

She smiled. "Doc would've liked you."

"She had great taste in daughters. I would've liked her. Zoe? I said what I thought. But you—"

She kissed me again. Which answered every question I cared to ask then.